Chapter 1

Erika parked her Mercedes AMG in the tiny garage behind the Logan Heights home. She walked across a well-tended yard to the rear kitchen door and knocked. Mr. Contreras immediately opened the door and ushered her in. "Please, sit here," he said. He pulled a worn wooden chair with a split plastic seat out from the scarred table where the family took their meals; or used to before his daughter was kidnapped and held for ransom across the border in Tijuana, Mexico.

The knock at the front door startled Mr. Contreras. Erika nodded to the small man; a directive to admit the visitors. She settled in her seat facing the kitchen entrance; her back against the wall next to the rear door.

The Contreras family lived in an old, but well-kept bungalow, built in the early 1950s. It was perhaps fifteen hundred square feet with a one-car garage that opened to the rear alleyway. There was fresh paint on the exterior, separating it from the rest of the dilapidated houses around it, and it featured a lush grass lawn, the only one in that neighborhood. A waist-high chain link fence surrounded the front yard.

Felix and Jorge parked their maroon BMW 750, with its oversized rims and skinny tires, in front of the Contreras home. Four of their best soldiers pulled up and parked behind them in a customized vintage Chevy. The four men spread out, taking up positions at the four points surrounding the house, both front and rear. It was obvious they had done this before.

Felix, with Jorge trailing, opened the chain link gate, walked up to the front door on the tiny porch and banged on the barred screen door. Mr. Contreras opened the door quickly. Even though he knew exactly who these two men were, he asked, "Can I help you?"

"Yes, you can open the door," Felix said. "We need to speak with you."

Mr. Contreras replied by unlocking the screen door and holding it open for the two men to pass. He noted the presence of the soldiers outside. He led the two men into the tiny kitchen in the rear of the house. The cooking area, refrigerator, and sink occupied only the first ten feet of space as they entered. An abbreviated formica-topped counter separated the rest of the room into an eating area with a table and four worn wooden chairs. The door to the backyard was situated just beyond the table. A dark-haired beauty smiled at them from her seat adjacent the door.

"Who is this?" Felix demanded.

"My name is unimportant, Senor Mendez," she responded for the frightened homeowner.

"I was not speaking to you."

"You are speaking to me now."

Jorge advanced on the seated woman, his aggressive demeanor telegraphed his intent. Erika produced a silenced weapon from beneath the table and pointed it at him, her smile still in place.

"Jorge, why don't you sit down? Right there, across from me. Felix, please join him."

"I will have you killed for this," Jorge spat in her direction.

"That is one possible outcome. Now sit down, please, with your hands flat on the table in plain sight. We need to talk."

Felix sat at the small table beside Jorge. Both men placed their hands on the scarred table surface.

"Mr. Contreras, would you be so kind as to step away from the table and stand near the back door?" The short man inched away from the line of fire that might become part of the discussion.

Jorge addressed him. "You are dead, too."

"Jorge! Please listen to me before you issue any more threats," Erika said. "I am trying to be polite."

The second installment of the Erika Johnson trilogy

EMERGENCE

Written by William S. Lawrence

Emergence

Written by William S. Lawrence
Cover Art and Layout by Helane Freeman

Lawrence Williams
Rancho Sante Fe, CA

For permission requests, sales to U.S. bookstores and wholesalers, or to inquire about quantity discounts, please contact the publisher.

Library of Congress Control Number: 2018907935

Printed in the United States of America
ISBN 978-1-7322112-0-9

First Edition
10 9 8 7 6 5 4 3 2 1

Felix addressed her, "If I call out, my soldiers will be inside this house in seconds."

"And you and your brother will be dead when they arrive, and I will kill them as well."

"Who are you?" Felix asked. He was becoming uncomfortable because of her calm demeanor. No woman had ever spoken to him like this. He was also intrigued. This young beauty certainly did not react to him as she should.

"Who I am is unimportant," she said. "What I do for a living is important. Let me explain. I work for the U.S. government as an agent charged with stopping the cross-border kidnap of American citizens for ransom."

" So, you are the person responsible for the pressure being applied to my business by the San Diego Police Department?" Felix asked.

"Yes, until now, I was content to leave your business organization alone, as long as you did not venture into my area of expertise. Then, your lower echelon began intimidating American citizens, kidnapping them for ransom and, now, raping a twelve-year-old girl just for fun."

Felix turned to Mr. Contreras. "Is that true?"

The man could only nod his head, not trusting his voice. Tears rolled down his cheeks. His fear of these men was palpable.

"This is not acceptable to me, Senor Contreras. I offer you my sincere apologies," he said. "The men responsible for this act will pay dearly."

The homeowner heaved a great sigh, but could not find the courage to look up from the floor.

Erika observed the two brothers closely. Felix Mendez's response had surprised her. Jorge, his shaved head sunk deep between his shoulders stared a hole through her, his hatred plain to see. He was the shorter of the two, maybe five feet nine, and built like a refrigerator.

Felix, on the other hand, was tall, and even more handsome in person, in a Zorro sort of way. He wore his black hair long, brushed back from a widow's peak that complimented a finely groomed goatee and mustache. She could understand why others would accept him as a natural leader. His presence commanded that sort of attention.

Once more, Felix addressed the frightened homeowner.

"Mr. Contreras, your family is no longer here, I see. Have you moved them somewhere safe?"

"Si, Patron," he managed.

"From now on, your family is safe anywhere, Senor," Felix said. "This home and your family are now under my protection. No one will harm you."

"Gracias."

Erika spoke up. "Senor Mendez."

"Felix, please." He was attempting to charm her. Erika filed that away.

"Felix," she continued. "Mr. Contreras is not telling you the entire story. You see, his little girl was so badly abused that she is in the hospital. Her wounds are not only physical, you understand? There is no way he could bring her back to this house, this neighborhood. The shame would kill her."

"I understand," he said.

"No, I don't think you do, Felix," she said." The Contreras family has no money, thus no choices. They can't just up and move. They can't even pay for the hospital bills. And coming back here to live is out of the question."

"What would you have me do?"

"First, you need to know who was involved," Erika said. "Then you need to remove them from the board."

"That is an interesting euphemism," Felix said. "I assume you mean permanently."

"Permanently, and as an example to everyone…THIS stops now," she said.

"I have already said the men responsible will pay for this outrage. They knew better than to do this where we live." The silence that ensued was ominous. It continued to lengthen until Felix realized what it meant. He turned to his brother. The look of pain etched into his handsome face was genuine.

"Jorge?"

His brother did not speak, did not lift his gaze from the table top.

"Tell me this is not true," he said.

Erika interrupted. "It is true; him and the two assholes standing out front."

"Jorge, you know I have forbidden this. This is bad for our business. I gave my word. No soldier was to do this."

Jorge still did not look up.

Erika interrupted once more. "Jorge, this stuff stops now."

Jorge exploded. "What?" He stood up in a rage. "Fucking puta! Who the fuck you think you're talking to? Stop? Stop our business? Are you fucking crazy?"

Erika's face remained calm, but somehow the familiar Glock had materialized in her hand once more. She fixed her gaze on Felix while the gun remained pointed at Jorge.

"Do you want me to address Jorge directly, or would you prefer me not to?"

"Go ahead," Felix said.

"Jorge, we're not talking about IF you're shutting down your kidnap enterprise. We're talking about HOW you're going to shut it down. We can shut it down by your direction, saving face for you and your brother, or we can do it the hard way."

"And how is that?"

"I shut it down for you."

Jorge stood there with both hands flat on the table, his body vibrating with the need to inflict damage, and stared at Erika, his face crimson. "I will die first."

"Another possible outcome," she said.

Before Jorge could react, Felix stopped him with an upraised hand. "Jorge," he said, his voice barely above a whisper, "stop."

Jorge froze, standing over the table, his body still quivering with rage.

"Please, Jorge, step outside. I will handle this matter." Felix's voice was calm, almost placating. He had seen his brother in this state of mind before. It was why he was such a feared enforcer. Once he got into this mood, it was nearly impossible to prevent the inevitable violence that followed.

"Jorge, do NOT speak of this to the others. You wait for me. Do you understand?"

Jorge never took his eyes off Erika. He nodded his understanding to his brother and stomped out of the front door, slamming it shut behind him.

"Senorita?" Felix said. "It is senorita, isn't it?" Here came the charm again.

"Yes." Erika knew he was interested. Her well-honed instincts, learned the hard way as a teen-age prostitute, picked up on the attraction even before Felix felt it. He had her interest, too.

"I would like to work this out somehow. But you have put me in a very difficult position."

"No, Senor. You put yourself there. I'm here to help you out of it."

"You came here to help me?" He was clearly amused. "How did you come to believe I need your help?"

"Felix, the cross-border stuff is what put you on the radar. Smuggling, dope, selling whores, killing each other doesn't interest us. But since 9/11, our borders are facing increasing scrutiny. Homeland Security has broad powers, even operational ones when it comes to our border issues. When your little gang-bangers started targeting American citizens, you moved up the priority ladder. If the media gets a sniff of this stuff, all hell will break loose. There will be no stopping it."

Felix recognized that truth. If the local news caught a whiff of what had gone on here, any hope of containing this situation would evaporate.

"Can you guarantee that our business ventures will be left alone if we curtail the cross-border kidnap of American citizens?"

"No, but I can guarantee a swift response if you don't."

The conversation came to an abrupt halt at the sound of the front door opening. Erika and Felix both turned their attention to the kitchen entryway.

Erika was up and moving in an instant. She pointed her silenced weapon at Felix, effectively freezing him in place the way a shortstop freezes a runner by turning the play towards him before throwing out the batter at first base. Jorge came through the kitchen door at a run, firing his pistol, the noise deafening in the small space. He got off one shot. Erika shot him twice in the chest, and then shot him in the forehead before he fell. She fired three rounds within one second.

She checked Felix in place by once again pointing her weapon at him, then immediately returned her attention to the front entrance of the kitchen. She shot the next man twice; the two muffled clicks so rapid, the human ear could not separate them and when he dropped, shot the last man, center mass with two more rounds. He fell atop the first two, piled up like cordwood.

The rear kitchen door reverberated from the impact of a body slamming into it, but held for a moment. It gave Erika just enough time to grab Felix by the collar and use him as a shield before the other two soldiers forced the door inward. Both men dove for the floor beneath the table before Erika could bring her weapon to bear. She backed Felix away from the table and maintained her position behind him.

One of the men grabbed Mr. Contreras and dragged him to the floor before Erika could react. He emerged from beneath the table with the frightened homeowner held before him, just as she had done with Felix.

"Let him go, or I shoot this little bastard," he threatened.

Erika maintained her distance and her silence. The other man stood up now, reinforcing his partner. He pointed his weapon in the general direction of Felix and Erika.

"Drop it," he said. "And you can leave."

Erika shot him just above his nose. He dropped to the floor in a heap. She still had not said a word to them. She turned to the last man standing behind Mr. Contreras.

The man was not showing any fear, and yet his movements were sporadic, jerky—like he wanted this dance to start. He may have been juiced up, high on something. Erika knew he was looking for any kind of sign from Felix about what to do.

She decided for him. She shot Mr. Contreras in the leg, above and to the outside of the right knee. As expected, he abruptly collapsed, leaving the soldier exposed. Erika shot him twice in the chest, dropping him right behind Mr. Contreras.

Felix hadn't moved, but she heard his voice now, full of pain, just above a whisper. "Mi hermano, mi hermano," he said. "Why? Why? I told you to stay outside. You were out of it, Jorge. Why?"

Without asking, he stepped away from Erika and went to his brother. She let him, not even realizing she had released him. She watched him kneel beside his fallen brother. Out of habit, she lined up on the back of his head, her finger on the trigger. Nothing there. She couldn't.

Instead she punched a single button on her cell, a direct connect.

"Yes?" Donny answered immediately.

"I need the team here, now."

"Two minutes out." The backup team of eight was parked four blocks away, on the other side of Highway 5. Two black Suburbans raced toward the home. The first team of four took the alley, the other team parked in front. All were equipped with mikes and ear pieces, along with black Kevlar vests with FBI boldly stenciled on the back in yellow. They surrounded the house and waited until Erika spoke.

"C'mon in. Five men down, another wounded. I have one

in custody."

Two pairs of agents entered simultaneously, guns pointed, from the rear and from the front door. The other four manned the perimeter.

"Shit, what happened here?" One agent blurted.

The scene looked like something out of a gangster movie. There were three men piled like Pick-up-stix in the front entrance to the kitchen, one down behind the table, another lying near the rear door, and Mr. Contreras sitting on the floor, his back against the wall holding his knee, blood welling up over his hands. Erika held another man by the collar, her gun in his back.

Erika responded. "The five down are gone. Check them. The one holding his knee is Mr. Contreras. He needs an ambulance in a hurry. This one is my prisoner. Cuff him and frisk him. I'll be back for him. I need to call this in."

She handed Felix over to the agent-in-charge and stepped out on the front porch. She redialed Donny.

"What happened?"

"It turned into a mess," Erika replied. "Jorge came in shooting and I put him down— four others, too. Felix is being processed by the backup. The homeowner is wounded."

"Who shot him?"

"I did."

"What?"

"There was no other choice."

"Shit. Mom won't be happy."

"I know."

"What are you going to do now?"

"Take Felix for a ride. I need to talk to him."

"Are you out of your mind?"

"Probably." She hung up.

After Erika retrieved her Mercedes E Class AMG from Mr. Contreras' garage, she took custody of the handcuffed Felix and walked him to her car. She put him in the passenger seat, fastened his cuffs to a U-bolt installed in the floor board with another pair of cuffs before climbing into the driver's seat and easing out into the street. The low rumble of the motor parted the gathering crowd like Moses at the Red Sea. The dark tinted windows hid the occupants from view as she headed for the freeway.

Felix stared ahead in silence, numb from the recent events. She headed north on the 5 Freeway and just drove, respecting his silence. They continued, without talking, for twenty minutes before she took the Manchester exit and drove west to the beach area of Cardiff. She parked just off the highway, facing the moonlit water.

"You okay?"

He stared at the water. "No."

"I had no choice."

"I know."

"I wish…"

"Yeah, me too," he said.

The unspoken words hung over them like the sword of Damocles. It was a delicate path on which to tread. Say the wrong thing, the sword falls; the right thing, maybe not. Once again, silence prevailed as the all-encompassing sadness permeated the cabin. The sound of the waves insinuated itself in the background.

Finally, he asked, "What now?"

"That's up to you," Erika answered. "My only focus was to put an end to the cross-border stuff. I figured you could do that."

"I could."

"And take care of Mr. Contreras. Maybe buy his house. Give him a new start, at least a chance."

"I could do that."

"Even after what happened?"

He took a moment to form his response. "It would have happened anyway. You see, once Jorge killed you back there, he would have killed me, too. He very badly wanted to be the Patron of Logan. With me gone, he would have all the power. You saved me from having to kill my own brother. And once my friends in Mexico found out what he did, the attention he brought to them, Jorge was dead. At least this way, it was quick. They would have made an example of him, stretched it out. Maybe me, too, if I survived."

"Because it would have threatened their business?" she asked.

"Yes, that is the only thing that matters to them."

"Do you have cover now?"

"If this does not become known to them."

"How could that happen?" She asked. "All the players are dead."

"There is you."

"There is no *me*. I don't exist."

"Who are you?" It was the second time today he had asked her that question. "What is your name?"

"My name doesn't matter. The Tijuana Cartel, the Mexican Mafia, don't know me—and they never will. If you and I come to an arrangement, they will never hear about what happened this evening. You tell them your brother died in a gun fight over a girl. That will be the official story. The newspapers will print it."

"And what do you want in return?"

"The cross-border stuff stops now. You are permanently out of the ransom business. Mr. Contreras sells his house to you at a premium—enough to start over."

"I can do that." He took a moment before asking. "But why are you doing this?"

"You're not going to like the answer."

"Tell me anyway."

"You're the devil I know."

"Meaning?"

"I know you control the four gangs in Barrio Logan, and you can put an immediate halt to the kidnap and ransom of American citizens. If I were to remove you from the equation, I'd have to start all over again. My agency frowns on me every time I shoot a bunch of people."

Felix shook his head as if to clear his thoughts. "You are a piece of work, lady."

"I've heard that," Erika said. "Now I have a question for you."

"Okay."

"I have a hard time believing you could just let your brother's death go unavenged. Why?"

Felix snorted. "If you only knew Jorge, you would understand. He was my brother, my half-brother, same mother. He was also the enforcer for the Tijuana Cartel. He kept the four gangs under control. But sometimes he was a bit, shall we say, heavy-handed. He had made many enemies among people who were supposed to be our friends. Enemies for me, and enemies for the Cartel. He was already dead—he just didn't know it yet."

"The Cartel?"

"Yes. The word was already out."

"He was interfering with their business?"

"Bringing them attention they did not want. They had warned him once already. Once is all you get from those people. Most would not even get a warning."

"So, you're clear?"

"Actually, better than clear. You did everyone a favor. You removed Jorge without requiring them to expend any resources or effort, and I'm free to run this enterprise as a business, not a gang."

"And the personal part of it? Between you and me?"

"That's over, too. You have my word."

Erika digested that for a few minutes, gazing out over the moonlit ocean. She wasn't a big fan of takings someone's word, but she was going to have to trust him a little. Finally, she turned to face him. "Okay, that works. You stay out of the kidnap for ransom business and buy Mr. Contreras' house."

"Done."

"I'll take you back now." She turned over the ignition, bringing the low rumble of the motor to life.

"How do I contact you in the future?"

"You don't."

"Why not?"

"That's just the way it has to be." She smiled. "Besides, I know how to find you."

She dropped the car into gear and pulled out onto Highway 1, heading south.

Felix kept silent until they were approaching Logan Heights, now back on the 5 Freeway, riding south. "I have to ask you something else."

"What is it?"

"Where did you learn to shoot like that?"

She thought of her two shooting instructors and smiled inwardly. They'd taken a young girl, born with an instinctive ability to point and shoot, and developed those skills to a degree that was unfathomable. Erika's speed and accuracy in employing a handgun was unique. Her instructors were both remarkable gunmen, possessing eight shooting records between them, both in combat trials and long-range target acquisition, earned over forty-five years. And yet, in their professional opinion, she had no equal.

If you googled quick-draw shooters, you'd find amazing video of shooters who could draw a single-action revolver and hit two separate targets, eight feet apart, in less than a second. The human ear would be incapable of separating the two shots. You could only see and hear the separate bullets hitting their targets if you slowed the video speed. The degree of difficulty is even more amazing when you consider the fact that the shooter must pull back the hammer to full-cock before the trigger assembly will engage and allow the shooter to fire.

Erika had no such encumbrances. Her weapons were tuned to her personally, the trigger pull reduced to a fraction required to discharge a weapon, the sights set at dead zero, by her former instructors. To Erika, drawing and firing a weapon was just a thought. Her reactions were a mere reflex—it just happened at lightning speed when the synapses fired. Once she sensed danger, her instincts took control. That was what Felix had witnessed.

"That's a long story, Felix," was all she said.

She pulled to the curb two blocks from his home, came around and unshackled him. She had no fear of him now and didn't quite understand why.

"I will arrange for you to be removed from the investigation into what took place at the Contreras residence. You were never there."

"You can do that?"

She didn't respond to his question. "Take care, Felix. And remember our deal."

"My word is good," he said. "Will I hear from you again?"

"Maybe."

Chapter 2

Erika drove through the ten-feet high iron gates that protected the Beverly Hills mansion from unwanted intruders. She parked her AMG Mercedes in the rear of the Spanish-styled estate and entered through the familiar kitchen door. Donny, her childhood friend and associate greeted her warmly. "Hey, Erika, how are you?"

"Fine, Donny. You?" She briefly hugged him and asked, "Where's the boss?"

"She's on the phone with the Senator. She said to wait in the conference room. She'll be down as soon as she's finished."

"Okay, let's go." They descended the rear staircase from the kitchen to the lower level and took their respective places at the enormous conference table. "I wonder what that piece of shit has in store for us now?" Erika said.

She was not a fan of Senator Ross ever since she viewed a secret video of him cavorting with Russian prostitutes and snorting cocaine at a strip club owned by the Russian mob. He was subsequently filmed engaging in sex with the two hookers before several thugs interrupted his dalliance with a camera and lights, deliberately humiliating the lawmaker and subjecting him to an ongoing blackmail scheme to protect their illegal enterprises. The discovery of that video led to an operation in Las Vegas that had cost the life of her one-time mentor, Richard, who was also the only father figure she had known since losing her biological father as a young girl to a tragic automobile accident. She was then sexually abused by a stepfather before running away from him and her alcoholic mother. She ran to Los Angeles, only to be abducted and turned out as a high-end prostitute for a savage pimp. She'd met Donny there. His story was much the same as hers, and they were thrown together as a package offered to clients who wished to experience the sensual delights the duo offered.

They met Sheila, and her husband, Richard, through an assignation that went horribly wrong. Richard was shot during the encounter, and his life was saved by Erika through a complicated series of events, in which she shot four intruders. After Richard recovered, he took the two homeless teens under his wing and turned them into formidable operatives in the secretive agency he oversaw. The agency was chartered to combat the growing numbers of victims of human slavery, their return to their loved ones, and the removal of the kidnappers. Erika was a special operator with an incredible facility with weapons, and Donny was the resident computer genius who planned and directed operations.

The Senator's sexual proclivities had put in motion a series of events that cost Richard his life during an operation to eliminate the same Russian gang. They preyed on young, attractive, East European women, brought them to America under the ruse they were to become high-fashion models, then drugged, threatened, and turned them out as indentured prostitutes with no hope of escape.

It had been eleven long, agonizing months since Richard had been murdered in Las Vegas. He'd been Sheila's husband, and her rescuer before that. He'd been the adopted father figure in Donny and Erika's sordid life, and their savior as well; their rock; their touchstone in a chaotic world. Revenge was the only option left to them; the only thing left after days and weeks of recrimination spent themselves. It was the only thing Erika lived for; all she thought about. She wanted to kill them all.

Donny broke from his reverie and answered her. "I don't know," he said. "But I doubt we'll be pleased with whatever Senator Ross has in mind."

"Our next operation should be to remove him."

"It would be best to keep that to yourself, Erika," Sheila said, as she entered the room.

Erika rose and gave her boss a hug. "I know, but it helps to envision it sometimes. It's cheaper than therapy."

The trio settled into their seats and Sheila began. "Before we get into a discussion of the Senator, I'd like to hear your report on Barrio Logan. I just got my ass handed to me by the esteemed Senator after he heard about what happened there."

"We haven't even issued a report through channels yet," Donny said.

"Well, it's obvious he has his own sources. Someone relayed the results to him already, probably someone from the FBI." She turned her attention to Erika. "What happened, Erika?"

"I arranged a meeting with Felix and Jorge to explain the facts of life to them in the hopes of ending their practice of kidnap and ransom without the need for a major operation. We have enough on our plate with the Russians, as it is. Unfortunately, Felix was unaware his brother, Jorge, was the chief architect of this little sideline and we spilled the beans. Jorge went into a rage and entered the house shooting. I put him down, and then his four friends. I had no choice in the matter. It was either shoot, or be shot."

"Did you have to shoot Mr. Contreras, too?"

"He was being held by one of Jorge's men. I thought it best to end the discussion at that point."

Sheila pursed her lips. "And I also understand you took Felix for a private conversation after the firefight."

"I did. I thought it was the best way to figure out the structure of the Barrio Logan gangs and get a sense of what needed to be done to end the kidnap enterprise. As it turned out, I did Felix a favor by eliminating his brother and gained significant intelligence into their operations."

"Please explain."

"Well, the pressure brought on by the San Diego Police Department worked beautifully. The Mendez brothers arrived at the Contreras home, as expected, with four soldiers posted outside. I was waiting in the kitchen when they arrived. When I explained to Felix what his brother Jorge, and two of his soldiers had been involved in, it was obvious he had no knowledge of their activities. He actually threatened to kill those involved before he learned Jorge was part of it."

"You're sure Felix had no hand in it?"

"Positive. He explained later that the Tijuana Cartel already had planned to eliminate Jorge and perhaps even Felix himself due to the increased attention from the authorities. He was relieved that I took his brother out cleanly before he had to. I got the distinct impression they were not close. It also strengthened his relationship with the Cartel and the Mexican Mafia."

"How?" Sheila asked.

"Apparently, Jorge had made a lot of enemies, both locally and in Mexico, by conducting an independent enterprise and not paying the required fee to operate. He was also attracting unwanted attention to Barrio Logan for what they saw as peanuts. He was slated to be taken out. I got there first."

"So now we're in the service business?"

"No, Sheila, we're not. I know what I did and I had no choice." Erika knew she had put Sheila in a difficult position because of the carnage she'd left behind. She had arranged to cordon off and sanitize the location. It looked like a gang war gone bad, but she still had a lot to explain to local law enforcement. They didn't tend to be understanding about gunfights on their turf. Sheila had to smooth out the wrinkles before presenting an official report.

"Erika, five of them? And you shot Mr. Contreras? You sure this wasn't personal?"

"I had no choice. Jorge stormed out of the house after Felix warned him to be quiet. He was back in two minutes and fired on me as he entered the kitchen. I put him down and then his two soldiers right behind him. Two more burst in the back door and took Mr. Contreras hostage. I shielded behind Felix and shot one of them. I had to shoot Mr. Contreras to get the other one."

"Oh, Christ!" Sheila said. "Donny, how do we explain this?"

"Easy; Mr. Contreras was caught in a cross-fire between brothers who had become rivals. Erika deserves a commendation for bravery under fire."

"You missed your calling," Sheila said. "You should write

fiction."

She turned back to Erika. "You took Felix for a ride. Why?"

"I saw how he reacted to his brother's death. I saw an opportunity and I took the initiative. As a result, he agreed to bring an immediate halt to the cross-border ransom schemes and to buy Mr. Contreras' home for cash. The Contreras' family can move on as best they can under the circumstances, the ransom business is finished, and we have a sort of loose ally in San Diego."

"An ally?"

"Too strong a word. Someone who has an interest in keeping Barrio Logan off the radar."

"Now we're in league with drug smugglers and killers?"

"Better the devil you know." It was becoming her favorite phrase.

"Okay." Sheila knew there was a lot left unsaid in Erika's report, but she felt this was not the time to complicate matters with Senator Ross any further. "Donny, you write it up for oversight. No names, no methodology, just the bare facts. Let's see what comes back to us."

"I need to call the Senator back, regarding my nomination," Sheila said. "You two wait until I finish. It shouldn't be too long. He had to attend to another matter before we continued our discussion."

"I thought that was a done deal," Erika said.

"With these people, there's never a done deal. There's always one more item to discuss," she replied. "He can also demonstrate his power over the nomination by making me wait like a recalcitrant child."

Donny said, "This is the same Senator featured in the videos, isn't it?"

"Yes," Sheila said, "the very same."

"Hmm. I would have thought our request would have eliminated any hesitancy from him," Donny said.

Sheila was not yet aware Donny had emailed the Senator

and attached a short film clip of him smoking crack and playing with two Russian prostitutes.

Erika understood his double meaning. "Perhaps he needs a refresher," she said.

"Let me call first and find out where we're at on this thing." Sheila left the room.

After being put on hold for several minutes, a familiar voice came over the line, oozing insincerity.

"Sheila, how are you?" The Senator asked. He acted as though they hadn't spoken earlier.

"Fine, sir. Thank you for asking."

"Terrific. Let me get you caught up," he said. "The committee met, and I'm pleased to inform you of your confirmation as Director of the agency. You will see the written appointment by next week."

"Thank you, Senator. That is good news."

"I'm glad you got the job," he said. "There is, however, an accommodation I was forced to accept from the committee."

"Really?" Sheila's radar was up now.

"Yes, the committee felt that, due to your relatively young age, it would be best for us to provide oversight of your decisions until we are convinced you're the right person for the job."

"Senator, is the committee aware that I was personally involved in the decision-making process over the last ten years, along with my late husband?"

"Of course, of course," he said. "It was precisely because of your experience that we nominated you in the first place. The agency has been so successful in its endeavors that we felt providing you with more continuity in the decision process would be wise for a short while."

"I see," Sheila said. "And would the entire committee or just one individual be providing this oversight?"

"Well, I'm pleased to tell you I was unanimously elected to serve the committee as your liaison," he said. "That will enable us to keep a lid on those items that require the utmost discretion and still fulfill the committee's wishes for oversight."

"That makes sense." Sheila was desperately trying to find the correct balance in what she was about to say. "It would be operationally dangerous, if not impossible, to include the entire committee in each decision. Our operatives' lives can be forfeited with just one leak."

"I understand," the Senator said. "The need for discretion goes both ways." This last comment contained an implied warning.

"Senator, thank you. You can be assured of my continued cooperation and discretion."

"I knew I could count on you, Sheila," he said. "Your appointment and future protocols between your office and mine will be forthcoming."

"Good-bye, Senator."

"Good-bye."

When Sheila returned to the conference room after her phone call, Erika could tell by her body language that she was upset.

"What's up?" Erika asked.

Sheila took a moment before answering, hoping to strike the right note.

"It seems the Senator will be providing oversight on any future decisions I make. He made it clear that he was elected unanimously by the committee to fill that role."

Donny said, "That's bullshit. He just doesn't want his video to resurface."

Sheila picked up on his comment immediately. "I thought you disposed of all the videos we collected."

"I did. Every single one in my possession," he said.

"Then how could it resurface? In fact, how would the Senator even know a video of his escapades still exists?"

Erika remained silent. Donny had stepped in it, so it was

his show now.

"I could think of a dozen ways," he said. "How do you know the Russians didn't contact the Senator with his own video? After all, he was the star performer."

"I don't," Sheila said.

"Then I think we should proceed as if he does know the video still exists and suspects that we do, too," Donny said.

Erika observed Sheila as she studied Donny's face for any telltale signs he was not being entirely truthful. To his credit, he never flinched.

Finally, Erika weighed in, saving Donny from any further scrutiny. "Let's all agree the Senator probably does know. Let's also agree the Senator believes we kept a copy of his dalliance. In our place, he would have. And it's not all bad to let him believe that. After all, he was briefed on the operation, and he is very aware of his own lack of discretion among the Russians. He has to assume we know about, or at least suspect, his involvement."

"Then he's sending me a message," Sheila said. "This political aspect of the job sucks. I don't know how Richard put up with it."

"C'mon, Sheila," Donny said. "It's a new position for you, no matter how much Richard shared. You were a sounding board; now you make the decisions. Just think of Richard and reverse the process. You're good at this. You know you are."

Sheila allowed a deep sigh to escape. "Okay, guys, thanks for the pep talk. I'm going to need to bounce things off both of you and you'll have to help me keep a tight rein on the Senator."

"Good luck with that. Hey, are we still on for the Maui trip?" Erika asked.

"You bet," Sheila said.

"This is the perfect time. Senator Ross won't be contacting us for a week or two. We are out of here on Monday morning."

Chapter 3

Sheila, Donny, and Erika had become inseparable since the Russian mafia had brutally murdered Sheila's husband. Donny, an administrator and resident computer genius, had been monitoring the operation from headquarters when Erika and Sheila witnessed Richard's cold-blooded execution at a warehouse in Las Vegas. Their ill-conceived operation against a Russian gang specializing in human trafficking and sexual slavery had cost them dearly.

They took comfort in one another's company during the endless de-briefing and subsequent nomination of Sheila to fill Richard's position as Director. Donny suggested ten days in Maui for some much needed and well-deserved R and R, while waiting for the Senate Panel in charge of U.S. Intelligence assets to confirm her appointment. Based on the sensitive nature of the Las Vegas operation involving at least one of those Senators, her appointment was expected to be a mere formality.

The vacation home was an elegant oceanfront estate located north of Black Rock, on Kaanapali Beach, on Maui's west shore. Exhausted from the time change, the 6-hour flight from Los Angeles to Maui, and the hour-long drive from Kahului Airport to Kaanapali, it was early evening by the time they unpacked.

Erika emerged from her ocean-front bedroom suite through the open glass wall of doors facing the pool and beach beyond. She mixed celebratory Mai Tai's and brought them to the lanai so they could watch the sunset. The sun retreating in and out of the billowing clouds between Lanai and Molokai always promised a spectacular light show. Tonight, it delivered on that promise, morphing the brilliant blue sky into a palette of gold, orange, red, and then purple. They all clinked glasses in a silent toast to the sunset and sipped their drinks as the light receded.

When the sun had finally disappeared, Erika peeled off her dress and undergarments and slipped into the warmth of the oceanfront swimming pool. Sheila followed suit, shed her clothing and dove in behind her.

"Well?" They asked Donny.

"Why not?"

As he stripped down, the women noted his handsome, exotic Filipino looks; the long, mussed black hair, deep brown eyes, and sensual lips on a 5'10" frame that combined to form an attractive package. The sinuous play of early starlight on the lean muscle and sinew of his body lent a cinematic quality to the moment. The startling size of his penis was no surprise to Erika and Sheila. It hung a good seven inches below his groin in a flaccid state, a thick ropey, extra-large appendage on a medium frame. While most men would be delighted to have been gifted with such size, they knew Donny was reticent, if not embarrassed by it. As an eleven-year-old, abandoned in Manila by a drug-addicted mother, he'd been sold to a local Madame and offered as a prostitute to adults of either gender as a freak of nature. His experience as an adolescent sexual plaything shaped his psychological outlook on the human reaction to his 'gift'. He was treated as something less than human; something to be used; something to be gawked at. He didn't feel special. He felt abused.

One such gentleman, a successful dot-com investor, unable to exist without Donny's considerable talents, brought him to America as his 'nephew'. After several years living like a young prince, a tragic automobile accident took the life of his benefactor, and once again, Donny found himself out on the street.

About the same time, Erika had been a fourteen-year-old runaway that thought she'd found her one true love on the streets of Los Angeles, only to be sold by that former lover to a vicious, sadistic pimp that drugged, raped and turned her out as his principal earner. Erika and Donny subsequently met as a tag team that offered a unique experience as a threesome to prospective customers, both male and female. Erika was the only person he shared his feelings with; the only person he was bonded to. Sheila was gradually becoming another.

Her story was almost commonplace; too commonplace. She had traveled to Japan as an eighteen-year-old, aspiring model only to be drugged, stripped of her passport, all her belongings and dignity, and turned out as a Western prostitute, an exotic delicacy. Two years later, she was rescued by her future husband in an international operation to return known kidnap victims to their families. Unfortunately for Sheila, there was no family to be returned to. Richard, her rescuer, became her husband and only family. Through a bizarre set of circumstances, the trio had met as lovers, and after a night of violence, became friends.

Thus, the women didn't have to wonder why Donny felt as he did about himself. Circumstance or physical threat had forced all three into prostitution at a tender age. They had lived the same horrors, the same treatment at the hands of others. Their shared experiences as young prostitutes bound them together on a level that was impossible for others to comprehend. They all bore the invisible scars from the damage. Unspoken as a vow, but nonetheless embraced by all, was the resolve to overcome those obstacles and fully enjoy their lives, emotionally and physically. They dispensed with allegiance to any societal norms guiding their behavior. They weren't promiscuous or predatory towards others. They simply enjoyed the physical sensations of the sex act with each other, and gave it no further consideration, commitment, or emotional attachment; three unconventional friends, sometimes lovers, who all sought the ultimate human fantasy…a true, honest relationship. They were indeed fortunate to have found this unique bond, saving one another from a lifetime of depression, sadness, and self-induced loneliness; human life rafts in a sea of personal turmoil.

Donny executed a perfect dive, cutting through the water to surface next to the women. Sheila slid over to him and took him in her arms. "Thank you, Donny, for being my friend— and for suggesting this."

Erika joined them in a three-way embrace. "I second that emotion," she laughed. "This is perfect." She kissed each of them and swam away. That was as close as she could come to expressing her love for them out loud.

After swimming for a short while, Sheila was the first to exit the pool. "I'm tired, guys. I'm going to lie down."

"Yeah, me too," Erika said. She followed in her wake, retiring to the same bedroom wrapped in a bath towel. They dried off and lay abed as Donny finished his swim.

"Damn, he looks good," Sheila whispered.

"Yes, he does," Erika said. "Let's get him in here."

"Oh, yeah."

"Donny," they chorused. "Come to bed."

They had a lot to consider during the next ten days, and they knew that their decisions would determine the shape of their future. However, they had agreed not to discuss any prior agency business during their stay in Maui, which pleased Erika no end. She did not want to get into the official debrief of the Logan Heights debacle until she was more prepared to defend her actions.

Their more immediate problem had started with U.S. Senator Jerry Ross and Rita Jackson. Mrs. Jackson was the CEO of a major banking institution that funneled and laundered large sums of U.S. tax dollars through the banking system until its origins were obliterated. The account at Rita's bank funded hostage negotiations or ransoms and kept democratic governments from appearing to be engaged in those practices. The monies were secretly funded through Senator Ross's Intelligence Committee. The Russian Mafia filmed them on video engaging in unconventional sex acts with a variety of players and subjected them to extortion. Erika stepped in to extricate Mrs. Jackson and the Senator, but the situation unraveled quickly and ended in violence.

The original operation was simple enough: recover the videos, destroy them, and punish the responsible parties. At the onset of the operation, they discovered additional videos of several well-known public figures, including the Senator from Oregon, a ranking member of the Senate Foreign Intelligence

Committee. Fearful this information could compromise the security of the United States, they attempted to eliminate anyone involved and capture any and all video evidence. They were successful in acquiring all the evidence, but four of the principals they were hunting escaped. The Russians would not likely forget the sting or the loss of three of their comrades killed during the operation.

Before they could worry about Russian vengeance, they needed the Senate to confirm Sheila as Director of their nonexistent agency. To guarantee her confirmation, Erika and Donny kept copies of the videos they recovered from the Russians. The graphic recordings would not amuse Mrs. Jackson's fellow board members or Senator Ross' political associates. Sheila wasn't aware of their insurance plan; she would have destroyed the video outright. Erika and Donny were hoping they wouldn't have to make the videos public.

Erika had a very personal stake in the outcome of the Director's appointment. With Sheila at the helm, eliminating the four remaining Russians would remain a priority for the team. But even if Sheila didn't receive the appointment as Director, Erika would still kill them. She had sworn to avenge Richard's death. Having Sheila as head of operations would make that eventuality much simpler. Richard's death would remain a priority. She had killed three of the seven Russians and would not stop until she had destroyed them all. The last four were just unfinished business for Erika. The likelihood they held the same intentions towards her never became part of her calculation. She accepted that premise in total as an eventuality in progress.

Chapter 4

On a 270-acre ranch, just down the valley from Aspen, Colorado, the four remaining Russians were having a meeting of their own. Leonid Utkin, the leader of their criminal group, along with his partner, Raina Polzin, sat with the two remaining principals in their gang. Fyodor Kaminski, the 6'7", 300-pound mountain of a man, was a former super-heavyweight wrestler. He had been banned from the sport for excessive brutality during his matches. At 6'3", and 225 pounds, Petro Sokoloff, wasn't quite as large, but he was extraordinarily athletic. He held black belts in four different martial arts disciplines and was a master with edged weapons. Both men were fiercely loyal to Utkin and took the loss of their three comrades personally.

Erika had first shot to death Sergei Markovic, a trained sniper and Petros' close friend, as he lay in wait for her. A single bullet to the head ended his criminal career. Then she and Sheila attacked several more gang members who had captured and tortured Richard in a Las Vegas warehouse. Upon learning his location, Erika killed Afanasi Lagunov, a master pimp and sadist. He ruled his collection of prostitutes and dancers through intimidation and brutality. She also killed Agnessa Koslov, Raina's crazed sexual pet, a second too late to prevent Agnessa from slitting Richards' throat. Raina had trained Agnessa as her personal slave, so her assassination represented a personal affront. Raina knew that it would be difficult to replace Agnessa with another woman who would enjoy both servicing Raina and watching her torture others.

At the moment, she was training another pet who sat at her feet wearing a dog collar. This woman was a classic beauty, blonde and statuesque, similar to Raina herself. Her name was Stasja Krupin. In Russian, her given name meant "resurrection." That was exactly what Raina had in mind—to mold her into the same sick plaything that Erika had snatched from her. Her humiliation in front of the others gathered around the table was simply the beginning of her new lessons in servitude.

The four of them were viewing still pictures of Erika and Sheila, screen grabs taken from the video that was running as the two women invaded their warehouse and murdered their friends. The brunette woman on the film had extended her middle finger to the camera before shutting it down, adding further insult.

Leonid sneered, "Now we know what they look like. Next, we find out who they are."

Through the windows they could see snow falling outside the stone and wood estate. They were used to the cold Russian winters, so the terrain and weather were familiar conditions. Only the opulence of their surroundings was at odds with their former lives. Crime in Europe and the United States paid well. Their criminal enterprise had profited upwards of two hundred million dollars with no end in sight. They would not allow these two agents to meddle in their affairs. They would have to pay.

"Leonid, if we capture either of these two alive, I want them for myself," Raina said as she stroked the blonde head of hair beneath her. *Pleasure before pain,* she thought.

"And you will have them," Leonid said.

"Do you know who they are?" Petro asked. He had his own reasons to find them. Sergei had been his best friend since their days together in the KGB.

"Not yet," Leonid replied. "But we will. It is only a matter of time. We still have our connections inside American Intelligence. Eventually their names will surface."

Fyodor, the giant asked, "Who is running the clubs in Las Vegas now that Afanasi is dead?" His voice reverberated through the great room.

"Oleg Yakolev," Raina said. "He is a capable administrator, and Maksima Orlov will keep the women in line. I think they will be more afraid of her than Afanasi. And she will keep the women away from Oleg. He likes a taste now and then."

"Is anyone watching their safe house in Los Angeles?" Petro asked.

"Yes, we have a remote camera attached to a light pole outside the home. If anyone visits, we will take them there," Leonid said.

"I hope it will be soon," Raina said. Her eyes radiated sparks of insanity. "Come, Leonid, our pet needs some lessons." She rose from the table and jerked the blonde beauty to her feet by the leash. "And I need some attention."

Raina led Stasja to the master bedroom. Leonid trailed behind the two women, curious to discover what perversions she had in mind for her new pet.

Fyodor and Petro remained silent. Discretion was best around Raina.

Chapter 5

The three friends drifted south along the Kaanapali shore, approximately two hundred yards from the vacationers frolicking on the beach. They formed a makeshift raft from their individual paddle boards by intersecting their paddles beneath each other's reclining bodies and drifted beyond the surf line to the calmer waters where the sailboats were tethered to buoys. The privacy allowed them to speak freely among one another.

"We should have done this a long time ago," Donny said. The calm water formed concentric ripples as he used his hands to spin their conjoined raft in lazy circles.

"You're just saying that because you're getting so much attention from two gorgeous women," Erika said.

"You figured that out all by yourself?" Donny laughed.

"Really! You two are shameless," Sheila said. She was tanned now, a light honey color compared to Erika's golden brown and Donny's deep umber. The past seven days had worked miracles for each of them. They were tanned from the sun, invigorated by the outdoor exercise of swimming, snorkeling, kayaking, and paddle boarding. They'd even surfed the small break nearby.

"You want to go to Hula Grill tonight?" Sheila asked. "Walk down the beach and back?"

"T-shirts and shorts," Donny said. "Sounds like a plan."

"I'm in," Erika said.

"Let's go," Sheila said.

Donny watched as the two women retrieved their paddles and easily stood up in the center of their boards. As they began paddling away, he wondered how he got so lucky. Sheila, in her thirties, still turned heads in her miniscule bikini, her fitness a testament to many hours spent in training. She could probably still compete favorably as a professional fitness contestant.

And Erika, although she didn't seem to care, commanded attention wherever she went. Her long limbs and graceful body, reminiscent of a ballerina, was the perfect counterpoint to Sheila's shorter frame. A Ferrari and a Porsche, both were perfect.

He stood and paddled after them, smiling at his good fortune.

Donny rinsed off the boards while the women showered, then took a hot shower outdoors. He put on board shorts and a T-shirt and found Sheila and Erika dressed casually in similar attire. Shoeless, they crossed the front lawn and walked down the beach to begin the short trek south along the shoreline. The warm water lapped at their feet, and the waves gently massaged the shore. The texture of the warm sand, the sparkling reflection of the late sun on the mellow surf, and the sailboats and catamarans at anchor with their sails reefed looked like a movie scene.

"How about we just stay here for another week or two?" Donny asked. It was impossible for him to ignore the startling beauty of this special place. It teased at his distant memories of his childhood in the Philippines. The weather and the population here resembled his native land, and staying here had awakened long dead memories of his life before he became a child prostitute in Manila.

The women only smiled in reply, a spoken answer not required for his musings. They felt at peace here for different reasons. This was a place of magic in the world. It provided a release from personal anxiety as the slow pace, mild temperature, and overwhelming natural beauty slowly peeled away worries.

They clambered up from the sand to the restaurant where they were seated in the barefoot section long before the sun lowered beyond the sailboat masts. No one wanted to break the spell by speaking. Too soon, a waiter appeared and Donny ordered a bottle of Chardonnay to toast the approaching sunset.

They enjoyed the wine and a selection of way too many appetizers, referred to as "pupus," before Donny broke the reverie. "Three more days, guys. Then back to civilization."

"Don't remind us," Erika groaned. "I was just getting used to this." She indicated the restaurant and its surroundings with a sweep of her hand.

The Hula Grill was a fixture on Kaanapali Beach, separated from the sand by only an abbreviated lawn and concrete walkway. It anchored Whaler's Village from the seaside and captured the lion's share of visitors due to its incredible location facing the famous Maui sunsets over Lanai and Molokai. The barefoot section fronting the beach boasted a floor of sand and actually meant shoes were not required while dining. There was no better place on the Island to enjoy a casual meal with friends.

Sheila said, "No matter what the decision is regarding the Directorship, let's agree to do this twice a year."

"Maui?" Donny asked.

"Not necessarily," she said. "Anywhere the three of us can be together. I feel like I'm alive again. I want more of it."

"Then let's do it," Erika said. "No matter what."

They raised their glasses in a toast.

"To future adventures," Donny said.

"No matter what," Erika said.

"No matter what," Sheila repeated.

A brisk tailwind ensured a short return flight to Los Angeles. Ninety minutes after deplaning, Donny, Erika and Sheila were once again ensconced in the lower conference room at the Bel Air estate.

Chapter 6

Sheila sat directly across from Donny and Erika. She still refused to sit in Richard's chair at the head of the table. Sheila had the title, but the three operatives were becoming co-directors of the agency, their relationship undocumented, but no less authentic because of it.

"So, how do we find the Russians?" Erika asked.

"That would be Donny's department," Sheila said, redirecting the question to him.

"I've identified several other strip clubs, bars, and restaurants owned through a series of corporations, all fronts for prostitution and drugs. It seems our Russians also have an impressive list of real estate and are collecting rents on top of the illicit enterprises. They must have protection at very high levels to have amassed the kind of wealth I'm discovering in plain sight. We should be careful," he said.

"You sound impressed," Erika said.

"I am," he admitted. "This level of sophistication is unusual in my experience, especially within such a short time frame. There has to be a legitimate source of funding to put all of this in place without appearing on the radar on any number of intelligence agencies."

"Then you suspect the same level of sophistication exists in their protection?" Sheila asked.

"Has to be," he said.

"Anything specific?" Sheila asked.

"Several people. Anyone of substance on the videos is suspect. Our banker is an obvious one. The Senator is also high on the list," Donny said. "The biggest problem, though, is we don't know what we don't know."

"What do you mean?" Sheila asked.

"There may be other videos in other clubs or warehouses that haven't surfaced yet. Any one of the other enterprises I've identified could house the same sort of video library we found in Las Vegas," he said. "In fact, there may be other victims, in other countries where the penalties for said behavior are far more serious, like Russia itself."

"People there disappear for much less egregious behavior than a sexual dalliance, let alone drug use." Donny was warming up now. "What if our Russian friends have documented proof of drug use by a highly placed Politburo member or Command General in the Russian military, or maybe someone similar in Great Britain or France? The consequences might not be as serious as in Russia, but anyone of importance would do almost anything to retain their status in the world."

Sheila was both impressed and amused. "I've never seen this side of you close up, Donny. Richard always shared the substance of your responsibilities with me, but hearing your assessments personally gives me a whole new appreciation of your abilities. I realize why Richard relied so heavily on your opinions."

If Donny was capable of blushing, he would have. Erika had never seen him so uncomfortable with a compliment. She enjoyed his discomfort.

"Thank you," was all he could manage.

Erika added, "You know, if we kill all the bad guys, none of this will matter..."

Sheila turned her attention to Erika. "And you always have the same solution for every problem."

"At least it's a permanent solution," Erika said.

Sheila smiled. She knew her friend intimately and was more tolerant of her because of it. "I can't argue with that."

Sheila returned her attention to Donny. "How do we locate the Russians?"

"I don't know, and that worries me," he said. "They could be anywhere, using any number of aliases."

"Why does that worry you so much?" Sheila asked.

"Because I think it's reasonable to assume they're looking for us," he said. "And they know what you two look like from the video feed. If I remember correctly, you were wearing a ball cap, Sheila. They may not be able to pick you out of a crowd, but Erika looked directly into the camera and flipped them off—a direct challenge. They won't forget that. They'll come for her."

"If I don't come for them first," Erika said.

There was no bravado in her words. She was dead serious.

Sheila absorbed her statement and turned to Donny. Sheila couldn't lose Erika…or Donny. "All the more reason for you to keep digging," she told Donny. "Let's find them first."

Chapter 7

Leonid and Raina were still living at the ranch in Aspen. Four months had passed since their associates had been killed in Las Vegas. It was late January and the heavy snows had arrived. They were drinking coffee together before an enormous plate glass window, watching the huge flakes blanket the mountain community in the valley below.

Stasja awaited instructions from her mistress in the lower level of the estate. Raina was pleased with Stasja's progress. Her new pet had evolved a nasty streak of sadism towards anyone other than Raina or Leonid, along with an eagerness to please the pair. Raina was transforming Stasja into quite a Doberman. She might never reach the depraved stature of Raina's previous pet, but she was getting close.

"Has Fyodor or Petro found those women yet?" Raina asked.

"No, not yet," Leonid replied. "But Petro thinks he has found a way to locate them."

"How?"

"The American training facilities," he said. "There are only so many of them and only so many trainers. If we find the trainer, we find the student."

Raina grinned wickedly. "That is one way, I suppose. There are others."

"Go on."

"What if we threaten the Senator or the lady banker with exposure? Wouldn't that be quicker?" She asked.

Leonid sipped his coffee. "We no longer have video of the Senator, so we have no leverage there. We still could bluff having copies of the woman since we emailed them, but she knows nothing of the operatives. She is not involved in that end of the business, only the financial elements."

"Can we use her to get to the Senator?" Raina asked.

Leonid almost laughed. "You are so devious, Raina."

"That's why you love me, Leonid."

"That and many other reasons," he said. "I will give it some thought."

Raina was pleased with herself. "She continued to stare out at the snow-covered panorama below while contemplating her revenge.

Petro and Fyodor were now living in New York City, sharing a five-thousand square foot luxury co-op overlooking Central Park from the lower East side. The apartment, situated on the 32nd floor, occupied the entire level and was accessible by a key controlled elevator for security. Not that they needed it. Anyone foolish enough to force entry into their home would come face to face with two of the most dangerous men Russia ever produced. Petro still practiced martial arts daily to hone his already impressive skills, and Fyodor was the definition of aggression with the disposition of a wounded Grizzly. His appearance caused all but the most intrepid to head in a different direction.

The two men sat at the kitchen table. Petro had a mug of black coffee and Fyodor was enjoying straight vodka over ice. The vodka had no discernible effect on him.

"I have a suggestion, my friend," Petro said.

"What?" Fyodor rarely used more words than necessary.

"No one in Los Angeles knows you. You were not part of the operation to return Helena to Las Vegas. I may have been seen there, maybe even recorded on video," Petro explained.

"So?"

"So, it might be productive to have you near the house where they took Helena. If you find one of their trainers or fellow agents, perhaps you could persuade them to tell us where we could find the two women who killed our friends."

"Have you discussed this idea with Leonid yet?" the giant asked.

"Of course; I would not undertake an operation without first getting his approval." Petro responded. "He would like us to work on this strategy while he and Raina try another approach. But whoever finds them first gets the first taste. I would like that to be us."

Fyodor did not answer, just stared out at the barren landscape of Central Park, the leafless trees and patches of dirty snow. Finally, he smiled and said, "Can you take care of all these clubs by yourself?" This was as close as he could come to making a joke.

Petro smiled in return, knowing this was his giant friend's attempt at humor.

"I will struggle without you, but I can manage," Petro returned the repartee.

"Then I will go. These two women should pray I find them before Raina does," Fyodor said. He returned to staring out the window and drinking his vodka.

"On that, we agree, my friend."

Chapter 8

Richard had used a small home in Thousand Oaks, California as a safe house to stash a Russian prostitute that he had abducted from a Las Vegas Strip Club controlled by the Russian mob. Richard had subsequently been taken from that same home by the Russians after they traced Helena, the prostitute, there through a GPS chip they had implanted in her. The Russians also killed two American agents left to guard them during the home invasion. They took Helena and Richard back to Las Vegas, where he was tortured and killed. A few miles from that very house, Fyodor Kaminski watched a video feed from the camera they'd mounted on a light pole across the street. The Americans were using the safe house again, only six months later. It made no sense to him. The home was obviously known to the Russians.

Maybe they want us to act. Maybe this is a trap.

Brooding, the giant studied the discs.

There were three agents featured in the videos. They were tall and very fit, and judging from their movements, very aware of their surroundings, scanning the area while not appearing to do so—obvious tradecraft to Fyodor.

For the next two weeks, he studied the videos of the safe house, noting their arrivals and departures, careful to log their every movement to discern a pattern and thus, a vulnerability. When he felt he found a weak point, he phoned Petro.

After the greetings were finished, Fyodor said, "I think the Americans have laid a trap for us."

"Why do you think that, my friend?" Petro asked.

"There are two agents in the home at all times who never go outdoors or answer the door. A third agent goes out for food or groceries at intermittent times with no obvious pattern.

We tried sending children selling cookies. We even sent an attractive female selling magazines. I confirmed they were in residence, but no one answered the door."

"They probably wired the house for outside cameras," Petro said.

"I believe that is correct," Fyodor concurred. "But there may be another way."

"How?"

"They have to eat. The next time the agent goes out for food, I will have a talk with him. Perhaps he will be willing to give us the names we want," Fyodor said.

"Are you sure there no patterns to their movements?"

"No, they are random, as though they know they're being watched."

"Do they ever go out together?" Petro asked.

"No. Two stay in the house at all times. It is never left unoccupied. It is the only time they are separated," Fyodor said. "It's almost an invitation."

"Then they probably have others watching the house from nearby," Petro said.

"I agree. The house across the street shows no lights and appears uninhabited," the giant said. "I believe they are watching from there."

"Has anyone followed the one who gets the food?"

"Just me," Fyodor laughed. "The next time he goes out, I will take him and see what he can tell us."

"Excellent."

Fyodor Kaminski settled his bulk in the front seat of the Black Lincoln Town car. It was one of the few sedans large enough to accommodate him behind the wheel. He was parked on the street three blocks from the safe house awaiting a cell phone call to inform him when an agent left the house. Less than an hour into his wait, his cell buzzed.

"Yes."

"He's moving. A gray sedan, license plate WRS024, is headed your way," said the voice.

Fyodor closed the phone and waited. One minute later, the sedan passed by. He allowed the car a one-block head start, and then pulled out into the residential street. He followed at a discreet distance until the agent turned into a strip mall anchored by a large grocery store. He drove past, circled back through the opposite end of the center, parked and watched the occupant of the gray sedan enter the grocery store.

Fifteen minutes later, the man emerged carrying two grocery bags, one in each arm. As he approached his vehicle, he clicked the automatic unlocking device with the key fob held in one hand, then shifted both bags into one arm as he opened the trunk. As he bent to deposit his purchases, he felt a sudden prick in his right buttock and a slight burning sensation, followed by the feeling of falling into the trunk; then, oblivion.

He never saw Fyodor. When he awoke, Fyodor had duct-taped his wrists, ankles and waist to a sturdy metal chair. He appeared to be in a house cellar.

"It says here that your name is Joseph Scott." The heavily accented Russian voice echoed, its deep bass bouncing over the hard surfaces of the basement. "I imagine you were hoping to meet me under different circumstances." Fyodor laughed. "But this will have to do."

The giant moved in front of Agent Scott, offering a first glimpse of his abductor. "You will talk to me now, if you want to live." He dropped the wallet and ID to the floor.

Scott sat there, mesmerized by the sheer size of the human being before him. He was still suffering the effects of the drug that Fyodor had injected into him. It seemed impossible to focus on the giant's words.

Fyodor slapped him, knocking the agent and the chair sideways onto the dirty cement floor. The agent's head bounced on the unyielding surface, before Fyodor yanked him upright as though he were weightless. He was clearly outclassed by this beast of a man.

Fyodor bent close to his face. "Do I have your attention now?"

The agent nodded vigorously.

Fyodor placed a picture of two women before him. "Good. I am looking for two women: one tall with dark hair and another short with blonde hair; both very pretty. You work with them, yes?"

"I don't know who…"

Fyodor picked Agent Scott up by his throat, cutting off his answer. He shook him like a rag doll, and then dropped him to the floor. Miraculously, the chair remained upright. Scott understood the man's brute strength and felt genuine fear.

"I did not ask what you do not know. I asked if you work with these two women."

Again, the agent nodded in affirmation.

"What are their names?"

"They work for another agency. We do not use names."

The giant did not speak. He reached out with two fingers, his index and middle digit, and hooked them over Scott's collar bone. With slow deliberation, he applied downward pressure to the fragile bone until it snapped cleanly in two. Scott screamed at the sudden pain.

When his cries subsided, Fyodor started in again. This time he held two fingers over the other collar bone as he spoke. "Surely you have heard a name, something on the telephone, perhaps?"

Slowly, he increased the pressure on the other scapula.

"I heard a name. I heard a name," he blurted.

"And what was it?"

"Erika."

"Erika what?"

"Only Erika; that's all I heard." By now he was rushing to speak, anything to stop the giant from doing that again.

"Which one is Erika?" Fyodor asked. "The dark one, or the blonde one?"

"I don't know."

Fyodor eased up on the pressure. Then he moved abruptly. Snap. The scream echoed off the walls. The break was sudden this time.

Once again, Fyodor waited in silence until his whimpers died out.

"You will tell me what I want to know, Agent Scott, sooner or later. Give me the other name."

"I don't know it."

"Are you sure?"

"Yes. I would tell you if I knew. Honest to God, I would." He was pleading now. "Please."

"Agent Scott, you are making me angry."

He took Scott's hand in one of his huge paws. He separated the man's index and middle fingers from the pinky and ring finger and held them in his left hand. Then he grasped the other two fingers in his right hand.

Scott felt his bladder release, the fear of what was about to happen overpowered his ability to control any bodily function. Fyodor ignored him.

"THE NAME!"

He couldn't make his tongue work. With a mighty pull, Fyodor separated the two pairs of digits, cracking all the bones in his hand, and then, with a tremendous effort, ripped the flesh all the way to the stump of his wrist. Blood fountained from the hideous wound, spraying everything in a four-foot arc.

Fyodor stepped back from the grisly scene. The agent shrieked an inhuman sound, and then passed out.

To no one, Fyodor mused, "I always wondered how that

would feel."

After Joseph Scott regained consciousness, Fyodor continued his assault until he was satisfied the man had no further information to surrender. He insinuated one knee between the agent's thighs, pinning the chair to the floor, then grabbed his head in his two huge hands, one on the chin, the other a pincer on the nape of his neck. With a violent twist, he spun his head to the side, breaking his neck and ending his torment. He continued twisting until the head hung loose, facing backwards on his neck.

That was how they found him in the grocery store parking lot. His seat belt propped him up with his torso posed in the appropriate driving position, while his face stared out the rear window.

Chapter 9

"That motherfucker!"

"Who?" Sheila asked.

"Fyodor. He's the only one who could have done this," Erika said.

Donny said nothing. He knew it was best to let her run on when Erika was in a mood like this.

They were in the downstairs conference room. Graphic pictures of Agent Scott littered the table. Night had overtaken the yard outside. It was pitch dark except for small garden lights outlining the path to the pool.

Sheila gathered up the photos and put them inside a folder, out of sight.

"Your anger is understandable," Sheila said. "But we have to put that aside and concentrate on finding them before they inflict any more damage."

Erika was brought up short by the remark. It gave birth to an idea.

"Why not do the same to them?" Erika asked. "Inflict our own brand of damage."

"How?"

"We know of several of their front businesses, like the strip club in Las Vegas," Erika said. "I'm sure Donny can come up with several ways to damage them, and I have some ideas of my own."

"That's what scares me," Sheila said. "I've seen what you're capable of when you get like this."

Sheila turned to Donny. "Please compile a list of their assets, ongoing enterprises, and anything else you can find.

Then provide me with a menu of possible actions that would interrupt or curtail their most profitable businesses."

"Will do," Donny said.

"I'd like the profile of who they put in the Las Vegas club to replace Afanasi and that crazy little bitch," Erika said.

"Why?" Sheila asked.

"I want to know who we're dealing with there."

"Just so long as you get my personal approval before any action."

"Absolutely," Erika said.

"Okay, let's get moving," Sheila said.

Chapter 10

"Did he give you a name, Fyodor?" Leonid asked.

"Yes. Erika."

"Just Erika? No last name?"

" No, sir. No other name. He did not know any more. Of that I am sure," the giant answered.

"Which one is Erika? The brunette? Or the blonde in the ball cap?"

"He did not know that either. He only heard that name used in his partner's phone call. Just Erika."

"You are certain?" Leonid pressed.

"Yes, he would have given me his mother by the time we finished. He did not know any more."

"Can you take one of his partners and find out?"

"I will try, if you wish it."

Fyodor would do anything to please his boss, but not out of fear. He feared no one. Leonid had seen Fyodor's value and given him a chance when everyone else in power dismissed the giant. Fyodor would walk through hell for him.

"Fyodor, would that put you in danger?" Leonid said.

"They have changed their security arrangements now. Food is delivered in an unmarked van. There are at least two men in the house that I can see. I think it is a trap for me. It feels that way. I think there are more agents that watch the van and the house."

Leonid paused for a few moments before deciding.

"Okay, go back to New York. Use private air travel. There is nothing more for you there. We will work with this name. There are other ways."

"Yes, sir. Oh, and I left them a message."

"What sort of message?" Leonid wasn't sure what to make of this last comment.

"I rearranged his anatomy before I put him in his car." Fyodor explained.

"You realize they will know immediately who did this?"

"Yes."

Leonid could visualize Fyodor's grin when he replied.

Putting down the phone, Leonid turned to Raina. She was seated before the roaring fire in the cavernous fireplace. Through the large pane of glass, the snow had stopped falling and the full moon lit up Aspen. A trail of lights lit up the ribbon of Highway 82 that meandered through town, a slipstream of red and white.

"We have a name."

"Who?" Raina asked, her eyes lighting up.

"Erika."

"Only Erika?"

"Yes."

Raina stood and paced to look out the window. "Which one is she?"

"We do not know yet, but we will."

"Where is Fyodor?"

"He is returning to New York. He cannot learn any more from the agents."

"Erika," she hissed the name. "Erika."

Leonid brought over the wine bottle and topped off her glass, refilled his, and kissed the top of her head.

"We will find her, Raina. We **will** find her." Walking over to join her and take in the spectacular night-time view, he said, "I promise."

Chapter 11

"Oleg Yakolev has replaced Afanasi in Las Vegas," Donny said. "Another woman is running the prostitution ring—Maksima Orlov. We don't have much intelligence on either one, but Oleg is ex-KGB, so we can assume a prior relationship with Leonid Utkin, and by extension, the others too."

He put photos up on the screen of the conference room. Oleg was an unremarkable man, six feet tall with bushy eyebrows that resembled baby caterpillars and a large push-broom mustache. His short-cropped brown hair sprouted over a pasty white complexion, and obsidian eyes placed his origins somewhere in the south of the former Soviet Union.

"At one time, he was a drill sergeant in the Russian Army, so we can also assume he is familiar with military weapons and tactics, and he probably enjoyed disciplining his troops. Drill sergeants over there are not known for their pleasant demeanor."

He clicked to the next picture. "This is Maksima Orlov. She does not pop up anywhere on our radar. She is an attractive woman. She may have been a former model brought in by this group, rising through the ranks to become one of them. We just don't know for sure."

The tall woman in the photo had long dark hair, and the black bangs that shaded her eyes gave her the appearance of a bird of prey. Her high cheekbones, perfect nose, and full lips reminded Erika of a high fashion model just past her prime.

"She appears to be the new manager of the Las Vegas club, while Oleg looks to be the enforcer. She is the liaison for the local politics and does their banking. She must have a business background or she would not be in that position."

"Not much there to go on," Erika said.

"Given what's transpired, that's exactly what I would expect," Sheila commented. "The FBI kept local law enforcement in the dark while cleaning up the Vegas incident. The FBI cordoned off the warehouse, took control of the premises, and secured the full cooperation of the police by labeling it a terrorist plot. The mayor of Las Vegas knew the negative impact a terrorist plot would have on tourism and was delighted to put an end to the local investigation into it. No one outside of this organization knows about the men Erika shot outside the strip club. Our team cleaned that up too. It appears our adversaries share our interest in discretion."

"So, you think they're putting semi-legit management in there to deflect any more local scrutiny?" Donny asked.

"That's exactly what I would do," Sheila said. "Make an attempt at legitimacy. Maybe make some political donations to both sides of the aisle."

"If they don't own them already," Erika said.

"What do you mean by that?" Sheila asked.

"We already know about the Senator's activities inside the club. He's probably not the only one."

"Meanwhile, we now have the beautiful, probably charming Maksima Orlov in charge of the club's management and presumably also acting as the liaison between the business and state politicians," Donny said.

"We really should keep an eye on Senator Ross going forward. If he is in their pocket, we're going to experience all sorts of problems," Erika said.

"Not to sound argumentative, but I think we should operate on the assumption he's already been in their pocket," Donny said.

"Are you referring to the film that started all this in the first place?" Sheila asked.

"Yes," Donny replied. "Think about it. The Senator is filmed smoking crack and cavorting with two known prostitutes. He never receives the film or a threat of blackmail and has only us to assure him we've destroyed the evidence."

"He can't be sure it doesn't exist," Sheila answered her own question.

Erika wisely kept silent. She knew Donny had sent a copy of the Senator's antics to him to guarantee Sheila's confirmation. But so far, Sheila was unaware of that strategy. And it appeared that the plan had backfired on them. The Senator was sure the evidence existed. He had a copy. It was certainly the reason he got himself appointed as oversight chairman of their agency.

"Let's operate from now on as if Senator Ross is not on our side. We have to assume he will protect his interests, which may not be ours."

"Agreed," Sheila said, "although, it will be a very fine line to walk."

Chapter 12

Rita Jackson, a forty-something mother of three, sat before her home computer. Her home was on one of the largest parcels left undivided in Montecito, a wealthy enclave just south of Santa Barbara, California. It comprised twenty-seven manicured acres surrounded by an eight-foot block wall. The house itself boasted an unnecessary sixteen thousand square feet, a seven-car garage, two guest homes, and impressive facilities for horses that no one rode.

A platoon of caregivers, maids and housemen raised Rita's children—ages fourteen, sixteen, and nineteen. The parents rarely interacted daily with their children as their respective careers required extensive travel and time away from Montecito. They gave generously to all the right charities, belonged to all the right clubs, and socialized regularly with high-ranking politicians and industry legends.

Rita enjoyed designer clothes, expensive jewelry, private air travel, and chauffeured automobiles. She could afford all these accoutrements since her annual salary and stock holdings ran well into eight figures. Her husband's income, as a captain of the aerospace industry was even more substantial.

Her husband, Wendell, was a quiet, well-respected visionary in the aerospace industry. He was well-liked by his peers and a very good friend to only a few people he trusted. His wife was not among his friends. They'd grown apart over the years since their children had been born. Gradually, they moved into different professional and personal orbits. After several years of not acknowledging the break in their relationship, Wendell began having an affair with his corporate secretary and Rita began taking a procession of lovers, both male and female. They simply drifted apart.

Although Wendell knew about her lovers, the email she had just opened threatened to expose her in very public ways.

She read the message for the fourth time, still wondering how a stranger could have acquired her private email address; only three of her intimate acquaintances had that address. And yet here it was—a message that detailed her recent engagement with a young man who possessed an amazing talent with blindfolds and fur cuffs. Her body still vibrated when she thought of him.

The email did not contain a direct threat. It posed several hypotheticals.

How would her family react if photos of her liaisons appeared in the world of social media? How would her business peers react? What financial impact would they have on her bank's revenue?

She knew the answer: it would be devastating!

The writer posed a solution; one that her good friend Jerry Ross could help with. If Rita replied with the names of the two women who had invaded the warehouse in Las Vegas, all of these questions would be rendered moot. Her secrets would be safe. The email's author would contact Rita in one week and would expect the names at that time.

Rita was a guiltless hedonist. She enjoyed her dalliances and lived for the next one, just as she would eagerly anticipate a new travel destination or business acquisition. Honesty never entered the equation—she was only honest when it suited her, and it rarely did. If it weren't for the negative impact it would have on her financially, she might post the photos herself. She didn't care what Wendell thought about her sexual life, and only cared a little bit what the children would think of her—they were almost grown now anyway. They would get over it.

No, this was a business problem, not a personal one, and she would approach it as such. She picked up her cell phone and called the esteemed Senator from Oregon, Jerry Ross. He was the Chairman of the Intelligence Committee that funded covert operations in the United States through her bank, and he was indebted to her on many levels, not just because of the millions she'd raised for his election campaigns, but also because she knew about his relationships with hookers and strip clubs. She had a lot of dirt on him. He would help her solve this problem.

"Hello, Rita, so nice to hear from you," Senator Ross personally answered his private line.

"Senator, how are you?"

"Fine, Rita, fine. And you?"

"I'm doing well, thank you. But I would like to ask your advice on a personal matter."

"Well, I hope I can help then."

"Oh, I'm sure you can," Rita said. "I need your expertise."

"What sort of expertise?"

"The most personal sort," she replied. "You see, there may be visual evidence of a very personal nature I would rather not surface in the public arena. It was suggested you might be able to ensure that never happens."

"And how would I be able to do that?"

"Well, I was given to understand that you may have a similar exposure issue with these people that you would prefer to remain private."

"Go on. "

"Our friends are looking for the names of two women who apparently invaded their business location in Las Vegas and took some of their property. They have assured me that upon the receipt of those two names, all visual references to either of us would disappear forever."

"If," the Senator emphasized, "If these two could be found, I take it your friends would do their utmost to get their 'property' back?"

"No question."

"And do you believe there would be some sort of retribution involved?"

"Knowing these folks, there most certainly would be some of that involved," she said. "I am assured that all of the participants involved, including you and me, would attain a permanent solution."

The Senator had a primordial instinct for survival and Rita had provided him with the solution to two very vexing problems: the existence of the videos themselves and the woman he suspected of sending it privately to his email, Sheila. He knew her as Sheila Gibbons. He didn't know the other woman's name, as an agent's true identity would be shielded even from him. If something were to occur that removed Sheila from the agency, he would be in a prime position to swoop in and install his own Director before anyone could stop him.

The videos and any other damning evidence could be either destroyed or used to his advantage. It took only a few scant seconds to recognize the gift he'd been presented. Once he was in charge, the other name would be simple for him to acquire.

"Unfortunately, Rita, I have no access to that sort of information, and if I did, I certainly would not 'publicly' disclose it, especially over a cell phone."

"I understand."

The Senator continued. "We're having a dinner for some friends here next month, and I thought I would send an invitation for you and Wendell to join us. Is your mailing address still the same?"

"Yes, it is."

"Great. I'll send the invitation by next week," he said. "I'm sorry I couldn't help you out with your problem."

"Don't give it a second thought, Senator. Good-bye."

"Good-bye, Rita."

The Senator sat for a moment, a smile fixed in place. She was such a harlot, so dishonest that even her lizard brain would have grasped the double meaning of his reply. He simply had to be certain that whatever happened could not be traced back to him. He would give it some consideration.

Rita Jackson sat at the desk of her huge home office. The custom marble-topped desk was centered across from an enormous stone fireplace, flanked by two chenille love seats. The coffered ceiling and full-length book shelves were constructed of rare zebra ebony wood that lent the room a masculine ambiance softened by silk drapery around the expansive view windows.

She was just about to leave the room when her cell phone buzzed, signaling an incoming text message. The caller ID read unknown, but she still took a moment to glance at the message.

Sheila Gibbons, Los Angeles

That was all it said. She scrolled through her messages to see if she could identify the sender by the area code or number, but her phone could not provide a clue.

In Fort Worth, Texas, an aide to Senator Ross, having finished fulfilling the strange request to text a name to a California cell number, dropped the throwaway cell in a dumpster. He'd bought the prepaid cell with cash, sent the text, removed the battery and disposed of the phone as directed.

He never gave it a second thought. The Senator was a very private man, and he'd issued far stranger instructions in the past. This errand didn't even make the top ten.

Leonid Utkin and Raina Polzin were sitting in the bar at Little Nell, the boutique hotel at the base of Aspen Mountain. They were both excellent skiers and had just finished a punishing afternoon of racing down the upper slopes before descending to the lower terrain and maneuvering through the throngs of less skilled skiers that always congested the base area near closing time.

They sat at a corner table nursing their drinks, vodka for

Raina, a single malt Scotch for Leonid. They'd stored their boots and jackets in personal lockers below the hotel, but they still wore waterproof ski pants and sweaters. In a town known for beauty and celebrity, they still made quite an impression. Raina, blonde, beautiful, and aloof, towered over most of the men and all the women. Leonid, only an inch or two taller, with a trim athletic body and a hint of grey seeping into his longish dark hair, projected an image of well-deserved success.

Hearing it buzz, Leonid studied an email on his cell phone and a wolfish grin appeared on his face. "If you order me another single-malt on the rocks, I'll give you a present."

"What kind of present?"

"Drink first, present after," he answered.

She raised her hand, caught the bartender's eye, and circled her finger over the table. He went to work on their drinks.

"Now, my present," she said, holding out her hand.

Leonid handed his cell phone over. She read. *Sheila Gibbons, Los Angeles.*

"It worked."

"Yes, it did."

As the waitress approached with their drinks, she noticed Raina's feverish look. The flush was not the result of an afternoon spent on the slopes. It went far deeper than that. It bordered on maniacal.

The waitress set their drinks on the table without comment before winding her way through the plush leather chairs and tables filling up with the Aspen ski crowd. The couple in the corner she'd just served hadn't even acknowledged her. They were in another world.

Chapter 13

Now that they were back from their Hawaiian vacation, Sheila summoned Erika to appear at the Bel Air estate to participate in an official debriefing regarding the Logan Heights operation. She drove through the familiar wrought iron security gates, shut down the deep rumble of the V-8 and entered the front door. She was greeted with a hug and a kiss by Donny and Sheila and excused herself to use the restroom. Refreshed, she left the bathroom to find the two of them still waiting for her.

Puzzled, she said, "What's up? I know where the conference room is."

"We won't be using the conference room today," Sheila said. "Come on out back."

Stifling her curiosity, Erika followed them out to the rear of the property. She never tired of the serenity that descended upon her when she spent time there. There was a large swimming pool designed as a Hawaiian grotto complete with large boulders, waterfalls, towering palms and spreading fichus trees. Riots of colorful flowerbeds exploded around the grounds. A gentle breeze carried the sweet smell of jasmine, and the sound of falling water soothed Erika.

They skirted the pool and sat at a bench where Donny and Erika had hatched many prior schemes together. Erika shot a questioning look at Donny.

Sheila smiled in answer. "C'mon Erika, you think Richard and I didn't know this was your private conference room with Donny?"

"That obvious?"

"The only reason Richard didn't put a recording device out here is because I asked him not to."

"They knew the whole time." Donny laughed.

"Okay, okay. I get it. Why are we out here now though?"

Sheila explained. "We're going to be doing things a bit differently now that Senator Ross has oversight of our operation. No more conference room debriefs since they're recorded on audio and video. No images of our agents or names are to be included in any report that he might view. I will not be responsible for any leaks that occur on my watch, and I can't be certain of our security where the Senator is concerned. As you recall, he has a certain fondness for young women and the occasional crack pipe."

"Thank you. That was going to be an issue for me, especially since we still have the Russian problem to deal with," Erika said.

"Let's discuss what happened in Barrio Logan," Donny said. "You can give us the authentic version of the events, and then I will distill it down to what we want the Senator to know."

Erika looked at Sheila through a different set of eyes now. "You really thought all this through, didn't you?"

"With Donny's help," she answered. "I didn't want to start my tenure as Director by compromising one of my best agents. That's the reason we didn't discuss this any further before we went to Maui. I had to be certain I was installed as Director before committing this to paper."

"The Senator will be receiving a standardized report on each operation, redirected by me personally, and traceable by its content to only the Senator's office. A sort of Trojan Horse in case something comes back to bite us," Donny added.

"Machiavelli would be proud," Erika said.

"So, what happened in Barrio Logan?"

"Just what I told you before."

"Nothing to add?"

"No," Erika answered.

"Are you okay with leaving it up to Donny to complete the

report?"

Erika couldn't suppress the grin. "Of course."

"Then we're done with that one. Try not to shoot any more bystanders, okay?"

"Okay." Erika hoped her relief wasn't as obvious as it felt.

"Any movement on the Russian thing?" she asked.

"Nothing," Sheila said. "Leonid and Raina must have gone underground. We've heard nothing of Petro, and even though Fyodor must have been here in Los Angeles, nothing of him either."

"Are you sure Fyodor was here?" Erika asked. "The broken neck could have been an intentional ploy to take us off the trail."

Donny answered. "We have a report of a large, bald man boarding a chartered jet out of Burbank the day after our agent was found. It landed at Teterboro, New Jersey, so he could be anywhere in the New York metropolitan area, or even New England, for that matter."

"A lot of big men are bald. Any photos?"

"No, but the credit card used to book the flight originated from a bank in Eastern Europe."

"That makes for a better case, I admit. But, it's not conclusive," Erika said.

"Erika, the horrific wound to our agent's hand was not the result of an incision. His fingers were pulled apart by someone, or something, capable of exerting enormous pressure. Your original instinct was correct."

"He has to be put down," she said.

"I agree," Sheila said. "But we have to find him first."

"Donny, can we put pressure on our people in New York? The Russians have to operate their business there somehow," Erika asked.

"So far, nothing has turned up," he said. "They use New York banks and lawyers to control those businesses.

Everything is legit. We can't touch them. If any of them show up though, we'll know immediately."

"What about Las Vegas?"

"What about it?"

"Can we pressure them there?" Erika was relentless.

"Same scenario," Donny said. "Local banks and attorneys. No prostitution, no extra- curricular activities by the dancers. They've all hunkered down. My guess is they'll stay that way until they get the opportunity to deal with us."

"We're obviously hurting them financially by curtailing the illegal stuff. Can we plant drugs on the premises, something like that?"

Sheila said, "We've discussed that. Too risky. All the clubs are under video surveillance 24/7. There's no way to plant anything. They'd also have irrefutable evidence of a frame-up."

Erika pondered these set-backs for a few moments. "If we can't hurt their physical locations, then we have to go after their people."

Sheila sighed. "You know how I feel about that sort of thing, Erika. It makes us no better than them. Unless, they're guilty of an offense that specifically falls within our agency charter, that's off the table."

"Okay."

"I mean it, Erika."

"I heard you."

Erika drove back to San Diego that evening. Donny would be crafting the written report for the Senator. Upon her arrival home, she booted up her agency computer to find an email from Ray, her long-range shooting instructor. He had received a Barrett 50 caliber, long-range sniper rifle and tuned it to Erika's specifications. He asked if she was available to come up to Owens Valley to qualify on it. Sheila had been copied, so Erika dialed her office.

"Hi Erika," Sheila said. "You miss us already?"

"Hey, Sheila," Erika replied. "Of course, I miss you guys already." The humor in her tone was obvious. "Did you see the email from Ray?"

"About the Barrett rifle?"

"Yes," Erika answered.

"Yes, I saw it."

"Any chance we could go up for a few days—get away for a while?"

"I'd like that, but I'm buried here. Why don't you go instead? It'll do you some good to get away and see the guys anyway."

"Okay. I think I will. I'm available on cell if you need me."

"No worries. I'll talk to you later."

"Bye."

"Bye."

Chapter 14

Erika made arrangements with the pilots who would fly her to the small Municipal airport in Independence, California. There were no commercial flights to that area of the Owens Valley and, besides, bringing home a .50 caliber Barrett rifle would prove problematic on a commercial airline. She made her flight arrangements for the next morning, and then emailed Ray with her arrival times. She shut down her computer and prepared for bed.

The next morning, she packed enough clothes for three days and drove to Palomar Airport in the North County of San Diego. She parked her car in the long-term lot at the fixed base operation, and waited in the small lounge for her flight. Within ten minutes, a Beechcraft King Air 350 descended from a cloudless sky and taxied over to General Aviation.

Two pilots emerged from the twin turbo prop and entered the lounge. Erika was very familiar with John and Eric from several previous trips. They hugged her and exchanged pleasantries. After excusing themselves for a restroom break, the three of them went directly to the plane.

It was bigger than Erika thought it would be, gleaming white paint with red trim, caramel leather interior, with seating for eight passengers. John pointed out the small lavatory in the rear, stowed her duffle bag, and closed the door.

"Ready?"

"Yep."

"Ok, buckle up, we'll head out. It should take us about forty-five minutes, door to door."

"Wow, that's pretty fast for a prop job."

"I know it's no Gulfstream, but this is one of the safest, most reliable planes in the air. It's rated for an altitude of

35,000 feet, with a range of 1500 miles. We can cruise at over 500 kilometers an hour and land and take off from some pretty short airfields. This plane has been a work horse for well over fifty years. And you'll love the ride."

"I'm not sure what you said, but I always feel safe with you guys," Erika said.

"Then sit back and enjoy. Can I get you anything before we take off?"

"No, John, I'm all set." She buckled herself in while he made his way to the cockpit.

As promised, the flight was smooth and quick. They were buffeted by the thermals during their descent, but that was normal for the Owens Valley. Several altitude records had been set here by glider pilots as the thermals rising off the 13,000-foot peaks created the perfect environment for motor-less aircraft.

Jim and Ray were both there to greet her, their familiar grey Suburban parked just off the tarmac. They didn't bother stopping at the small, green wooden structure that served as the Independence Airport. They threw her duffle bag in the rear cargo area and drove south onto Highway 395.

She'd greeted both men warmly, having formed close bonds with each after some initial awkward moments in the years before. After dozens of shooting lessons from the two men, Ericka learned to trust them implicitly in any situation. Jim had won two national long-range shooting contests, and Ray had won more pistol combat contests than he cared to remember. In fact, he wasn't even required to be present for this lesson.

Ray simply enjoyed Erika's company almost as much as he liked to watch her shoot. He drove, and Jim sat in the front passenger seat, while Erika sat behind Ray to converse easily with Jim.

"So, you found me a new toy?" Erika asked.

"Oh, yeah!" Jim's enthusiasm was obvious. He was acting like a ten-year old with a new bicycle. "This baby will put a .50 caliber round out to an effective range of 2,000 yards."

"That's over a mile!" Erika said, her eyes lighting up. "How do you know what you're shooting at?"

"The optics are incredible," he said. "There's also a mini-computer that mounts directly on the scope that factors in temperature and barometric pressure and calculates angle cosine and displays rifle cant. After you determine range to your target, you just turn the elevation knob until the Barrett Optical Ranging System, BORS, screen matches the target distance. The ballistic solution is calculated automatically by a Windows software program to put you right on your target."

"This is exciting," she said. "I've never heard of such a rifle. Do you laser for distance first or does it do that, too?"

"I like to laser it independent of the system to be certain, but I believe there's a program for that also," he explained. "In this case, I've put human-size targets at 400, 600, 800 and 1000 yards. We'll spend the next two days putting holes in them."

"Is there a suppressor for that large a caliber?"

"Yes, and they also make a BORS for night force, in case you want to shoot in the dark."

By now they were on the dirt road heading west, off the highway. They would be at the range in just a few minutes. Erika sat back in her seat and tried to contain her excitement. *This would be fun!*

They parked under the now familiar grove of willow trees that grew along a seasonal stream, fed by the snow melt from the towering mountains to the west. She helped to unload the gear and set up at the shooting station. Today, they would be shooting from a bench rest until Erika became intimate with the new weapon. Then she would practice from a variety of positions; prone, kneeling, sitting, lying flat, and perhaps even off hand, meaning standing upright with nothing to lean against or steady the weapon with.

Once they were settled around a wooden picnic table, Jim removed the substantial rifle from its protective case and set it on the table, resting on a retractable bipod under the barrel and the rifle butt that featured a built-in handle at the rear. Its sheer size and obvious weight were necessary to accommodate the .50 caliber ammunition and propel a bullet of that size accurately to ranges exceeding one mile. In fact, the bullet could travel up to 7000 yards when shot in an arc before that incredible amount of energy was expended, thus, the need for a minimum of a five-mile safe zone when practicing at long range.

Jim began explaining the rifle and its capabilities. "This is a Barrett M107A1, .50 caliber rifle designed to be used with a suppressor, increasing its effectiveness as a sniper rifle. Without it, the sound alone is distinctive enough to give away the shooter's location. It has a four-port cylindrical muzzle break designed to work with the quick attach suppressor to reduce recoil. Erika, this rifle packs quite a wallop. I brought some extra shoulder padding for you, by the way."

He handed her a padded shooting vest with the extra shoulder pads.

"This is a semi-automatic rifle with a ten-round magazine. Unloaded, it weighs 27.4 lbs. with an overall length of 57 inches, with a 29-mil barrel length. It propels a 661-grain bullet at a muzzle velocity of 2,750 feet per second. Even a mile out, it retains a muzzle velocity slightly over 1100 feet per second, enough to do some serious damage. A loaded ten-round magazine weighs another four pounds bringing the total weight to over thirty lbs. Not something you want to haul around all day."

Jim handed a mammoth cartridge to Erika. "Shit, that's almost as long as my whole hand," she said.

Jim stifled his amusement at her remark and continued, "This is a .50 BMG cartridge. It is 5.45 inches in length with a .804-inch diameter. This round can produce between 10,000 and 15,000-foot pounds of energy against whatever it hits. It was first produced as an anti-vehicle round. A standard hunting rifle produces muzzle energies between 2,000 and 3,000-foot pounds, so you can imagine what a .50 BMG, at six times that level, would do to a human body. It wouldn't matter what part of the human anatomy it hits. The resulting damage would be fatal."

"How much does wind affect a round of this size?" Erika asked. She was hefting its weight in her hand. It was easily longer and thicker than her fingers.

"That's what makes it so effective at long range. Because of its high ballistic coefficient, it suffers less drift from a cross-wind than a smaller caliber. This afternoon, when the wind kicks up, you'll be amazed how little it moves even at extreme ranges."

"Will I have to compensate for windage?"

"Yes, that's the only calculation the BORS system attached to a scope won't give you. The rest, as you'll see, is almost automatic."

Jim pointed to the rectangular green screen mounted atop the scope on the black rifle. "This is the BORS system I was explaining in the car. It's like having a mini-computer on your rifle. You enter the cartridge specified—in this case, the .50 BMG, distance to target, and target size, and the internal sensors calculate the ballistic solution. At that point, you match your sight picture to the resolution and squeeze off the round. Assuming you're on target, you get a first-shot-on-target capability that was unheard of before this system was developed."

Erika had a competitive streak. "Any confirmed records with that weapon?"

"Bob Furlong, a Canadian Army sniper has the longest confirmed kill of a Taliban Commander in Afghanistan at 2,657 yards!"

"Oh, c'mon. You're kidding. A mile and a half?"

"Not at all. It was even farther than that. There have been similar shots made in combat as well. Not too long ago, an Army Ranger Instructor in Texas hit a 1,000-yard target, off hand, in front of nine witnesses. It was also videotaped for confirmation."

"Off hand? Standing up? No leaning against anything or propping up the weapon?"

"That's right. Completely off hand."

Erika pointed to the scope. "What is it?"

"A Schmidt Bender 5-25 x 56 mm scope. It's tuned to the BORS system."

"This is incredible. You think I can handle a weapon this size?"

"That's what we're here to find out," Jim said, a huge smile on his face. "Erika, you look like a five-year-old on Christmas Eve."

"Is it that obvious?"

"Yep."

"Then let's get started."

Jim directed her attention to the weapon, pointing out the safety and bolt mechanism to seat the first round and the massive ten round magazine. He instructed Erika to practice dry firing the weapon while unloaded, to get a feel for its size, weight, trigger resistance, and personal fit. Once he was satisfied, he had her unload the magazine and reload it, so she was certain about the number of cartridges she had ready to fire.

He asked her to pick up the weapon and take it to the shooting bench situated ten yards away. Hefting the weapon in two hands, Erika exclaimed, "Wow, this *is* heavy!"

"Over thirty pounds, loaded," Jim agreed. "Not something you want to carry around on maneuvers."

She lugged it over to the bench, which resembled an elementary school desk on steroids, designed so the shooter could slide in from the left side. There was an elongated bench to set the rifle on and a built-in arm rest on the right for a shooter's elbow.

Once Erika was situated behind the rifle, Jim had her dial the knob on the BORS system atop the scope to set the target distance at 400 yards and recheck the ammunition type against the catalogue contained in the miniature computer. Once all the parameters were matched up, he handed over the loaded magazine.

"Arm the weapon and seat a round." With a wry smile he added, "Oh, wait. Put on the extra padding. You can thank me later."

Erika shrugged into the padded vest and racked the slide to seat the first round. Everyone put on their ear protection and safety glasses.

"Now line up the scope with the BORS input until both lines overlap perfectly and prepare to fire."

"Any windage?" She asked.

"Not at this range. You can adjust as we move farther out," Jim said. "Do you have the 400-yard target acquired?"

"I do."

"Fire when ready."

"Off safe." Erika snuggled into a familiar position.

"Firing," she said.

The concussion, even though she was expecting it, jolted her backwards. The kinetic energy, even ameliorated by the automatic bolt system designed to absorb the kick along with the ported barrel, was still enough to move her body back against her seat. Her eye never left the scope, though, as she maintained constant contact with the weapon, a habit with all good snipers. She was rewarded with a perfect hit, dead center.

She looked up at Jim, returning his huge smile. "Thought you'd like that!" She heard his loud guffaws through the sound-deadening ear muffs.

"Oh, yeah. Dead center," she crowed.

Jim patted her on the shoulder, one of the few human beings allowed that privilege. "Put nine more on the 400, and we'll move out. I want you real confident of your bullet placement. We can adjust for windage as we progress."

"Will do."

Erika took her time sighting and putting the remaining rounds on target at about 20- to 30-second intervals, checking the bullet placement after each shot. Satisfied by her newly-found comfort level and having obliterated most of the center of the cardboard target, she removed the empty magazine, made sure the rifle was racked back to an empty chamber and stood up, removing her ear protection. She couldn't, however, remove her huge grin.

"That is a serious weapon," she said rolling her right shoulder, knowing she would be sore the next day.

"I brought Advil," Ray said, handing her three pills and a bottle of water. "You can thank me for that later, too." He laughed.

The three of them belonged to a unique, politically incorrect group that enjoyed the precision equipment of their trade, respected the capability and responsibility that went with it, and reveled in the private company of their fellow shooters. It was even more special to the three of them since Erika's unique abilities with weapons were known to only those within her agency cell, these two men, Donny, and Sheila.

In Las Vegas, there were four more who had witnessed Erika's startling ability with a gun through a video feed. All four were Russians. There was also Felix...

Chapter 15

Over the next two days, Erika practiced using the .50 caliber Barrett Rifle at 400, 600, 800, and 1,000 yards and from a variety of positions until both she and Jim were satisfied with her performance. She was living on Advil and her shoulder was already black and blue. She mentally thanked Jim for the extra padding each night. The following morning, Ray and Jim drove her back to the range for a more competitive type of shooting. When they retrieved the gear from the Suburban's cargo compartment, Erika discovered three Barrett Rifles instead of one. There were also three shooting benches set up facing no discernible targets.

"Ok, guys, what's up?" She asked.

"Oh, you thought you were going to be the only one having any fun out here?" Jim asked.

"I guess not," Erika said. "Where are the targets?"

Ray pointed west to the mountains. "Out there, in the scrub brush, at 1,500 yards. There are three of them, ten yards apart; one for each of us. Yours is in the center, painted red. Mine is white, on the right. Jim's is yellow, on the left. I'll show you through a spotting scope."

Erika had perfect vision, but she couldn't discern either color or shape at that distance. They each set up their own weapon on a shooting bench, and then Ray affixed a spotting scope to the distant targets and invited Erika to look through the glass.

"Ok, now I see them," she said. "You're sure of the yardage?"

"Yeah, we lasered it to be sure," Jim said. They're all at 1,500 yards exactly."

Erika was wearing an old Army ball cap Jim had given to

her years before. She spun the battered cap backwards on her head and peered up at Jim. "So how are we going to do this?"

"We'll each take fifteen shots, no warm up shots. I want to see how well you shoot cold at this distance using the BORS System. Total number of hits wins."

"Wins what?"

"Dinner and drinks tonight," Jim answered. "Ray's going to go first." Five shots each, then we rotate. The two losers pay for the winner."

"I can taste that prime rib already," Erika said.

"We shall see," Jim said.

Ray took his position at the bench and everyone donned safety glasses and ear protection. Jim and Erika lined up their spotting scopes on Ray's target. The white shape was in the outline of a man.

"Off safe," Ray said. "Ready to fire."

"Fire," Jim replied.

The .50 caliber Barrett roared, and Jim called out, "Miss, one yard right, correct elevation."

Ray clicked his scope dial to accommodate for a north/south breeze. "Two clicks," he said. At this range, the adjustment of only one degree could conceivably put him left of his target, so he was making only minute adjustments until he was on target. One degree off at 100 yards would still be on the target, highly doubtful at 1,000 yards and 1,500 yards was anyone's guess.

Ray settled in and fired again. "Hit. Right edge of target, about six inches below the center line," Jim said.

Ray clicked the windage dial one more click. "Should be on," he said.

His next shot was center mass, a little high. Two more rounds hit his target for a total of four, but the pattern was sporadic, leaving holes everywhere on the white silhouette.

"Not bad, for a pistolero," Jim said.

"Erika, you're up," Ray said. "Mind the wind."

She took up her position on the bench and dialed two clicks on her weapon before the first shot. "Off safe." Erika repeated. "Ready to fire."

"Fire," Jim said.

She relaxed into the weapon, slowed her breathing and heart rate until she couldn't feel the pulse in her wrist any longer. She squeezed off her first shot between heartbeats.

"Hit," Jim said. "Center line, left, almost off the target."

"Shit," Erika whispered. She adjusted the scope two more clicks, then reacquired the red target. Again, she slowed her bodily functions and squeezed off another round.

"Miss," Jim said. "Center line, six inches right. You over compensated."

Erika didn't reply. She re-adjusted back one click and settled in. She fired.

"Hit. Center line. Center mass. That's more like it," Jim said.

Erika took her time and put the remaining two rounds into a close grouping of roughly eighteen inches near center. Four hits, the same as Ray."

"Nice grouping," Ray said. "Jim, you're up."

Jim took his position. "Off safe," he said. "Ready to fire."

"Fire," Ray said.

With no adjustment to the scope, Jim settled in and took his first shot. "Hit. Center line. Center mass."

Ray and Erika exchanged a look of puzzlement. Jim fired again with the same result. Three more rounds pierced his yellow silhouette with a one-foot grouping of four shots, only one shot a foot higher than the pattern. "Nice shooting," Ray said.

Jim smiled, but said nothing.

They rotated through two more times. Erika missed three more times, once in the second round and twice in the third.

Ray missed two additional shots, giving him a total of 12 hits and 3 misses, compared to Erika's 11 hits and 4 misses. Jim never missed.

Late spring in the high desert of the Owens Valley brought out its best attributes. The cold nights gave way to cool mornings, and then morphed into warm, sunny days, the clouds out of the west piled up against the 13,000-foot peaks, allowing for perfect temperatures in the valley below. Then the cycle of cool nights began all over again, as the sun set behind those same peaks, providing clear views of both the eastern moonrise and startlingly close stars.

Ansell Adams had catalogued much of the area in his famous black and white photographs, from the towering mountains to the valley floor where remnants of the Japanese Internment Camp at Manzanar struggled for survival. Several of his photos hung in the small Independence museum founded by a former internee, Shiro Nomura. The photographs demonstrated that the landscape changed very slowly in this part of the world.

The streams ran full and high from the Sierra snow melt, and the huge willow trees lining the streambeds drank greedily while the liquid bounty lasted. Their broad leaves spread a canopy of shade that shielded them from the relentless sun, while the cool water provided an additional reprieve from the rising temperatures. This time of year, temperatures could range from the mild sixties to the more aggressive nineties. Today was perfect—a cloudless deep blue sky, a slight breeze, and temperatures in the mid-seventies.

Erika, Jim, and Ray packed up their gear and carried their cooler over to a picnic table beneath the willows. Crystal-clear water slipped through the nearby ponds. They spread out an old blanket and piled their plates high with mounds of sliced roast beef, turkey, and ham along with three different cheeses, apples, pears and grapes, and a host of condiments.

Ray sliced up raw vegetables, while Jim cut a loaf of

French baguette into slim, bite-sized pieces. Erika uncorked a bottle of Chardonnay and a bottle of Cabernet, pouring a glass of white for herself and two glasses of red for the guys. She deposited the corked bottles in a still pool of the stream to keep them chilled, before joining the men for their feast.

They toasted the afternoon's adventures and got down to the serious business of eating. Erika rarely felt this content or safe. Here were two capable, quiet men she could trust with anything, including her life. Neither asked anything of her, other than her friendship. In fact, they had tolerated her sullen, childish behavior when they first met, hoping to see a capable young woman emerge from that unattractive shell. As their relationship grew over the years, Erika resolved they would never regret their patience with her.

"You ever been up there?" Erika asked, indicating with a nod the towering jagged peaks to the west.

"Every year in the fall," Jim said.

"You, too?" She asked Ray.

"Yep."

"Hunting?"

"Yep."

"What for?"

Jim said, "There's mule deer that come over the top from Kings Canyon National Park and black tail still up there, too. Most have been taken by mountain lions now that some judge put the lion hunters out of business."

"How's that work?" She asked.

"Oh, some well-meaning environmentalists got together and convinced a judge to rule that lion hunting with dogs was unfair and inhumane, so all the dog owners moved east to Colorado or other states where they could make a living. The cats take about one deer per week, so they've pretty much decimated the herds up there. Twenty years ago, it wouldn't be unusual to see a couple thousand deer over a week-long hunt. Now you're lucky to see one hundred, if that," Ray explained.

"Now the cats are coming down into Round Valley above Bishop and taking people's dogs and cats," Jim added.

"Don't the dogs fight back?"

"Sure, but it's not much of a fight. I met a rancher up there on horseback who told me he watched a cat jump over his stock fence with his Doberman in his mouth," Jim answered. "I know they don't let their young ones out at dusk anymore. They just don't want to take a chance with their kids."

"Is it pretty up there?" She asked.

"God, yes,' Ray said. "You take 158 West out of Bishop to the end of the trailhead, where there's a pack station if you want to ride up on a horse or a mule. Or you can walk. It's about five hours, give or take, either way to the valley. There are mountain lakes in front of a cathedral of mountains and waterfalls that plummet over 400 feet. If you kept on going west, you'd wind up in Fresno."

"Sounds incredible," Erika said.

"Come hunting with us in the fall. See for yourself," Ray said. "We'll take you up to Honeymoon Lake to see one of the prettiest places God ever made, or French Canyon to see the falls."

"I've never been on a horse."

"Then it's about time," Jim said. "Besides, we'll put you on Auto."

"Otto?"

"No, Auto. As in automatic. You could close your eyes, and he'll take you right over the pass at about 11,000 feet, across the top, and down into the valley."

Erika was close to outright laughter at this point, she was so happy. "I might just do that."

"You let me know," Jim said. "We'd be proud to have you."

They'd put a dent in the feast and drank half of the wine. Too soon, it was time to head back to town. They packed up the remnants of their meal, leaving no trace behind.

Erika hugged each of them in turn. "Thanks guys. I love being with you."

"Thanks for coming. We love having you around, too," Ray said.

"And thanks for the new toy." She indicated the Suburban, where her new rifle was stowed.

"Use it wisely," Jim said, "and carefully."

"I will," Erika said.

Dinner was a casual affair at the local diner, where they'd eaten many times over the years. Everyone had showered and put on clean clothes. The common theme was blue jeans. They asked for and received the corner booth, so they could talk undisturbed. Jim and Ray ordered their usual, a single malt Scotch. Erika requested red wine.

Once the waitress brought the drinks, Erika said, "You never told me you could shoot at extreme distances like that."

Jim smiled, "I've had reason to practice at those ranges."

Erika knew better than to pursue that line of questioning. Instead, she asked, "Do you think it's possible for me to get that good?"

"Sure," Jim answered. "But, the opportunity to use that skill would be rare and usually done in places you wouldn't want to visit."

"How'd you get so good?"

"Practice," he said, "hours and hours of practice."

"Would you teach me?"

"Of course—anytime you can come up," Jim said. "But, let me explain something to you. Remember the first time we met?"

"Uh, yeah. Some of that I'd rather forget. As I remember, I was pretty rude and childish," she answered.

"Yes, you were, but that's not what I wanted you to remember. Focus in on how you felt with a handgun, how quick you were, how simple it seemed. Ray and I have never seen your equal, before or since. The speed and accuracy you demonstrated after four days was nothing short of remarkable. Do you know why?" Jim asked.

"No."

"You were connected. That weapon was a part of you, an extension of your will. You don't even think about missing a target with a handgun, do you?"

Erika contemplated the question for a few seconds, trying to dredge up a memory of doubt. "No, I guess I don't."

"Did you experience any doubt with the Barrett today?"

Again, she gave the question some thought. "I guess I did. Yes, I did."

"There you go. You're not connected yet. This type of shooting is far more technical. It requires far more discipline; a much longer learning curve; a lot more practice," he said.

Erika nodded.

"Let me know when your shoulder heals up and we'll schedule some more sessions." He grinned.

"Funny, Jim."

Their meals arrived and the conversation trailed off as they were served rare prime rib, mashed potatoes, and green beans. It got very quiet in a hurry as the trio dug in. Erika was in heaven: the food, the company, the day spent together.

"So, how's that prime rib taste?" Jim asked.

"Very funny, shooter," Erika answered. "I'm happy to buy your dinner, Jim."

Chapter 16

The return flight to San Diego was uneventful. At home, Erika stored her new weapon in a basement vault, the entrance hidden behind a retractable bookcase in her bedroom. Once again, as she did each time she entered the vault, she took out her most prized possession, her father's wedding ring. She'd taken it from her childhood home after settling the score with her step-father—his life for seven years of physical, emotional, and sexual abuse.

She gazed at the large, simple gold band, full of scratches, thin with erosion, and thought how different her life could have been, had he lived. Cruelly, fate had snatched him away in the form of a car accident with a drunk driver. Her life had turned upside down as a result. After running away from home at the age of fourteen, Erika had spent the next year searching for that special someone she could trust, spend her life with, and develop the type of relationship she had always imagined her father had. She had been sold to a vicious pimp instead and used in horrendous fashion because of her naiveté. She knew better, but could not help entertaining the notion that Felix, this attractive Mexican from Logan Heights, might be the one. His quiet acceptance of their bizarre circumstances reminded her of her father, Carl, accepting his wife's drunken escapades and continuing to love her despite it. She returned the ring to its special place with a deep sigh and went back upstairs.

She checked in with Sheila and Donny and discovered there had been no new developments with the Russian gang. She had the remainder of the week, four days, to spend as she wished.

After spending three days with Jim and Ray, then seeing and holding her father's scarred wedding ring again, Erika felt a sense of melancholy. Why didn't she have a relationship with the kind of depth they had with their families? What was wrong with her? Was she so damaged that no one would love her with the same intensity and commitment she remembered from her father?

In her fragile state of mind, she dialed Felix's cell with a prepaid throw away of her own. This was the only phone she would use, and he was the only one she would call with it.

"Hello?" She let the deep voice with a smooth overtone wash over her. Thinking for a moment, she realized she never heard his voice in any other context. He was never down, never excited, always controlled, devoid of passion.

"Felix?"

"Yes. Is this who I think it is?" he asked; the hope in his voice obvious.

"Yes, hello to you," Erika said. She had a difficult time rationalizing the call. She knew she was about to complicate her life in ways she couldn't possibly foresee, but she simply could not help herself. She knew he felt something that night and there was no doubt that hope had raised its ugly head once again in her heart. It was the only thing that reminded her of her own humanity. His voice was all it took for her to realize she had to find out if what she felt was genuine.

"I'm glad you called," Felix said. "I've been thinking a lot about you."

"Me, too." It was out before she could catch it.

"Can I see you?"

This was moving way too fast. What was she thinking?

"Is that wise?" She responded, trying to slow things down when deep inside, she didn't want to.

"I don't care about wise. I want to see you again. Any way you wish. You say when and where."

She was going to pretend she was checking up on him and his organization, to be sure the cross-border kidnap ransom had been stopped, but they were well past that ruse already. This was personal.

"You sure about this, Felix?"

"I'm sure."

"Okay. How about lunch tomorrow? Do you know where Pacifica Grill is on Pacific Coast Highway in Cardiff?"

"I'll find it."

"I'll meet you there at noon. The reservation will be in your name," she explained.

"I'll see you there."

"Bye."

"Bye."

Erika stared at the dead cell for a moment. She had this giddy feeling she would have recognized as that of a fifteen-year-old on her first date—if she'd ever had a normal experience like that growing up. And although it was a heady feeling, she wouldn't lose sight of her need for security. She chose this particular restaurant because she could perch above the eatery from the bluff across the highway to ensure Felix came alone and unarmed.

She hadn't intended to kill his brother. And even though it was in self-defense, she wasn't sure he truly would forgive such an action. And yet, she was willing to walk into the proverbial lion's den on some faint hope that what she was feeling was genuine—on both their parts.

Tomorrow would tell.

Chapter 17

A recently notorious hotspot in Manhattan was the strip club, Delilah's. The New York press had blasted several professional athletes for excessive alcohol and drug use in that club, as well as the occasional weapons charge. The club was huge by real estate standards in New York, spanning seven thousand square feet of basement level on 8th Avenue near Times Square. Mayor Giuliani had gentrified the neighborhood, clearing it of drugs and prostitution. A more stable element had materialized as a result, including better restaurants and high-end hotels. The theatre district aided the neighborhood's renaissance.

And yet, if you strayed more than three blocks in any direction, the drug addicts, pimps, prostitutes, and muggers circled Times Square like sharks. Nothing ever changed, it just moved outwards like ripples. Delilah's was only two blocks from 42nd Street, close enough to the Square to seem safe, but far enough away that the sharks could pick off the unwary.

Since Delilah's opened, however, the four blocks that stretched away from Times Square on 8th Avenue had become the safest place in Manhattan. The Russians treated the desperate drug addicts and opportunistic robbers with vicious disregard if they interfered with the patrons of the club.

Twelve steps led down beneath a discreet bronze plaque that read "Delilah's: A Gentleman's Club." A four-foot wide, bright red door admitted patrons into an ante-room where the $100 cover charge was collected, before patrons were subjected to a thorough pat down for weapons or drugs, which would become a liability if discovered on the premises. Patrons stepped through a heavy curtain into an atmosphere of decadence that assailed the senses. Loud, throbbing music, four different bars, and women of every color paraded through a gauntlet of testosterone-laden men, their inhibitions lowered by alcohol.

Strobe lights painted the dim interior in alternating bands of light, briefly exposing the perspiring table dancers before moving on to the stage presentation, a pantomime of sexuality presented to a packed house of enthusiastic drunks. The bright spotlights were trained on three different elevated stages, each equipped with a dance pole, on a raised promenade. Many patrons were able to have ringside seats. Famous stars and athletes could appreciate the female form cloistered away within the privacy of the VIP sections.

In one such section, two rookie professional football players celebrated the finalization of their first multi-million-dollar contracts for the New York franchise. Kyle McLachland, an inside linebacker and Damian Horton, a pass rushing defensive end, combined for nearly six hundred pounds of aggressive, alcohol-fueled bravado. They were loud, offensive brutes and no one wanted to tangle with them. They were throwing money at the dancers and at their bar tab, so club management sanctioned their obnoxious celebration.

Trying to pull a nearly naked dancer onto his lap, Horton broke a wooden chair. Kyle laughed uproariously at his teammate who was sprawled on the dirty floor. Embarrassed, Horton reacted angrily by kicking the dancer away and flinging pieces of the broken chair into the crowd. Enough was enough. Four security guards descended upon the pair to end their party and escort them from the club. A melee ensued. Two of the guards were beaten severely with the broken chair legs and a quart of premium Vodka that Horton wielded like a club. The heavy bottle did not shatter when he assailed the hapless security guards. With two of their coworkers down and bloodied, the other two guards maintained a safe distance from the berserk football players, who drank from the bottle, laughed and exchanged high fives; just a little manly fun for them.

Fyodor Kaminski was in the club nursing his own Vodka. He was in a foul mood since he'd accomplished nothing in Los Angeles except obtaining a useless first name. He was not supposed to make his presence known to the club's clientele.

He was there only to ensure no one was helping themselves to the large sums of cash generated by the club and to remind club management to maintain their business at the highest level.

But when Fyodor witnessed the brutal treatment of his security team from behind the one-way glass of his elevated office, something snapped. He drained his shot of Vodka and stormed out of the office, heading directly for the young football players. The onlookers quickly moved out of the way as the giant approached and just as quickly suctioned back into place, as though a vacuum was created by his passage, eager to witness what was to come.

Fyodor strode over to the posturing defensive end, his massive chest puffed out as he glared at the approaching Russian. Without breaking stride, Fyodor walked to within inches of Horton, wrapped him in a bear hug, lifted him off his feet, dropped his left shoulder, spun to the left on his heel and in a twisting throw called a "Suplex," slammed him head first into the cement floor, fracturing two vertebrae in his neck, rendering him immobile and unconscious.

He was the lucky one.

Before Kyle could react, Fyodor was up and moving. He grabbed the linebacker by his shoulder-length brown hair and head-butted him in the nose, shattering the bone and flattening the once attractive face. McLachland hadn't been manhandled by anyone since he'd received a beating from his father at age twelve. By the time he was thirteen, not even his father dared to discipline him. And now, before he could even attempt a defense, this giant systematically beat him to a pulp.

Fyodor grabbed him around the neck with both hands, picked up his 265-pound body as though he were a child, ran him backwards some twenty feet in the air before slamming him so hard into a wall he broke two of the young man's teeth. Fyodor pummeled the athlete with the chair leg, eventually using boots, chair parts, the intact Vodka bottle, and finally the table itself to finish the assault. By the time Fyodor's temper ran its course, Kyle would never play another down of professional football. One of his knees was badly damaged, and he had a dislocated elbow, which would require months of physical therapy. The broken ribs and shattered forearm would heal eventually, but the onslaught would leave Kyle McLachland emotionally devastated for the remainder of his life.

It took less than two minutes. His rage spent, Fyodor walked casually through the crowded room as everyone gave way in awe. A group of almost two hundred people had witnessed the most savage beating they were ever likely to see. More than a few were physically ill. Fyodor walked through to the rear of the club to the alley where his town car and driver were waiting. He opened the rear door himself and sat there seething for a moment, before saying, "Take me home."

The driver pulled out and headed for the Central Park area.

Chapter 18

Erika sat in her parked Mercedes, on a bluff across the highway from the Pacifica Grill. Through a small pair of binoculars, she watched Felix Mendez emerge from a black 600 series, BMW coupe. Apparently, he was into automotive performance, as well. He was wearing expensive tan slacks, a form-fitting cream-colored silk shirt, sleeves rolled up to expose his forearms, and cognac loafers with no socks. She could detect no weapon.

Turning over the car to the valet, his long dark hair flirted with the ocean breeze. He took a moment to appreciate the steel grey ocean shrouded beneath the heavy fog hugging the Southern California coast before entering the restaurant.

Erika started her car and eased down to the restaurant. She valeted her car and entered the restaurant, her purse strapped diagonally across her body, her hand on the Glock concealed within, the familiar handle her security blanket. She was wearing a simple long-sleeved, white blouse with a modest black skirt and sensible low heels. Her long dark hair hung loose, imperfect and naturally styled by the breeze, making her even more attractive.

As usual, she ignored the attention she commanded when entering a room, but Felix didn't. Standing as she approached, it struck him anew just how beautiful this dangerous woman was. She shook his hand as if this was a business meeting, before she took the chair the hostess held for her.

"How are you?" Felix asked.

"Fine, Felix. How are you?"

"I'm doing well, thanks."

The awkwardness between them was a rare experience for Erika. She tackled most challenges head on with a directness that made most adversaries uncomfortable. But Felix was no adversary. She didn't know what he was, but she wanted to find out.

He took matters into his own hands, literally. "Give me your hand, please."

"Why?"

"Just trust me for a moment—just this once."

Erika complied, resting her left hand on the table between them. Her right hand automatically went to the familiar weapon in her purse. This could turn out to be the world's shortest lunch date, she thought.

Felix took her hand in both of his and idly caressed the back. "If we are going to be friends, we need to establish trust between us. To establish trust, we need to speak openly and at length. I want to know you, know who you really are."

Erika thought she was the direct one. Felix has already taken the initiative, but she was no shrinking violet, by any stretch of the imagination. She left her hand between his.

"I would like that," she said, surprising herself. "But there are a lot of complicated issues to work through before that can happen."

"I know. I want you to know who I am, too." He let go of her hand. "You can release the gun now," he said quietly.

Erika clasped both hands together on the table and studied the handsome Chicano. His face was perfectly formed, almost beautiful instead of handsome. Long dark hair framed his chiseled face beneath a prominent widow's peak, impossibly long eyelashes, almost black eyes, olive skin and a generous mouth. When he smiled, brilliant white teeth framed by a serene countenance gave no hint to the kind of violent life he must have lived. Obviously at peace, he was smiling now.

"Where do we start?" Erika asked. She could be direct with him too. It was an odd feeling…but pleasant.

"You ask a question. I answer truthfully. Then I ask a question. You answer truthfully."

"What if I can't answer your question?"

"You tell me you can't answer the question," he said. "In

fact, you may be getting the same answer from me."

"And I go first?" She asked.

"Of course."

They were interrupted by their waitress and ordered quickly—iced tea, halibut and salad for him and an Arnold Palmer, salmon and salad for her. At least they were compatible diners.

"Okay, how old are you?" Erika began.

"Thirty-one. How old are you?"

"Twenty-seven. Where were you born?"

"Here in National City. You?"

"El Cajon. Any family?"

"None. You?"

"None," she said. "How long have you been running Logan Heights?"

"Since leaving the military, seven years ago."

"You were in the military, what branch?"

He laughed. "Yes, to the first question. Navy Seals to the second. Now I get two questions."

"Oops, sorry. Go ahead and ask."

"How long have you been doing what you do?" Felix asked.

"Forever. It's the only thing I've ever done."

"How'd you get started?"

"I can't answer that."

"Who taught you to shoot?"

"Two dear friends. My coaches. My turn."

"How did you wind up in the Seals?"

"Good one," Felix said. "My brother and I were left in the foster care system. My mother was a heroin addict. She overdosed when I was ten and Jorge was only four. I used to ride my bike up from Imperial Beach and watch the Seals train on the sand dunes. It became the only thing I wanted to do. I joined when I turned eighteen."

"Where did you grow up?" He asked.

"El Cajon, initially. Then my parents died in an automobile accident, and I moved in with an uncle in L.A." The small lie would have to suffice for the time being.

"What was foster care like?" She asked.

"About what you'd think. At first, they placed Jorge and I as a pair—brothers. Then we were separated. I was taken in by a childless couple in Imperial Beach. Jorge was left to deal with the system."

"How could they separate brothers?"

"Two different last names. We were only half-brothers. We reclaimed our family name, Mendez, after I got him out of the system. The foster care system seemed to lose track of that little detail."

Their food arrived and Felix said, "Now you owe me two more questions again. Let's eat first, and then we'll explore some more. Deal?"

"Deal."

They finished their meal, but neither of them really wanted this first date to end. A unique chemistry was developing a life of its own that overpowered their natural wariness. Felix looked out at the beach and the ocean beyond. He again took the lead. "Would you like to walk the beach? I'd like to talk some more."

"Me, too," Erika answered. "C'mon."

They exited through a beachside door, kicked off their shoes, walked barefoot across the loose sand to the hard pack near the water, and headed north. There was a campground on a bluff above them to the right where dedicated surfers could pitch a tent or operate out of a mobile home, to catch the mostly gentle waves on what the locals considered a family beach.

Even though the low fog persisted along the coast and the waves were miniscule thrashers, it seemed the surfers just needed to be in the water. There were dozens of them sitting on their boards outside the break, hoping for a wave of any consequential size.

"Have you ever surfed?" Erika asked.

"I was a Seal," Felix said. "I've done anything you could possibly do in the ocean and a few things I'd rather not admit. You?"

"No, I've never seriously pursued it, but I have tried small waves on vacation. I do like the standup paddle boards, though."

"Good, we should do that sometime," he said.

"Okay."

They walked for a while, not touching, just being together. Somehow, even with their limited interaction, both knew the other had suffered significant psychological trauma as a child. There was an internal radar that people like them possessed that was unexplainable, but no less genuine because of it. They just knew.

"How about if we just talk?" Erika asked.

"Works for me," Felix said. He offered his arm and she took it in hers, snuggled up hip to hip now. "Much better."

"Are you close to your foster parents?" Erika sensed something there.

"Not really. My foster dad was ex-Navy, strict taskmaster— good guy. He got me out of the system and I'll always be grateful for that. He died of cancer when I was fifteen and then it was just Sarah and I."

"Sarah was your foster mom?"

"Yeah."

"It turned into something else, didn't it?" She posed it as a statement, not a question.

"Yeah." He turned to look at her. "How'd you know?"

"It's not hard to imagine. A widow living with a young man who looks like you. I couldn't imagine it *not* happening."

"How do you know these things?"

Erika stopped and turned them to the sea. "I had a step-father once, but not a good one." No other explanation was needed.

He put his arm around her shoulders and stared out to sea with her for what seemed like minutes. "I understand. In foster care, there are many 'step-fathers'. After I enlisted in the Navy, I gained custody of Jorge. He was almost thirteen and the damage was already done. I was too late."

The real conversation was buried within the words they shared. Neither required a translator and they both knew this was the glue that would bind them together much faster than a physical attraction. They resumed walking. "I need to know something," Erika said. "I need to know that what happened between Jorge and I is over. That it's resolved in your mind."

The campground gave way to a deserted stretch of beach sandwiched between the highway and the ocean. They continued their walk. "You need to understand who Jorge was, and then you'll understand why it's over," he said. "The foster care system is a breeding ground for juvenile offenders. Juvie is a breeding ground for adult prison. Jorge was a victim of each of them. Everyone is brutalized somehow in foster care: by the foster parents, the administrators, or the older kids. That's just the way it is. Juvie is even worse. And prison, shit, forget about it."

He stopped walking, turned to Erika. "By the time I got to Jorge, he was already lost. He'd been beaten and brutalized in every way possible. He blamed me for deserting him. Then, over time, he became them. He did the beating. He did the brutalizing. And he was good at it. Everyone was afraid of Jorge."

"Were you?"

"Afraid? I don't know. I guess I was. I knew that someday we would have to find out. Then word got out he wanted to take over Logan. Force me out."

"Does that mean what I think it does?" Erika asked.

"Yes. It was coming to a head. Him or me. He made many enemies for us. It was known to my friends in Mexico. They were waiting to see what I would do: if I had the *cojones* to do what was required. He had to go. This was clean. No torture. No beheading. Just gone. It was a mercy you did for me."

"I have a hard time considering it a mercy."

"Erika, look at me." He stood still, holding her eyes with his. "Jorge loved me when he was a child. I was his brother, his friend, his protector. After I left foster care, he lost all that. Bad things happened. He blamed me. He came to hate me. And finally, he made plans to kill me. That's what you walked into. By the end of the week, one of us would have been gone. You saved me from killing my own brother."

"Okay, Felix, I just needed to be sure." She didn't know what else to say.

"Let's head back," he said. The confession seemed to have diminished him somehow, taken the lightness from the air, and turned the fog into an oppressive shroud.

Finally, he said, "Now, what about you? What's your story?"

She knew she owed him an explanation, a return gift. "Like you, I was damaged by people who were supposed to protect me, love me. I left home when I was fourteen. Then I met even worse people, experienced the worst that humans can do." It was all coming out in a rush, as though a psychological dam had burst. "I took revenge on those people, then on my stepfather when I became an adult. Do you understand what I'm saying?"

"Yes."

"And you still want to know me?"

"Yes." He stopped and took her in his arms. "Even more now."

His acceptance was her undoing. She couldn't help herself.

She began to cry, her head buried in his chest, her body heaving in great sobs as he held her. They didn't speak. He just held her for a long time. For the first time since Hawaii, Erika felt peace and hope.

"I'm a mess," she whispered into his shirt. She stepped back. "And so is your shirt."

They both looked at the mascara, lipstick, and tear-stained silk, then at each other. He kissed her slowly, gently; the perfect combination for the moment.

He turned her back south, toward the restaurant. "C'mon; enough for today."

"I need one more thing from you, Felix."

"Name it."

"I need to know the kidnap ransom thing is over."

"My word to you is good. For as long as I am breathing, there will be no more of this in Logan."

"Thank you."

When the valets brought their cars around, Felix turned to her and asked, "How can I reach you?"

"The cell I called you on. It's only for you."

"Perfect." He kissed her quickly. "Bye, Beautiful."

"Bye."

Chapter 19

Donny buzzed Sheila over the intercom and she picked up. "Can you come downstairs? I think I've located one of our friends."

"Be right there."

She could tell Donny was excited as she entered his basement lair. "What do you have?"

Donny swiveled from behind a bank of computer screens and scooted his chair out from behind his desk. Sheila took a seat opposite him.

"There's a report out of Manhattan, near Times Square, that two professional football players were nearly beaten to death in a strip club called Delilah's."

"What's the significance?"

"According to several eye witnesses, the two pros were having a great time until they decided to rough up a security team that was sent to escort them out of the club. After they beat up the guards, a large bald man picked one of them up like a rag doll, and used a classic Russian wrestling move called the "Suplex." He slammed him into the floor head first, breaking his neck. That is Fyodor's signature move, the one that got him barred from the Olympics. Then he grabbed the other player and beat him to within an inch of his life. The onlookers said it was the most brutal thing they'd ever witnessed."

"Do you have anything else to go on?"

"Well, aside from the fact that two very large men, weighing almost three hundred pounds each, were overpowered and literally destroyed in seconds, Delilah's has been on my list of possible assets of Leonid's Russian organization. The coincidence is just too overwhelming. It has to be them."

"We need to confirm this. Let's get an observation team in there. And you start digging into the company that owns the club. See what other assets are owned by the same corporations."

"Already on it."

It was early, as the sun struggled to make its appearance through a muted glow filtering its way down 8th Avenue from the east. A New York Edison van with two technicians that did not work at that company was parked across the street from Delilah's Gentleman's Club. They put the final touches on an installation requested by a government agency out of Washington D.C. on an electric pole that stood like a sentinel at the mouth of an alley across the street from the club. The installation consisted of a high-resolution camera attached to a satellite feed that could be downloaded in real-time to a remote location. There was a second camera installed on a building that overlooked the alley behind the club. The feeds led to a computer in Bel Air, accessed by Donny, equipped with facial recognition software developed by the NSA. If any of the Russian principals appeared on either camera, that information would automatically be transmitted by email to Donny's agency account.

Now the wait began.

Chapter 20

In Aspen, Colorado, snow still blanketed the higher elevations, but the spring runoff had turned the lower slopes into a season of mud. Everything was wet. Last month's gurgling streams became rushing rivers of cold mountain runoff, the pristine water seemingly in a panic to join the already swollen Roaring Fork and White Rivers. Down valley from Snow Mass Ski Resort, the small towns of Rifle, Glenwood Springs, and Grand Junction settled in to wait for full summer, when the crowds of hikers, fisherman, and other outdoor enthusiasts descended on the valley. It was some of the prettiest country that existed in the Western United States, leading further west to the deep canyons and impossible red stone architecture of eastern Utah.

Leonid Utkin and Raina Polzin spent the past winter on their 270-acre ranch overlooking the Aspen Valley. Leonid, when he wasn't on the slopes, oversaw his vast empire through a series of intermediaries that kept him isolated from the day to day concerns that affected the profitability of his legal and illegal enterprises. Strip clubs, bars, small hotels, and night clubs, all tangentially connected by the sale of alcohol, comprised his legal empire. His illegal enterprises depended on the sale of illicit drugs, prostitution, and gambling. His illicit businesses were the most profitable. Now that ski season was over, Leonid was anxious to put both sides of his business interests back in a growth pattern that had been interrupted by the American agency looking into his past dealings.

He was concerned over reports that a large bald man had destroyed two promising pro football stars. The reports had titillated New York sports fans for over two weeks. Several follow up stories about the rehabilitation of the two players continued to surface. Leonid instructed Fyodor to lay low at the apartment and stay away from the New York establishments until he could be relocated to Atlanta or Dallas. No one was pleased.

Raina, although second in command to only Leonid, filled her time quite differently. She was six months into training her new slave. Raina still yearned to meet the woman who had killed her former pet. For now, she amused herself by alternately heaping pain and humiliation upon her new protégé, a statuesque young blonde Russian model, before rewarding her with the jolting release of sexual orgasm. Stasja, the new recipient of Raina's perverted ministrations, was developing quickly into a cruel, subservient replica of her last pet, willing to do her bidding without restraint, without question. She existed only for the approval and intimate attention she received from Raina.

Raina sat at her desk, studying the latest financial statements from their European holdings. Her office was a blend of stone and dark wooden shelves laden with books she'd never read, Persian carpets, and large glass windows that captured the expansive mountain vistas. Stasja knelt at her feet, clothed in a short silk robe, wearing a leash and collar. Leonid entered and took a seat opposite her desk.

Raina turned from her desk, a wicked grin hinting at the cruel nature within. "Which one is this Sheila Gibbons?"

"The blonde woman in the baseball cap," Leonid said. "The other must be Erika, no last name, the brunette shooter."

"I want them both," Raina said. There was a sordid intensity in that simple statement, a declaration of evil intent.

"As do I," Leonid said. "One will get us the other. I'm sure of it."

"You will give them to me?" It was posed as a question only to show respect. It was a foregone conclusion that Raina would get her opportunity. "You did promise."

"Of course, Raina. Of course."

Chapter 21

"I think we've located Fyodor," Donny said to Sheila. She turned from the correspondence she was reading in the conference room.

"Show me," she said. They'd been trying to locate the Russian giant ever since reports had surfaced regarding the club beatings.

"The same LLC based out of London not only owns and operates Delilah's, but seven other clubs in the New York Metro area. They also own two nightclubs, several low-end bars, and two residential buildings. One of the buildings is on East 60th, overlooking Central Park. The 32nd floor is leased to the same LLC, Lion Trust, LTD," Donny explained. "Leonid means Lion in Russian. It's just too much of a coincidence, so I put in a surveillance request from our friends at NSA, and here's what we received this morning."

He handed over some grainy black and white photos that were time stamped with a date from the previous month. "It seems the NSA had an interest in our friends that was unrelated to our situation."

The photos showed a larger man bundled up against the winter temperatures in a black calf-length cashmere car coat. He would have resembled the height and girth of a grizzly bear if it weren't for the bald pate and ridged brows protruding from a woolen scarf encircling his neck. It could certainly be Fyodor.

"Has Erika seen this yet?" Sheila asked.

"No."

"Please call her and have her come up in the morning. Then get any confirmations from anywhere else you can in the meantime," she said.

"Will do."

Erika arrived at seven a.m. the following morning. She'd gotten an early start to avoid the inevitable workday traffic, but suffered gridlock when she reached the area around Los Angeles International Airport. It broke loose just long enough for her to drive a few miles at normal speeds before once again becoming enmeshed in the bumper-to-bumper crawl that was now the norm between the 10 Freeway and Sunset Boulevard. She exited at Mulholland and headed up into the hills of Bel Air.

Donny was already in his basement office, engrossed in his computer screen, when Erika crept up behind him and planted a kiss on the top of his head.

"How are you doing, Donny?"

A genuine smile erupted at the early surprise. He rose and gave her a hug and a return kiss. "I'm fine, Erika. How was the drive?"

"Boring, with the usual stops. It sounds like you found something interesting. Huh?"

"We did. I'm working on my presentation now," Donny said. "Have you had breakfast yet?"

"Not yet. Are you going to feed me?"

"Yeah. C'mon to the kitchen, and I'll scramble some messy eggs."

"Messy eggs? What's that?"

"Ham, eggs, cheese and whatever else I find that looks good. You like hot sauce?"

"Yes."

"Good, I'll add some Red Rooster."

Erika poured juice for each of them. When Donny noticed, he said. "Pour a third one. Sheila will be down in a minute."

"Oops, I forgot the boss." She laughed.

"So, I'm the boss now, huh?" Sheila said as she entered

the kitchen. The room was enormous, featuring a central granite island flanked by long granite-topped counters, walk-in refrigerator and freezer, dual sinks, dishwashers and ovens, along with a cook top you could roast half a beef over. The room swallowed the three of them.

Sheila maneuvered around the island to greet Erika with a hug and kiss. "I think you're going to like this meeting," Sheila said.

"Good, I could use a lift about now." Erika continued pouring the juice while Sheila set up the place mats and silverware.

"Why? Is there something going on?" Sheila asked.

"Naw…just life sometimes, you know." There was no way Erika was going to discuss Felix or the obvious complications that could result if the relationship progressed. Besides, Sheila lost her husband, Richard, in a particularly gruesome manner little more than a year ago. Erika's situation, by comparison, was a non-event.

"Yeah, I do," Sheila said. She was aware of what each of them had to contend with as adults due to the abuse they'd suffered as children and young adults. Nothing seemed normal or simple, especially relationships. It was probably why the three of them clung to each other in difficult times. Losing Richard had been her cross to bear. Erika and Donny had stood by her ever since.

"Food's up," Donny said. He filled the plates with heaping portions of eggs, scrambled with ham, cheese, shallots, onions, and mushrooms, then added his favorite hot sauce, Red Rooster, for flavor and the orange tint it lent to the eggs.

They sat down to eat, content as they consumed the breakfast. Afterwards, Donny took a carafe of coffee and three cups in hand and said, "C'mon. Let's go downstairs to the video player so I can share this information with you."

Once they were all settled, Donny pushed a button and the video screen at the end of the table rose from a cabinet. A still shot of Central Park in Manhattan appeared. Several more clicks took them around the south end of the Park in a series of still shots until the scene stopped and rested upon an older high rise in the Southeast corner.

"This is where two of our Russian friends are now," Donny said.

"Which ones?" Erika asked. Donny had her focused attention now.

"Petro Sokolof and Fyodor Kaminski," he said. He clicked the remote and picture of Fyodor materialized that showed him entering the building in a long black coat and scarf. His size and bearing was unmistakable. Another photo of his face, full on, confirmed his identity. Donny advanced the film through several more stills until he got to the one of Petro Sokolof entering the same building. It was a great shot, leaving no doubt as to his identity either.

"Do you know which floor—which apartment?" Erika asked.

"Yes, it's the 32nd floor, one story below the top of the building. There are thirty-three stories total; the top one is used for mechanics, the water tower, and roof access. Got it? It's accessed by a private key-controlled elevator that opens directly on a vestibule that services the apartment. No other entry other than the fire escape, and even if you could get up that way, you'd be facing a three-inch steel fire door that's impenetrable," he said.

"Do you have the floor plans?" Sheila asked.

Donny looked at her with an amused look on his face. "Of course. It's in your folder," he said. "Along with aerial photos of the building from every angle and the surrounding neighborhood as well."

"Okay, sorr-r-r-y." Sheila laughed.

"No worries," Donny said. "What I was about to say was there's no way to gain entrance to the apartment without raising an alarm. Remember, the building is owned by Lion Trust, LTD, the same corporation that owns all those other properties. Every attempt we've used to gain access to the building has been politely, but firmly denied. They've actively isolated that building and particularly that apartment, by installing their own security force around it. And before you ask about roof access, that area has a permanent video feed and rotating guards. These guys are serious."

"So how do we get to them?" Erika asked.

"You have to get them coming or going," Donny said, "which brings up another problem. Their garage is located beneath the building, also guarded, so we're never certain who is in the vehicles that emerge, since they use blacked out Town Cars to travel around the city."

"Have you followed them?" Sheila asked.

"Yes, that's how we picked up on Sokolof. Kaminski hasn't been seen on the street since the incident at the strip club."

"What incident?" Erika asked.

Sheila responded. "About a month ago, two young professional football players got out of hand in a New York strip club, 'Delilah's', and beat up two security guards. A minute later, a huge, bald man dumped one of them on his head in a classic Russian wrestling move that Kaminski was known for. In fact, that's why he was banned from Olympic competition. The ball player suffered a broken neck. The other one was then beaten so severely, he'll never play again. Donny picked up on the news article and started considering it. It took him a while to connect the dots, but between researching the incident and the foreign ownership of the club, our suspicions grew. Then the NSA got photos of both men and forwarded them here at my request."

"Where are they now?" Erika asked.

"Kaminski is holed up in the apartment…"

Erika interrupted him. "How can you be sure of that?"

Donny said," We have a spotter with high-powered binoculars, watching them from an apartment across the park, on the West side. Kaminski occasionally comes out on the veranda to get his fresh air and down a few vodkas. There are some photos in your folder. He doesn't look happy."

"When did he ever?" Erika asked.

"Good point," Donny said. "And now there are some further complications."

"Such as?"

"We can't locate Sokolof," Donny said. "We were hoping to take him entering one of their establishments, but he hasn't been seen there in two weeks. And we haven't seen him on the veranda either. It appears he's moved out of the area."

It should have been a simple operation to isolate the two Russians and eliminate them if they were able to bring the full talents of the intelligence community to bear, but this was an off-the-record operation. They were not officially involved in foreign intelligence if the operation did not fit within the guidelines of their charter, which was strictly limited to the rescue or ransom of individuals belonging to the Democratic governments that funded them. This was revenge for Richard, pure and simple. It had to remain with the three of them exclusively. They were also concerned about involving the Senator in any operation that involved the Russians. He was an obvious security risk. This one had to be off the books.

"Can't you trace their phones?" Sheila asked.

"They're way too smart for that. They must be using throwaways or some other form of communication. Until we get our hands on one of their phones, we just don't know," Donny answered.

"How far away is the apartment we're using to observe Kaminski now?" Erika asked.

"Without measuring exactly, somewhere between a quarter and half a mile," Donny said.

"Can you get me access to the observation post without anyone else around?" Erika asked.

"Sure. That's no problem," Sheila said, "but, why?"

"I think I have a response for Kaminski," Erika said.

"One that won't put this agency in jeopardy?" Sheila asked. "Or my directorship?"

"Neither one," Erika replied. "But it might be nice if you

had some level of deniability."

"Okay, but I'm trusting you on this one," Sheila said.

"I know. I won't let you down."

"When do you want to go?" Sheila asked.

"Right away. I don't want to lose this chance," Erika said.

"Ok, I'll set it up."

Donny just looked on silently. He already had an idea of what Erika might do.

Sheila said, "Donny, none of this leaves this room."

"No worries, boss. I got it covered."

Once again, Erika appeared at Palomar Airport in the early morning to meet the familiar agency pilots, Eric and John. They escorted her out to a Gulfstream 550 this time, a far more sophisticated jet with international range that could comfortably accommodate fifteen adult passengers. It boasted a full lavatory with shower and a private bedroom in the rear, satellite television and communication, and it was capable of traveling thousands of feet above regular air traffic and at greater speeds.

She settled into the overstuffed suede passenger seat as the two pilots went over their checklist.

"Buckle up, Erika. We're out of here," said the voice over the intercom. "Once we're at altitude, I'll come back and chat. ETA to Teterboro: four hours, twenty minutes."

Erika relaxed as the big jet taxied to the end of the tarmac, accelerated like a shot down the runway and lifted off at an upwards angle you would never experience on a commercial airliner. The boys were showing off.

In addition to her normal baggage, John had stowed another silver-metal case measuring three by two feet and ten inches thick. It contained Erika's new form of communication.

Chapter 22

Now in Dallas, Texas, Petro Sokolof carefully put down his disposable cell phone as though it would explode on contact with the wooden table. It was early evening. The weather outside was crackling with lightning strikes, punctuated by thunderous booms—a perfect accompaniment to his mood. The huge picture windows faced west, challenging the oncoming storm with bravado that was unwarranted by the slim protection afforded by the glass and steel high rise. Peter felt exhilarated by the feeling the storm would march through the building, not around it.

Springtime in Texas could produce anything from hail the size of baseballs, to hundred-degree temperatures, sometimes both in the same day. Petro did not enjoy any part of it. He preferred the reliably cold climate of his native Russia or the cooler mountainous regions of any country. He detested the schizophrenic unpredictability of Texas weather.

After Fyodor's outburst at Delilah's Club, Leonid had ordered Petro out of New York. Fyodor was under wraps at the New York apartment. After the melee in the club, drawings of his likeness had circulated around the city. He might be recognized by anyone in Manhattan since the topic of the day was the identity of the giant that had so casually destroyed two professional football players. Half of the city wanted him arrested and the other half wanted him to play for their team. If he fled, he would be recognized and reported to the police. Leonid wanted to keep his men safe and still be able to continue searching for the two women who had killed their friends, so he separated them and relocated Petro to Texas. Petro hated the decision, but he respected Leonid.

Petro brooded over his isolation a moment, but Leonid's call had brought welcome news. They now had a name—something for him to work with. They wanted him in

Colorado, a little closer to California, where they could plan their next steps. Tomorrow he would board a private jet for Aspen, Colorado. He hoped the weather would be cooler than Texas.

Fyodor was to be left out of it.

Chapter 23

After landing, Erika climbed into a non-descript black town car parked at Teterboro Airport. Her driver stowed her luggage in the trunk, and forty minutes later, she arrived at the Four Seasons Hotel on East 57th. Manhattan's elite visitors frequented the hotel: investment bankers, athletes, clothing designers, models, and cinema and stage stars. The food and service levels were impeccable and the prices reflected that incredible service. The hotel was the best New York could offer.

Erika breezed through registration and the bellhop took her bags to her large suite. She called Donny on her cell. "I'm settled in at the Four Seasons. When can I get a look at the apartment?"

"A key will be delivered to your hotel room within the hour. They've been instructed to slip it under your door along with the address and directions. No face-to-face meetings in the city. Please call me and confirm when you have it," he said.

"Okay." She hung up.

Ninety minutes later, Erika phoned Donny again.

"I'm at the location, but now I need you to explain which apartment building I'm supposed to be looking at."

"Okay, go out on the balcony."

"I'm there."

"Now, open the photo attachment I just sent your email."

"Just a sec."

She opened the attachment to find a photo, obviously taken

from this exact vantage point, featuring a group of buildings on the other side of Central Park.

"Okay, got it," she said.

"Now, scroll through all the photos. There should be ten of them."

"They're all here. What am I looking for?"

"The first photo is of the Southeast portion of the Park. Hold it up and orient yourself to the same view."

"Got it."

"The next photo is a close-up of the building exactly in the corner. The southern-most building is the shortest. The center one is the tallest. The East building is the middle height. Do you have that orientation?"

"Yes."

"Go to the next photo. That's the tallest building in the cluster of three on that corner."

It took a few seconds for Erika to be certain she was looking at the correct building. Once she matched the details of the photo to the actual building she said, "Okay, got it."

"Next photo," Donny said.

"Got it."

"That's the top eight floors of the same building in the center."

"Okay, but I can't make out that level of detail from this far away," Erika explained. "Let me set up a spotting scope and get it focused on those floors and I'll call you back."

"I'll be waiting."

"Okay."

Erika opened her silver case. In addition to the Barrett rifle, the case contained a collapsible tripod with a set screw on top to accommodate an attachment. In this instance, she removed a spotting scope and screwed it down on the tripod at eye level from inside the apartment. Once she oriented the scope to her object building, she focused in on her target. Now she had the top eight floors captured within the scope in greater detail.

She called Donny back. I'm all set up, and I have the top eight floors in the lens."

"You're not out on the balcony, are you?"

"No, Donny. I've done this once or twice before. I'm at least ten feet inside the apartment with no backlight." Her voice wasn't reflecting any testiness, but it was close.

"Okay, sorry," he said, "next photo."

"Go ahead."

She brought up the next one, which showed a wide veranda that stretched across the center of the building. The outside corners were comprised of old fashioned dormer windows, four to a side.

"That's a shot of the thirty-second floor, one story below the top of the building. There are thirty-three floors total, plus the water tower and the small roof access structure on top. Got it?"

"Got it."

"I know it looks level to you from that distance, but you're actually on the thirty-fourth floor of your building which puts them some twenty feet below you, maybe a few more."

"Understood," Erika said.

"Next photo."

Erika scrolled down. "Go ahead."

On most nights, that's the veranda where he's appeared. He hasn't established any clear pattern to appearing outside, but he's come out five of the last seven nights. He has a few drinks before returning inside for the night, sometimes twice on the same night, but never more than that," Donny said.

"Let me focus down on that, Donny. Hold on." She turned the elevation knob down a few clicks until she had the veranda isolated. "Okay, I've got it."

"Now compare the curtains and furniture you can see to the next photo to be sure you have the right one," Donny said.

"Done. I've got it."

"Now leave the scope there and look at the next two photos."

Erika did as instructed. The first photo showed Fyodor standing at the rail, the identical curtains and furnishings appeared behind him in the photo. The last photo was of the roof top above the apartment. It showed a man standing on the roof near the parapet overlooking Central Park. Hanging from his neck were binoculars large enough to be captured in the photograph.

"I recognize Fyodor, but who's on the roof?" Erika asked.

"We don't have a name. We assume he's connected to the Russians. There's no other reason for the increased security. They're clearly concerned about the football player incident. Fyodor is staying in place and Petro is nowhere to be found," Donny said.

"Okay, I'll set up here. Have you cleared everyone from the premises?"

"Absolutely."

"I'll keep in touch," Erika said.

"Please do, Erika. This is important to Sheila and me, too."

"No worries."

Erika began her preparations. It was now late in the afternoon and the light would fade much quicker down below, inside the skyscraper's concrete canyons. Like a giant spotlight, the last rays of the setting sun were concentrated on the upper third of the tall buildings fronting Central Park.

First, she took out a laser range finder to pair with the spotting scope on the tripod in the living room. After coupling the two devices, she activated the range finder and committed the distance to memory, to be input later in the BORS system attached to the Barrett Rifle. The display read seven-hundred-twenty-two yards. That translated to 2,166 feet, approximately 500 feet short of half a mile. She performed the procedure two more times to be certain of her distance and obtained the identical reading each time. Satisfied, she turned to the Barrett and removed it from the case.

Sitting cross-legged on the carpet, she assembled the rifle. She mated the barrel to the receiver, attached the scope with the integrated BORS system, and then fitted the flash suppressor and silencer. Putting on latex gloves, she inserted ten .50 caliber rounds into the magazine and married it to the undercarriage of the receiver with a resounding click. If, for some reason, she lost one of the spent casings, no fingerprints would be found. Jim had drilled the habit into her.

Next, she removed the spotting scope from the tripod and placed the thirty-pound Barrett atop it, screwing it securely into place. She adjusted the height of the tripod until she could square her eye perfectly behind the scope before activating the BORS system. When the tiny screen glowed green, she would input the critical data, yardage being the most important.

She set the distance for 722 yards, then reacquired Fyodor's apartment and let the BORS set all the other elements for target resolution automatically. The only other element that concerned her was windage. How a bullet travelling at 2,720 feet per second would be affected by the wind as it traversed the nearly half mile distance through Central Park was critical.

Making sure all the lights in the apartment were extinguished, Erika went out onto the balcony and held a tiny transmitter out as far as her reach allowed. It was an electronic wind gauge capable of detecting even miniscule movement of air. The display detected a 4.2 mph north-south wind, negligible for her purposes, perhaps one click at that range. She silently hoped her luck would hold, allowing her to hold right on target before firing. She went back inside, pulled a chair up next to the tripod and settled in to wait.

Chapter 24

Butting up against the Buttermilk Ski area, the runway of the Aspen airport runs parallel to Highway 82, just west of the town. Because of the wind, planes usually take off and land in the same direction, facing the mountains. In the winter, you could flip a coin and be just as accurate as any weather forecaster as to whether you'd be able to land there or not.

Petro landed in Aspen on a brilliant spring morning without a bump in the air, a rare occurrence for the airport situated at 8,000 feet in the Alpine Valley. Exiting the plane with his duffle bag thrown over his shoulder, he walked toward the black suburban waiting just outside the gate at General Aviation. Fifteen minutes later they reached the ranch where Leonid and Raina waited. The driver dropped him at a log cabin guest house, just out of sight of the main house.

Shouldering his duffle bag, he entered the two-bedroom cabin. It was quite opulent, with an ensuite bathroom, full kitchen, study and great room with a river rock fireplace and granite topped bar. Petro, however, had no need for alcohol. He was unique in that regard; a Russian who didn't drink alcohol.

After unpacking, he walked directly to the main house. He was anxious to learn about any developments in their search for the two women.

Leonid greeted him with a bear hug. "How are you, my friend?"

"Better now," Petro grinned. "It's good to be back in the mountains."

"Come," Leonid said. "Raina is waiting for us."

Leonid led the way to the living room where Raina was seated. She rose to greet him with a perfunctory and insincere hug and air kisses. Warmth was not her strong point.

"Would you like some coffee?" Leonid asked.

"Yes, please."

"Raina?"

"Yes."

Leonid went to the kitchen and returned with a tray of coffee, cups, cream and sugar. He did this service as a reminder to himself: never to be above his fellow members, but to be one of them. He believed that to be an effective leader, he had to be willing to perform the same duties he expected of others. He gained their respect as a result.

Raina sat in silence, slowly sipping her coffee. She radiated eagerness.

"Raina, would you like to bring Petro up to date?"

"Yes," she said. It all came out in a rush. "We now have a name to investigate. The blonde woman in the video has been identified as Sheila Gibbons, of Los Angeles." Her excitement was obvious.

"Then we have a place to start," Petro commented. "How do you want to proceed?"

"We've already scoured the internet, Google, social media, and found nothing. We've looked at credit card companies, DMV records, passports, birth certificates, academic records, employment history, military service and social security. Nothing came back positive. It's as though she never existed," Raina said.

"And this Erika person?" Petro asked. "Anything on her?"

"No," Leonid interrupted. "With only a first name, we have nowhere to begin. We need to find this Sheila Gibbons. She will give us the other one."

"And how do you propose we do that?"

"We are not sure yet," Leonid said. "But we would like to send you to Las Vegas, back to the club. Perhaps we can entice this woman to come to us."

"With me as the bait?"

"It worked once," Raina said. "Seeing you there is the last thing they would expect."

"You think they will come for me?"

"Without a doubt," she said.

"Will I have Fyodor with me?" Petro asked. Having the Russian giant with him would give him a measure of security no one else could provide.

"I'm sorry, no," Leonid said. "His likeness is all over New York and the national news now. It is not a perfect likeness, but it is close enough. I want him to stay in the New York apartment until this story dies down. Then I will send him to Europe when the opportunity arises."

"Who will I use as my security team?"

"I have already sent six of my best men to Las Vegas. They will watch your every move in shifts. You will never be alone. If we attract the prey we seek, I will send more," Leonid said. "This is our most important priority. If we allow these women to kill our brothers, soon we will be nothing to our competitors. They will nip at our heels like rabid dogs until we are no longer feared by them. I intend to make an example of these two as a lesson to those who would seek to infringe on our interests."

"I understand," Petro said. He knew that once Leonid felt insulted, he would not rest until the personal affront was avenged. Petro felt the same way. It was part of their bond.

In an eerily seductive, whispered voice, Raina said, "And if you keep her alive, I want her brought to me."

"I will see to it," Petro promised.

Petro arrived at McCarron International Airport in Las Vegas the next morning. The Citation X taxied to the Fixed Base Operations Center where he was met by two Russians that he realized he had met briefly once or twice in the past.

One was a short barrel of a man, his facial features squished down so that his eyes overhung a short nose and blubbery lips; he resembled an overfed hog. The other was tall, with lean, rangy arms punctuated by hands that appeared several sizes too large for his height. He had fierce blue eyes, a long, perfect nose, thin lips, no facial hair, and only a close-cropped fringe of blonde hair on an otherwise bald head. Petro remembered where they'd met.

The pair had accompanied Leonid during an operation in Rome, at the famous Spanish Steppes. They'd met Boris Alkaev, a Russian mobster and two of his men, both Italians, at the base of the steps near the fountain there. The meeting had been arranged for 2am when the tourist attraction and the church at the top of the steps would be deserted. Boris was to turn over keys to a travel locker in the train station containing two-million Euros, the price agreed upon for the delivery of a cocaine shipment in another locker at his hotel. The keys were to be exchanged and the two principals were to remain together while the contents of each locker were verified by a third party as they waited.

Sergei Markovic, whom Erika had killed in Las Vegas less than a year ago, had been secreted atop an apartment building with a clear field of fire to the train station. Petro had been sent to retrieve the two-million Euros payment. When he opened the locker, he found the money packed in a large duffle bag as expected. What he didn't expect, however, were the four men who braced him with drawn weapons held low against their legs. His cell phone was turned on and transmitting continuously to Sergei on the other end. When one of the men instructed Petro to walk out of the station ahead of them, Sergei was waiting.

Two men were walking behind Petro and two kept pace on either side. Sergei shot the man to Petro's left with a silenced rifle. Petro spun on his left foot and kicked the man to his right with a crushing blow that snapped the knee back at an angle nature never intended. A third man fell as Sergei put a round through his chest. The fourth and last man looked up, desperate to locate the shooter as Petro produced a wicked double-edged knife from his sleeve and stabbed him in the throat. He turned back to the man he'd kicked, intending to cut his throat, when another of Sergei's rounds took him in the head. Petro picked up the duffle bag and walked away from the carnage. It only took seven seconds.

Sergei reported the incident to Leonid, who had a receiver attached to his ear. Without warning, Leonid produced a silenced handgun and shot the two Italian guards point blank. Boris turned and bolted up the Steppes, attempting to put as much distance between him and the three Russians.

The short Russian produced a silenced Israeli Uzi as a black Mercedes sedan roared up to the fountain. The submachine gun sprayed a ribbon of brass onto the pavement as he emptied the weapon into the car, ejected the spent magazine and inserted a full one with a practiced ease that belied his bulk. Not a trace of emotion impeded his actions. He was on automatic.

The thin, rangy Russian vaulted up the marble steps four at a time before Boris had ascended a third of the way, slapped his large meat hook of a hand around Boris' face and drove him backwards to the unforgiving granite with a resounding crack as his head met the hard surface. Without a moment's hesitation, he encircled the fallen man's ankle and dragged him, feet first, back down the granite stairs, his head bouncing off each riser as they descended. Boris was stunned, bloody, and unresponsive as the two Russians bundled him into the back of the silver Range Rover waiting at the curb, sandwiching him between Leonid and "The Bear."

The two Italian guards Boris stationed at the top of the Steppes were already dead. They'd been shot by two of Leonid's men, stationed expressly for that contingency at the same instant Leonid killed the others below.

As the memory came flooding back to Petro, he realized why. These men were former Spetznatz, Russia's equivalent of Special Forces, the unit responsible for the brutal repression of Afghanistan decades ago. If the other four men assigned to this operation were like these two, Leonid was pulling out all the stops to find and punish these two American women. He settled back into his seat, satisfied with Leonid's choices.

Alexei, the short one, and Dimitri, the tall man with the

huge hands, brought another memory back along with those names. It was particularly bothersome pictures of them in blood-spattered butcher's aprons, their sleeves rolled up, their hands and arms painted red with Boris' blood, whose remains then left that warehouse in eight separate garbage bags, to be delivered to his friends in exchange for the cocaine they'd sold them in the first place. It would not do to let their rivals think them weak.

Chapter 25

Erika sat in the darkened apartment for two consecutive nights, scanning the building across Central Park with night vision binoculars. She had only seen the rooftop guard pacing the perimeter of the building. Fyodor had yet to make an appearance. The guard made it obvious the Russians considered the premises worth the added security, but it was still not proof Fyodor was in residence. In fact, the appearance of security might have been installed as a ruse to make them believe he was there. At this point, it was a coin toss.

On the third night, her thoughts wandered back to California—back to Felix. She still wasn't sure what it was about him that had so inexplicably drawn her interest. He was beautiful, certainly. The restaurant patrons and the waitress could barely take their eyes off him. But no, it was something else. Something she could sense, but not see. She felt it the first time they met, in that tiny kitchen. He had looked at her directly, frankly, without guile. With most men she met casually, there was an instant interest in her looks and her physical being as they took a lascivious assessment of her body. With Felix, she felt he was looking inward, intensely curious as to what she was thinking, what she was feeling— like he had a sixth sense. She felt he understood there was something deeper, something special, when he looked at her.

Could she ever truly trust that killing Jorge would never become an issue between them? Could she trust her life to his explanation of their relationship? She couldn't possibly know the answers to these questions. She wanted to find out.

As she focused the binoculars across the park once more, a light came on and behind the curtains and she saw blurred movement from right to left. She slowed her breathing, gradually bringing her heart rate down to normal, mentally going through the necessary steps in her mind, rehearsing them over and over.

Ten minutes later, her patience was rewarded. The curtains pulled aside to reveal Fyodor Kaminski. His three-hundred-pound frame filled the lens. Erika remained still, the binoculars focused on him.

Even at that distance, she could sense the power of his pent-up violence. Like a caged tiger or a grizzly bear, he walked and breathed like a predator. He turned away from the sliding glass door and dropped the curtain back into place. Erika watched the curtained shadow retreat into the apartment. She took the opportunity to move to the Barrett Rifle atop the tripod, locked in on the apartment. She turned on the BORS system, wary of the green display screen casting a muted glow within her surroundings.

Erika was ten feet inside the apartment, with another ten feet of space across the veranda through the open slider. She doubted the tiny screen would produce enough light to attract attention from almost a half mile away, but it still bothered her. She wanted Fyodor so badly that no detail escaped unnoticed, even one so miniscule. She lined up the scope on the balcony across the park and waited.

She noted the sentry atop the roof through her night vision binoculars. The man had appeared at the parapet twice since she saw Fyodor, giving rise to the thought that the increased distance to that target was negligible, in case he became an issue. She put away that thought and concentrated on the veranda below. The giant Russian was all that mattered.

Erika sat in a padded rocking chair, expending nervous energy by staying in motion. It calmed her to be immersed in a benign activity that kept her brain in neutral. Her eyes, however, remained fixed on the apartment building across Central Park.

The light in the target apartment went dark. Erika rose and took her position behind the scoped rifle, her eye affixed to the starlight scope aimed at the veranda. Night vision had progressed from the multi-hued green imagery of a decade ago. Now the optical relief was so stark, it resembled the sharp focus of a video game.

She watched the curtains pull aside; the sliding glass door open, and the larger than life image of Fyodor Kaminski emerge onto the darkened veranda. He held a drink in hand as he approached the railing to scan the surrounding area. Based on the darkened veranda and the absence of back light, Fyodor was still behaving with a great deal of caution.

She checked the BORS shooting system atop the scope, confirming her target resolution at the appropriate yardage, and matched the parallel lines of the BORS to indicate she was dead on target. Fyodor rested his giant frame against the rail, sipped his drink and stared out at the night vista.

Erika took three deep breathes, filling her lungs to capacity, and slowly emptied them in a controlled exhale. As she got to the end of her third exhale, she pictured the .50 caliber bullet leaving the muzzle of her weapon, travelling across the Park for almost two full seconds before impacting Fyodor in the chest. Time stood still.

She squeezed.

Two seconds felt like two minutes. Erika watched through the scope as Fyodor reacted, his body jerked as though someone punched him in the solar plexus, before he crumpled backwards, out of her scope picture as the kinetic energy of the huge round slammed through his chest cavity, eviscerated the organs within, and continued on through the apartment and presumably, most of the building.

Another message would be sent.

She lined the scope up with the roofline of the building, checked the BORS system for a resolution and waited. It only took a few seconds until the guard appeared at the parapet, perhaps alerted by sounds from below. At this distance, Erika had no way of knowing. She relaxed into her shooting stance, legs braced, eye on the target, slowly exhaled and squeezed.

The man disappeared from her scope as though yanked from behind by a tremendous force. That would be her only evidence of a hit. No human being could move that fast of its own accord. It was all the proof she required.

She closed the sliding door and began packing, breaking down the weapon, stowing each piece carefully in the padded case, along with her spotting scope and laser range finder. She retrieved her spent brass and put them in the case before breaking down the tripod, which she laid alongside the closed case. She called for her town car and began wiping down every surface in the room, even though she wore gloves during her stay.

Habits.

On the ride back to the hotel, Erika sent Donny and Sheila a text.

Message sent to FK. See you tomorrow.

Four down. Three to go.

Chapter 26

The return flight to San Diego was pleasant and uneventful. The Gulfstream 550 ate up the miles with a speed and efficiency most people would never experience in a lifetime, but had become commonplace for Erika.

Her mind wandered from the operation she'd just completed. She never invested any emotion in her operations. She seemed to be missing that piece of DNA. She did make a mental note to let Jim know the Barrett had been a timely gift, but that was the extent of her introspection. Perhaps, events in her life had robbed her of empathy. She certainly did not dwell on it. Her mind wandered back to Felix. She hadn't felt an unbidden spark of attraction like this since she was fifteen and met her first love, Dana. He later sold her to a vicious pimp named Moby. Those memories were hard for her to bear. Moby and Dana had paid for their crimes with their lives.

She was no longer a child. This was different. She was grown a woman with a wealth of highly specialized experience normal people could not relate to. She loved and trusted Dana, and he sold her like property to Moby, who subjected her to beatings, gang rape, and forcibly injected her with heroin... Moby's proven method for breaking her and turning her into a high-end prostitute—an oxymoron from Erika's perspective. She'd become Moby's top whore, bringing in more money than the rest of his stable combined. She learned to use sex to get what she wanted at an early age.

After she gained her freedom from that life, she was lost—literally and figuratively. Her return to a semblance of a normal life first came with the aid of Donny, a male prostitute she'd bonded with after a horrendous night of violence. They'd escaped together and formed a lifelong relationship that would never be broken. They'd shared living quarters, meals, a bed, and everything else two people could...along with some shared experiences no one would want.

Sheila and Richard Gibbons came next. They hired, sheltered, and trained Erika and Donny in the art of rescue and ransom. They'd given them their dignity and a renewed sense of purpose that was critical to their recovery as human beings. She would never admit the depth of her love for all three of them, but that love was her touchstone to reality.

Erika never told Richard how much she loved him when he was alive. But now that love formed the core of her personal vendetta; she was focused on exterminating those responsible for his death. When Richard was abducted in Las Vegas, she'd killed three of the seven Russian mobsters responsible for his death. Fyodor Kaminski was the fourth. She would not rest until she found the last three.

Now Felix had come into her life. He was an obviously attractive man, but she felt drawn to him because of the experiences that haunted him too. A former Navy Seal, he served four tours in Iraq and Afghanistan. He was no stranger to discipline, loyalty, or killing. Now he ruled the four gangs that ran Logan Heights and, by extension, had an impact on organized crime in many U.S. cities as a major source of narcotics smuggled into the country from Mexico. It was a complex, dangerous business to operate. The price of success was incredible wealth and power. The price of failure was death. Erika knew the truth. Felix was an arbiter of crime and violence, and apparently, he was very good at it. She knew where that life led and she wanted no part of it.

During their previous lunch, she discovered Felix was a complicated man, with a personal code of conduct, a self-deprecating sense of humor, and an interesting past. She knew that he yearned to belong, and the attraction between them had erupted with an intensity and urgency that was unexpected and overwhelming for them both. She resolved to explore the breadth and depth of their nascent relationship.

Once again, Erika, Sheila, and Donny were meeting behind the swimming pool grotto in the rear yard of the Bel Air mansion. The operation in New York had to be discussed and a strategy developed to report the operation to Senator Jerry Ross without exposing Erika's participation. Sheila needed to confirm the kill first-hand.

"You're certain he's dead, Erika?"

"Positive."

"Please explain how you can be so sure from over half a mile away?" Sheila asked.

Erika straightened in her chair. "I hit him in the center of his chest with a .50 caliber bullet, almost the size of your middle finger. On contact, the kinetic energy contained in a round that size, with that velocity, would punch a hole through his chest so large you could push your arm through up to the elbow. I never took my eye off the target. There was blood spatter behind him on the sliding glass door about three feet in diameter and a hole in the center of it the size of your fist. The target never got up, never moved from where he fell. I watched for a good twenty seconds before I shot that imbecile on the roof. I'm sure, Sheila. Fyodor Kaminski is as dead as it gets."

"Good enough for me," Donny said.

"It has to be," Sheila said, "because we're not going to get any form of objective verification from the other side. They'll just sanitize the building and dispose of the bodies so that no one ever finds them."

"Sheila, I'm positive. He's gone."

"Okay, Erika. I'm convinced. Now how do we report this to the esteemed Senator?" Sheila asked. "He's supposed to be in the loop on our operations, particularly those that include the Russian Mafia."

"Do we need to report it at all?" Donny asked. "It seems to me this is an ongoing operation and should not be divulged to anyone until it's completed." He allowed a barely discernable smirk to appear.

Thinking for a moment, Sheila said, "I suppose I could build a case for that. *We don't comment on open operations,* is a typical response in the intelligence community. Unfortunately, the Senator is a member of that community, a ranking member. He will probably point that out to me."

"Only if he finds out from someone else," Erika said. "And it might be interesting—no; *important* to find out if he has an independent source for his intelligence."

"It's probably worth the slap in the face you'll receive if he brings it up," Donny added.

"And if he does confirm a kill, it could only come from one source—the other side. There was no one else on our side from either support or logistics there to confirm the kill. He might stumble on the private air travel to New York, but that won't put him inside the operation," Erika said. "And the distance I made that shot from will only confuse matters. That's specialized knowledge. It's not even likely he'll connect the two."

"Okay, let's go with this," Sheila said. "Donny, you write up an ongoing operations report, for internal use only, to be delivered to the oversight committee upon conclusion of the operation. Mark it clearly that way, so that a three-year-old would recognize that was our intent. No names, of course. That way the agency is covered if this matter goes beyond this discussion."

"I'll take care of it," Donny said. "And I like the way you think. Richard would be proud."

"I hope you're right."

Erika kept silent. She didn't like having to hide details of an important operation from the very people who were supposed to be supporting them. Her inner radar told her this was a potentially dangerous predicament. It unsettled her.

Donny noticed. "Erika, what is it?"

"I don't know," she said. "This just smells bad. I don't trust the Senator one bit."

"We agree," Sheila said. "But, there doesn't seem to be

anything we can do about it now."

"I know what I'd like to do..."

"Stop, Erika, don't say it."

Donny just shook his head. He could have finished Erika's sentence for her.

Chapter 27

"If that bitch is responsible for this, I will flay her alive and make her eat her own flesh. That fucking bitch!" Raina roared, pacing back and forth through the great room. "I want her. I want her more than anything I've ever wanted. Find her, Leonid. Find her, I beg you!"

He knew better than to respond to Raina when she was delirious with rage. Better to wait until she wound down and spent her anger before even considering a plan. Leonid sat in an overstuffed arm chair, seething in silence. Staring out the window, he thought of his lost comrades:

Sergei, the polite young man with the boyish face, a deadly sniper with the patience of a rock.

Afanasi, a bull of a man who ran his clubs and his whores with an iron fist and the occasional branding iron.

Agnessa, a cute pixie of a girl, used as both pet and tool, had been trained in violence and perversion by Raina herself.

And now, Fyodor, a mountain of a man who had been seemingly indestructible, had been assassinated.

One American Intelligence officer, a woman, was responsible for the first three and probably Fyodor as well. Lost in his hatred of this brash American, he stared out the window.

"We shall see," he vowed. "We shall see." He possessed actionable intelligence that he would not share; not even with Raina.

Aleksi Kaminski was a large man like his brother Fyodor. Even at five years his senior, Aleksi resembled his younger sibling so closely they could have been twins. The same height, 6'7", nearly the same weight at 270 pounds, the same bald head and deep-set eyes beneath protruding brows.

But the similarities ended there. Aleksi was a gentle bear of a man, an academic professor of economics at the University of Moscow. He eschewed politics and all its complications, preferring the quiet life on campus, interacting with the intellectual youth of Russia, challenging them to better themselves, cheering when appropriate and expressing his disappointment with a saddened demeanor when one of his pupils did not put forth their best effort. He was universally loved by all his students and respected by his fellow faculty members for his quick wit and forgiving nature.

He married a simple woman from the forested central region over twenty years ago and brought her to Moscow with him to live. His wife, Olga, gave him three beautiful daughters and a son, all nearly grown now. His world revolved around the five of them, his island of peace in the seemingly endless discord of the smog-choked city. To say his wife and children loved him was a grave understatement; they worshipped him. He had never struck one of them in anger, preferring to sit down and explain the consequences of their behavior with limitless patience. It only took that disappointed look on his face to remind the children their actions required improvement. He had fought for and earned a profound sense of peace in his life.

Shortly after the birth of young Fyodor, their mother died from complications related to the enormous size of the infant, an injury their father would neither forget nor forgive. When Aleksi was a teen, he became responsible for the care of his younger brother, Fyodor, an aggressive, athletic child whose abnormally large frame and great strength landed him in trouble at school on a daily basis.

Thankfully, their father, a coal miner, was absent most of the day, working 12-hour shifts, 6 days a week. After work, he arrived home covered in soot that collected permanently beneath his fingernails, eyelids and skin folds. He was rarely in a good mood. If everything was not up to his expectations, his two sons suffered his wrath. The beatings were so severe, both boys suffered broken bones and contusions that ran the gamut from surface injuries to extreme internal pain. By the time Aleksi was fourteen, he was already inserting himself between his father and young Fyodor, absorbing most of the beatings himself. He was a savior to his younger brother—the only human being who loved and protected him from the world. The younger sibling could only look on as Aleksi took the punishment meant for him.

When Aleksi was recognized for his intellect and academic achievements, he was selected for advanced education by the State to attend the University of Moscow. At this point, the die was cast. There was no way he could leave the thirteen-year-old Fyodor to suffer his father's rage on his own. Something needed to be done.

The evening he was preparing a bag with his meager belongings for his departure, their father came home later than usual. He was drunk and began berating Aleksi for abandoning them, and then he started on Fyodor, explaining what his additional responsibilities would be once his brother left. When it became apparent it would be impossible for the younger brother to accomplish the long list of daily tasks, Aleksi spoke up. He begged his father to stop and think. His father reacted by slugging him in the solar plexus, doubling him over, then pummeling him to the ground.

Fyodor snapped. He grabbed the iron fireplace poker and bashed his father over the back of his head, again and again and again, until his arm was tired--- and his father was dead, blood sprayed all over the room from the hideous wounds.

When Aleksi recovered enough to rise and view the carnage, he knew they were done. Minutes later, the authorities burst in because of the loud noises emanating from the small stone house. The boys' fate was sealed. There was nothing he could do any longer to protect Fyodor. Aleksi was sent away to the University, and Fyodor was shipped to a youth detention center. Fyodor began his initiation into a life of violence and crime.

During the years they were separated, Aleksi continued to monitor his brother's progress through the system. When Fyodor was selected for an advanced athletic training program, Aleksi breathed a huge sigh of relief. The National Government had found Fyodor useful; therefore, his health and welfare would be protected by the State. In actuality, his athletic prowess and psychological profile had been widely documented by the trail of broken bodies he'd left behind in every reform school where he'd been bullied. Once his dominance of every physical threat he encountered was discovered by the Russian Junior Olympic Team, his ascendance in the wrestling world began.

Aleksi kept in contact with his younger sibling through letters and phone calls. He sent money when he could and attended every wrestling match within travelling distance. His was the only voice Fyodor heard cheering, the only man to show him love and support. The only man he would willingly die for.

When Fyodor heard the sliding glass door shatter in the New York apartment, he dropped to the floor on instinct. It took only moments for his surprise to turn to horror, when he realized Aleksi was on the veranda looking out at the night lights of New York. They hadn't seen each other in over two years and true to his generous nature, Aleksi had arrived to visit and spend time with his little brother. He'd only been outside a minute, sipping his vodka when the glass door exploded into shards.

Fyodor crawled through the broken glass, paying no attention to the dozens of cuts being opened on his elbows and knees, only to find Aleksi on his back, a huge pool of blood spreading ominously beneath him. He knew it. He really did know it, but he would not accept it. This could not be. Not Aleksi. Not his protector: his mother, father, his brother. No. Not him. No.

He felt his neck for a pulse and found nothing. His eyes stared upwards, seeing nothing. Slowly, lovingly, he gathered

Aleksi's head in his lap and kissed his forehead, stroked his cheeks and crooned like a baby. The soft mewing sounds of agony mixed with his tears as he cradled his brother. It was the worst moment of his life.

Chapter 28

Erika dialed Felix's cell number. She felt the adolescent sense of giddiness once more.

"Hello, Erika."

"Hello, Felix."

"How are you?" He asked.

"Fine. Fine. How are you?"

"I'm doing well, Guapa."

"Guapa? What's that?"

"A term of endearment, Erika. It's nothing, really." He shrugged it off.

"It doesn't sound like a term of endearment. You sure?"

"Okay, it means beautiful," he said. "You satisfied now?"

"Immensely," she said. "Are you available for another meal? Dinner this time."

"Just say where and when."

"There's an Italian restaurant on Coronado Island called, *Prima Donna.* Do you know it?" She asked.

"Very well, Erika. Coronado is where I trained as a Seal. It's an excellent restaurant," he said.

"How about tomorrow night, seven pm?"

"Done," he said. "I'll see you there."

"Bye, Guapo," she said.

"Funny. Bye, Erika."

Erika clicked off, realizing that for the first time, she had a life separate from Donny and Sheila. They didn't know about Felix. It was a step away from them. She wasn't sure how to feel about that, so she put it in the back of her mind. She would deal with that issue if and when it materialized.

When Erika arrived, Felix was already seated near the rear of the restaurant. A handsome, Italian Maître 'D in a beautifully tailored dark suit escorted her through the long narrow restaurant to where Felix waited. He rose and kissed her lightly on the lips, a gesture she casually returned without any thought. Felix had that impact on people.

The Maître 'D seated Erika, nodded his approval to Felix and left.

"He knows you?" She asked.

"Oh, yes. We've known each other for years."

"So that's how you got the power table, huh?"

"Well, they take care of me, and I take care of them," he said. "I ordered a bottle of Italian red wine. Is that alright?"

"Of course."

He poured them each a glass and saluted Erika. "To new beginnings."

"New beginnings," she repeated, raising her glass.

They enjoyed a fabulous meal and casual conversation, before ordering coffee. Neither of them wanted the date to end. Gradually, the wall Erika kept between herself and the outside world was crumbling. She felt powerless to stop it.

Finally, she broached a subject that required very careful navigation. "You know what I do, right?"

"I've seen what you do, Erika. I've done similar things, in the military and outside of it."

"I'd like to pose a hypothetical, to get your take on it. Is that okay?"

"Of course," he said. "I'm capable of reading between the lines."

"If you suspected someone in your organization, someone high up, was supplying information to a third party that could prove dangerous to people you cared about, how would you handle it?"

She hoped that was enough information to provide a response.

Felix must have sensed that. "First, I would have to be certain who it was, then evaluate the information that was passed on. How dangerous it was. How immediate the concern. Then you must consider how highly placed the individual is. If he can't be removed directly, then you send a message. You remove the person acting in his stead. Or, you leave that person in place and turn him back on his controller, after convincing him there was no other way out. Does that make sense to you?"

"Perfectly," Erika said. "You've confirmed what I already thought and given me a bigger picture to evaluate. You've done this sort of thing before. You're good at this."

"Thank you, Erika. Is this something I could help you with?"

"No. No, it isn't. I may have said too much already. It's something I have to do myself," she explained.

"Well, the offer still stands. Anything you need."

"Thank you."

Felix signaled for the check. Leaving a generous amount of cash on the table, he asked, "Would you walk with me?"

"Yes, I'd like that."

The Maître 'D flashed Felix a look of *well done* as they left. Erika pretended not to notice.

They walked South on Orange Avenue. A right turn a few blocks later had them heading for the beach. The Coronado shores boasted several miles of beach from the North Island Naval Air Station, all the way down the Strand to Imperial Beach.

The sky was clear and an almost full moon illuminated

the shore. The stars punctuated the sky's black canopy, lending a romantic air to their stroll. They continued south toward the oasis of light that illuminated the famous Hotel Del Coronado. They held hands as they walked. First date awkwardness vanished in an instant. She wore a black skirt and a grey blouse. Felix wore jeans, sneakers, powder blue shirt and a navy blazer. Sensing the cool ocean breeze, he took off his coat and wrapped it around her shoulders.

"Where are we going?" She asked.

"I'm not sure," Felix stopped and took her in his arms. "I know where I would like to take you." He nodded toward the hotel lights.

She stared into his eyes, searching for the truth about if she could really trust him, hoping it was there. She wasn't sure yet.

"There's nothing I would like better, Felix," she said. "I'm just not ready yet. There's a lot you need to know about me first." She was on a roll now, and it all came out in a rush. "I've done things—bad things. Things I can't tell you yet, maybe not ever."

He held her. He wanted her to purge, get it all out. Take a step. She didn't. She just held on, desperate to find words. None came.

Finally, he said, "Don't worry. I'm not going anywhere. I'll be here when you're ready."

She kissed him with the sort of promise that made him weak in the knees. Inexplicably, a tear fell, released without conscious thought. Hope reared its head once more in her life. In her past, it had been a bitter promise and an even more bitter result. Once again, Felix held her in silence until she was finished then turned her back towards the restaurant. The kiss told him all he needed to know.

She was worth the wait.

Chapter 29

Erika woke Sunday morning to find a text from Donny.

CALL ME ASAP.

She dialed his cell.

"Hi, Erika. Where are you?"

"Home. What's up?"

"We need to meet as soon as possible. Something's come up. It's important."

"Are you in Bel Air?" Erika asked.

"No, I'm home. This needs to be private," he explained. "Can you come to my place?"

"Sure. When?"

"Now."

"That urgent?"

"Yes."

"I'll be there in an hour or so."

"I'll be waiting." Donny hung up.

An hour and a half later, Donny heard the familiar rumble as Erika's Mercedes approached. He greeted her at the door and ushered her into the small, two-bedroom condo in Irvine. After a perfunctory hug, he brought Erika into the tiny kitchen to sit at the table.

"Donny, what's going on?"

"I need to tell you something, something I did that Sheila and you knew nothing about," he said.

"Donny, just spit it out," Erika said. "You're starting to piss me off."

"You're not going to like it," he warned.

"I already figured that much out, Donny. Tell me what it is."

"I put in a request with NSA to alert me if any key words I submitted to them came up in any context. They were to alert me if and when they did."

"What were the terms?" Erika still had no idea where this was going. She'd assumed this had something to do with the forty-seven million dollars missing in Brunei.

"Sheila's full name—and yours," he said.

"What? You did what? Who the fuck told you that you could use my name for any reason, let alone Sheila's?" Erika was furious and, for the first time, furious at Donny.

"Please, calm down," he began.

"Don't tell me to calm down, Donny. Tell me what the fuck happened," Erika demanded.

"Ok, just listen," he said. "I tagged your full name and Sheila's in case the NSA got any hits on either one, foreign or domestic."

"When?"

"When Richard was killed."

"God damnit, Donny! You better have a good reason for this," she said.

"I do. I do. Just listen, okay?" He was almost pleading with her now. She'd never gone off on him like this before.

"Look, both of you appeared on tape in that Las Vegas building; especially you. The Russians knew what both of you looked like. It was only a matter of time before they would try to put names with the faces. Their organization is too large and too sophisticated to just let it go. I knew they would try, and they did."

"What did they get?"

"Sheila's name," he said.

Erika felt her stomach drop. "Not mine?"

"No, nothing has appeared related to you."

"Okay, explain what this means. How'd they get it?" She asked.

"Erika, I need you to relax and just listen. Please. I never expected your name to come up at all. You're an operative, not an administrator, and as such, you're not required to appear before any Intelligence Committees or individual senators that sit on or head those committees. No one knows your name outside of this agency. It appears nowhere. Even your medical records are redacted. In the system, you're only a number, but socially, those people who you've interacted with on missions or trained you, *do* know your name. Financial records, asset ownership--all these things require a name. You're buried deep, but you're not invisible. You have to understand that."

Erika was quiet now. She was quick to understand the implications of this new information. A few moments passed before she asked the obvious. "What about Sheila?"

"That's a problem. She is an administrator now, as Richard was. In her new position, she is required to interface with Senator Ross and presumably, his office and staff. She is also required, on occasion, to appear before a closed-door session of the full Intelligence Committee, either to report on operations or justify budgets. Even though these are closed door appearances, that term is not worth the time it takes to say it. The place leaks like a sieve."

"How did they get her name?"

"Let me explain a few things first, so you understand what we're up against. Do you remember when Agent Scott was taken from the Westlake safe haven and tortured?"

"Yes," Erika said.

"Well, I assumed he was tortured for information, not as a reprisal, so I acted accordingly. Did you have any personal contact with that man?" Donny asked.

"No, none that I can think of."

"And no one there ever heard your name?"

She gave her answer some thought. "I don't think so. I never went there. I don't even know who was assigned to that ops, so I can't be 100% sure, but I don't think so. Why?"

"I'm just covering the bases on you first. Your name has never surfaced," he answered.

"Okay. Tell me about Sheila."

"Her name, her full name, was texted from a cell phone in Dallas, Texas to a cell phone in Montecito, California two days ago. No other message, just her name."

"Who sent the text?"

"We don't know. The cell phone ceased to operate as soon as the text was sent. It was a prepaid phone paid for in cash in the Dallas area, then presumably destroyed after it was used. There's no way to find it now," Donny explained. "They probably pulled it apart and threw it in a river. It's a dead end."

"Who received the text?" Erika asked.

"Rita Jackson, our CEO of the sex tapes," Donny said.

"Where the hell would she get Sheila's name?" Erika looked about to explode. "That fucking snake!"

Both of them remained silent for a few minutes, brooding while the severity of their predicament descended upon them. Finally, Erika broke the ice.

"Donny, I'm sorry I was angry with you. You did the right thing. But, please-never-ever-do something like this without telling me first."

"Okay, Erika. I was just trying to protect you the best way I knew how. Sheila, too," he said.

"I know. I know. But promise me that we'll always do these things together, like we used to."

"I promise."

The personal crisis was past. Now it was back to business. "How do you think our CEO got Sheila's name?"

"Well, since it came to her from an outside source, it

was not through her banking activities for the intelligence community. Besides, no names are attached to those accounts. That leaves only one source: Senator Jerry Ross."

"I should have known," Erika said. "Those sick sons-of-bitches."

"Erika?" Donny's tone was ominous.

"It gets worse."

"What?"

"Her name was texted to a place in Aspen, Colorado from the same cell in Montecito."

This problem just went from severe to critical.

"You get a name or address from that?" Erika asked.

"No name. The address is a ranch, a large, expensive ranch in the hills above Aspen, owned by a corporation."

"Does anyone else know about this?" she asked.

"Just you. I haven't talked to anyone else yet," he said. "But I have to tell Sheila. She has to know."

"I know, Donny. I know." Erika hesitated. "Let's think about this for a moment then we'll call her down here."

"Here?"

"She's never been here?"

"No, you're the only one."

"Ok, we'll do it up in Bel Air, when the time is right."

Chapter 30

Petro had been summoned back to Aspen for a personal meeting with Leonid. He was surprised at such a quick turnaround, but knew his boss rarely did anything without reason. Waiting for their meeting to begin, he sat in the great room with Leonid and Raina.

Leonid rose, picked up the house phone and dialed one of the outlying guest cabins. "Come, now," was all he said.

He turned to Raina. "Your new pet is locked away for the night?"

"Don't worry, Leonid. She will do as she was told. No one will disturb us."

Five minutes later, the front door opened and the huge frame of Fyodor filled the entrance. Leonid rose to greet him. Petro and Raina were rooted to their chairs, astonished. Fyodor lifted Leonid off his feet in a fierce bear hug, a gesture of love and respect no one had ever witnessed from the giant, and then gently set him back down and entered the room. He hugged Petro and then Raina, the latter to everyone's surprise, because he had never done so before.

Looks of bewilderment fluttered about the room until Leonid broke the spell. "Sit, my friend," he said to Fyodor, "while I explain."

"We lost two good men last week, a soldier and presumably, our friend, Fyodor. They found us in New York, as I feared they would. The man assassinated on the rooftop was our security agent. The man killed in the apartment was Fyodor's brother, Aleksi, a man we all loved and respected. He was not a part of our organization. He was an innocent."

Hunched forward, Fyodor stared at his huge hands draped across his knees. He was too overcome with emotion to meet anyone's eyes as his brother's name was said aloud. He was too close to tears. It was his fault. He never should have let Aleksi visit.

Leonid continued. "As he should have, Fyodor contacted me immediately. I decided to keep this between Fyodor and myself as a precaution. I want all communication on this to cease as of now. The only people who know Fyodor is alive are all in this room. I want it to stay that way. Aleksi's body has been flown back to Moscow where he will be treated with the respect he deserves. His family will be taken care of for the rest of their lives. Fyodor was flown directly here by private jet under an assumed name. I picked him up myself."

No one spoke. They knew not to. Leonid was focused on only one thing: revenge. Once he was certain they knew and had absorbed the gravity of the situation, he outlined their responsibilities.

"Petro, you will return to Las Vegas, as the bait. I want you surrounded by the six men I assigned you at all times, but not obviously so. Give them jobs that keep them near you, as drivers, cooks, housemen, etc. You will keep the others hidden, but nearby, as if unconnected to you. When I send word, allow yourself to become conspicuous: visit the club, go to dinner on the Strip, and live at the home in Henderson. At the end of the cul-de-sac, it is well protected and isolated. One of the homes at the inlet to the dead end will be occupied by our own men. If they come for you there, I want them bottled up and eliminated. I want anyone who survives brought here. Understood?" Leonid asked.

"Perfectly," Petro said. "What about Fyodor?"

"Don't worry about Fyodor. When the time comes, he will be there waiting," Leonid said. "I prefer him to be a surprise."

"And me? What will I do?" Raina asked.

"You will stay with me. We will be there when it is time. For now, we need to work on developing more information from our banker in Montecito," Leonid explained. "She will be the key to finding both of them."

Raina didn't answer. Her macabre smile said it all.

Chapter 31

Erika's cell designated solely for Felix chimed. That tiny spark of hope grew into a flame.

"Hello," she said.

"Hello, yourself, Erika. I want to see you. Can you get away?"

She had to stop herself from blurting out 'yes'. She hesitated for only a moment. "I'd like that. Are you free tomorrow?"

"I'm free whenever you'd like me to be," he said. "What would you like to do?"

She thought for a few moments. She wanted to know more about him, his background, and his time in the Seals. Actually, she wanted to learn everything she could about this new man in her life.

"Do you ever work out? Run, maybe?"

"Almost every day," he answered. "I have some healthy habits from my time in the service. I usually split my time between running, swimming and resistance training. What do you do?"

"I love to run. I'm a less than average swimmer. I use weights four times a week when I can."

"Would you like to try a five-mile run, and then lunch afterwards?"

"That sounds perfect. Do you know Torrey Pines State Park in Del Mar?" Erika asked.

"Yes, I've been there."

"Let's meet tomorrow morning in the upper parking lot at 10," she suggested. "And bring your 'A' game."

He laughed. "See you there."

She was eager to see Felix again, to see if what she was feeling was genuine. It had been so long since she felt this way. Tomorrow morning couldn't come fast enough. Felix was waiting when she pulled into the parking lot. Leaning against the fender of his black BMW, dressed in a sleeveless white T-shirt, black shorts, and well-worn grey New Balance running shoes. With so little clothing, his wide shoulders, broad chest, small waist and long muscular limbs were on display. He was so impossibly gorgeous. A pulse-quickening smile erupted when he spied her.

She parked next to him and got out. She was dressed similarly in black spandex shorts, grey Nikes and halter top, her pony tail pulled through a battered ball cap. Without any thought, he gave her a hug and briefly kissed her lips. It seemed like they'd been doing it for years. She liked it.

He led her up the pavement to where the trails began. "So, you want to see my 'A' game, Erika?"

"Do you have one?" She teased.

"That's what we're here to find out, Senorita. Which trail do you want to run?" He asked as they studied the sign describing the trail loops.

She pointed. "This one, two miles down to the beach and three back up the long way."

"Okay, but start slow. I am an older fellow, you know."

"Yeah, right," she said.

They walked down the uneven dirt path until they warmed up, then Erika broke into a slow jog as the trail narrowed, so that Felix trailed behind.

"Let me know if I'm going too fast," she chided over her shoulder.

"I'll try to keep up."

She quickened the pace, picking her way through the low mesquite bordering the undulating trail winding through the uneven terrain, switching back on itself as they gradually descended to the beach. The sun was just pushing the fog back off the cliffs with a promise of the heat to come. They made it to the sand in fourteen minutes, passing several hikers going both directions. Both were glistening with perspiration by the time they reached the hard-packed sand near the water, happy to share a common bond.

"Was that your 'A' game?" Felix teased as they jogged along the wet shoreline.

"I was trying to take it easy on you. You are a bit older, you know." Without warning, she took off at a sprint.

Felix responded, digging in behind her, the sand flying off his heels. He'd run too many miles on too many beaches while a Seal, to let this girl pull away from him. But, no matter what gear he put it in, she found another one; just enough to stay a few yards ahead of him. Ever so gradually her pace slowed, so Felix slowed with her, keeping them in a rhythm as they turned for the torturous climb from the beach back up to the road.

As the path steepened, Erika's pace slowed further as her lungs and buttocks screamed from oxygen depletion. Felix whacked her on the butt with the flat of his hand as he passed her. This was a walk in the park compared to his days as a Seal. This didn't even qualify as a warm- up. The Seals have a mantra: *The only easy day was yesterday.*

Now it was Erika's turn to keep up, and she did, staying within ten yards of the automaton Adonis in front of her. When they reached the road at the crest of the hill, Felix stopped and offered her a very tired high five and gave her that great smile of his. She half-heartedly smacked his hand and bent over, hands on her knees, recovering. She was happy, so happy!

Felix walked in circles, slowing his heart rate, catching his breath. "C'mon, Erika, let's walk it off."

He pulled off his shirt, displaying his chiseled abdominals and chest, toweling the sweat off his face with his shirt as they walked back to the car. She couldn't take her eyes off him. *Where was this heading?*

They reached the cars and toweled off, letting the sun finish the job as they leaned on the trunk, hip to hip, recovering. "Where to, now?" Felix asked.

"Let's drive into Del Mar for an early lunch," Erika suggested. "There's a great place on the beach called Jakes."

"Great, I'll follow you," he said. "But I have to do something first."

"What?" Erika was puzzled.

"This." He turned to her, pinning her against the warm steel of the car with his pelvis, his arms planted on both sides of her, his naked torso only inches from her. His lips hovered inches from her mouth, daring her to complete the circle. She moved to him. When she kissed him, a hunger she hadn't known took over, tenderly at first, and then heated up, leaving them breathless, smiling at each other. Taking his face in her hands, she whispered, "Is this real? Are you sure?"

Putting his finger to her lips he said, "As real as life. Let's not question it." He kissed her again, this time his strong arms around her, molding their bodies together, his desire obvious. There was a bit of privacy behind the car for the two lovers, but their passion acquired a life of its own by the time they broke apart.

"C'mon," Erika said. "We'll do Jakes another time. The Lodge is less than a mile from here.'

"Are you sure, Guapa?"

"I'm sure."

They broke apart and grabbed fresh t-shirts, pulled them on as quickly as they could and jumped into their cars, eager as teenagers.

Less than ten minutes later, Felix signed for a suite overlooking the Torrey Pines Golf Course and the Pacific Ocean. They didn't care about the manicured grass, the deep blue sky, or the two gliders sailing over the cliffs. They were in each other's arms, frantic to get their clothes off. Erika was the byproduct of too many sexual encounters over her life, many forced, and far too many for monetary reward. This was different: this held hope and the promise of love, the most fragile of human emotions.

"Just let it go, Erika," he whispered into her hair. "Trust yourself first, and then trust me."

And she did. They made love with a tenderness she'd never experienced, as his eyes locked on hers, they melded together, their bodies becoming one as he entered her. He never took his eyes off her, trying to drink all of her in. They took their time, reveling in each new sensation until their heat built to a crescendo and burst, leaving them spent, panting for breath.

Neither moved, nor spoke. They fell asleep, Felix still inside her. Twenty minutes later, he spooned behind her, pulling the duvet over them. Erika felt him growing again and adjusted her posture to admit him once more. This time they went even slower, stretching it out, barely moving. Afterwards, they slept again.

Felix slipped from bed and ordered a late brunch of juice, fruit, bacon and eggs with coffee. She rose to the sound of running water, and joined him in the shower. Erika was well beyond questioning her feelings for Felix and the obvious complications a relationship with him would present. Their unexpected attraction to one another had taken on a life of its own. She willingly walked into his arms beneath the warm spray of water.

Clad only in terry cloth robes when room service arrived, Felix tipped the man who served their meal on the veranda. Ravenous, they dug into the food.

Erika was so happy she was beaming. "What are we doing here, Felix?" There was no way she could remove the smile from her question.

"Enjoying one another."

"I'd say this is a good start then." She shook her head in wonder.

"I always knew it would be," Felix said. "I wanted this to

happen long ago."

"Even though you know what I do?"

"That would be preaching to the choir," he said. "You know what I do, too. Neither of us leads a conventional life style. There's a lot of baggage on both sides."

"There's a lot more you don't know about," Erika said. "We'd have to go slow."

"Erika, I don't come with any guarantees. I doubt there's a white picket fence, two and a half kids and a mortgage in our future. I don't know your past. You don't know mine either. All I care about is what I see ahead of us. What each of us has done is behind us. What's in front of us is what we make of it. I see tremendous value in you as a friend, a confidante, and now," he smiled, "a lover."

Erika digested his statement for a moment, then, as was her habit, asked the most direct question. "What do you want out of this? What do you want from me?"

"The truth. From this day forward, we are the architects of our relationship. I want an honest relationship with a woman who will speak only the truth to me, never betray my trust or confidence, and protect me as her family. When we are together, we treat one another with respect. When we are apart, we handle our business as we see fit. No promises. We do what we have to do."

"Felix, we're both involved in things that could get us hurt or killed. There's a lot we don't know about one another. I like you. I like what you stand for, but there's a lot to work out in the future. I don't come with guarantees either."

"I know that, Erika. Figuring this out together is what makes it worthwhile. I've never felt this way before. I want to see where it leads," he said. "Does that work for you?"

"Yes, one step at a time," she said. "But you need to understand something. The people I'm dealing with right now are dangerous people with no conscience. If you were in the wrong place at the wrong time, they wouldn't think twice about killing you."

"Erika, I understand that and it changes nothing. I'm in a fluid situation, too. Since Jorge died, there are many soldiers who think I'm vulnerable now. Some of these men were sworn to my little brother, and they feel entitled to his position. I must change that perception or remove them. You understand?"

"Yes."

"And it doesn't matter?"

"No."

Felix held her and kissed the top of her head. "You're a piece of work, lady."

"I've heard that before." She laughed. "From you, I think."

Soon enough, they would have several reasons to recall this conversation.

Chapter 32

Donny and Erika met at the Bel Air estate in the early afternoon. As agreed, they took care to omit any unofficial discussions from their reports when they submitted their requests to the Senate Oversight Committee. Erika and Donny knew that Sheila's full name had been transmitted via email between Montecito, California and Aspen, Colorado. They knew Rita Jackson, the CEO of the bank that funded intelligence operations was the sender, and they assumed the receiver was someone they were searching for within the Russian Mafia. They had not, as yet, shared that information with Sheila.

Additional information had come to light that took precedence. Petro Sokolof had been positively identified at the strip club in Las Vegas. They were meeting to decide what action to take.

"I don't get it," Erika said. "He shows up, bold as brass, knowing we're trying to locate him."

"I agree," Donny said. "He knows we have nothing on him that he could be arrested for, but to appear so openly, knowing what other options are open to us, makes me suspicious."

"Obviously, they're expecting a response. They have to realize we'd pick up on this quickly. Somehow, they want us to react. They're baiting us, trying to draw us in," Sheila said.

"Where is he living?" Erika asked.

Donny provided an aerial perspective of a tract home situated at the end of a cul-de-sac in Northeast Henderson, a suburb of Las Vegas. A dozen or so similar homes flanked either side of Petro's home. Beyond the backyard were miles of desert that led to the mountains and Lake Mead. It would be a simple matter for Petro to disappear into the barren desert on a moment's notice. It was also an area that could conceal a small squad off Russians lying in wait. The homes leading up to the cul-de-sac also had to be considered potential threats. This would not be simple.

"Do you have any sense of his movements? Any consistent habits?" Erika asked.

"Not yet," Donny said. "He does go out in the back yard for a dip in the pool in the late afternoon, but I think that's to lure us in the back door. There are at least two others living in the home, and a driver in a blacked-out Range Rover appears at random times. He's gone to dinner several times, always with two men escorting him, and twice he met Maksima Orlov, the woman who runs the club now. He usually goes to the club after dinner and stays there until late. The same Range Rover returns him to the house in Henderson afterwards."

"You think he has the desert behind the house under observation?" Erika asked.

"Without a doubt," Donny said. "You'd need an army to take him at the house. The desert is an open invitation to disaster. We can't be sure he's in the Range Rover until he reaches his intended destination and executing him in a public venue would create insurmountable political problems for this agency, so that's off the table."

"What's left?" Erika asked.

"The club is a possibility, but if any harm came to Petro there, I doubt anyone would get out in one piece. I have the feeling they're trying to herd us into an attempt they'll be prepared for. I'm wary of the entire setup."

"Can we draw him out?" Erika asked.

"How?" Sheila asked.

"I'm not sure."

"Erika, you know better than to do something without my express approval, right?" Sheila asked.

"Yes," Erika answered. "Don't worry, boss. I wouldn't put you in that position."

Sheila turned to Donny. "For now, I want 24/7 observation

of the house. Task a drone out of Nellis Air Force Base. I want that intelligence analyzed for any opening that seems feasible and reported directly to me or Donny; no one else. This stays with the three of us."

"Okay," he said.

"Erika, you stay close. If we get any actionable intelligence, we'll act on it."

"Alright, I'll head home. I'd like to go over these reports on my own, take some time with them."

"I'll walk you out," Donny said.

Erika kissed Sheila good-bye, noting her friend looked like the weight of the world was on her shoulders. "It'll work out, Sheila. Don't worry so much. It'll age you."

"I'll try."

Donny escorted her to her car. When they were out of earshot, he said, "Don't you think we should tell her that her name has been exposed?" He was clearly worried.

"Not yet, Donny. I want to try something first," Erika replied. "I'll let you know the second I have something."

"Please make it soon. I don't like this."

"Me neither."

Donny watched the gray Mercedes disappear beyond the gates, shaking his head. He had the feeling things were about to change and not for the better.

Chapter 33

In the basement of the Henderson house, Petro was sweating profusely, gripping his knees as he recovered from his exertions. Weary from two hours of practice, he pushed himself upright once more on the balls of his feet, knees slightly bent, arms loose at his sides. He faced the man standing ten feet away who was holding an empty revolver pointed at his chest.

"Again," he said. "When I move, you pull the trigger."

The man said nothing, all his concentration was directed on Petro, all his senses primed to react to any movement, eager to shoot. He was the third opponent Petro had drafted in this deadly game. If he pulled the trigger before Petro closed the ten feet of space between them and disarmed him, he would be awarded one thousand dollars. So far, no one had collected.

Petro calmed himself, willing his body to experience complete relaxation, a state he could most effectively explode from. When he felt his opponent begin to tense in expectation of an attack, he burst forward below the level of the revolver like he was shot from a cannon, his left hand gripped the floor and swiveled his legs forward in an arc, sweeping the man's legs out from under him, causing his back to impact the cement floor before his head slammed backwards with a resounding crack as it bounced off the hard surface. Petro removed the revolver by twisting the backside of his adversary's right hand inward toward his body and pulling the handgun upwards out of his hand. He sent it skittering across the basement floor until it came to rest against the stairs. Petro knelt over his opponent and gently slapped him in the face to bring him to his senses.

"Just lay there for a moment, Yuri. You're a little disoriented."

When he recovered sufficiently, he said, "I am done with this game, Petro. This is not for me."

"I know, my friend. I'm sorry. Let's get some ice for your head."

He pulled his friend upright and helped him upstairs to the kitchen, sat him in a chair, filled a large Ziploc bag with ice and held it to the back of his head for him. "Hold this a moment, Yuri. I need some water."

While filling two glasses from the tap, his mind wandered to the dark-haired American woman. *If only I can get within ten feet of her.*

Chapter 34

For the first time in recent memory, Felix was happy; no, not happy—enthusiastic, full of hope—looking forward to each day. His life had always been filled with confrontation. It began with his mother, who was never there for him, leaving him to fend for himself and his little brother. It was a fearful existence, stealing enough food for two and hiding it from their mother. When she returned, often with a strange man, they hid, crawling through the broken latticework beneath the back porch and huddling together in the dirt for warmth, waiting, while their mother entertained her guest. Often, Felix would rock young Jorge to sleep, caressing his forehead as he silently cried.

Then one day, two uniforms appeared; an older white man with gray hair and tired eyes, and an oversized black woman with a buzz cut. They took the two boys and drove straight to McDonald's, where they each devoured two Big Macs, a large order of fries, and two cokes. Sadly, the adults looked on, their suspicions confirmed by the amount of food the boys inhaled. And then they took them to an orphanage. It was the first time an adult could not meet Felix's eyes as they left. It would not be the last. He could still see that tired, defeated slouch of their shoulders as they ambled off, too worn down to care, time and time again.

Finally, with Erika, a woman had come into his life that asked for nothing, looked him straight in the eye and said exactly what she was feeling. He didn't know where their relationship was headed, but he was eager and anxious to find out. A friend once told him that a beautiful woman was a fine thing to be seen with, but he would love and hold dear the woman who would sell stolen oranges on the roadside with him, if circumstances warranted. Felix felt like he had the best of both.

He called Erika and invited her to dinner at Prima Donna, his favorite Italian restaurant on Coronado Island, and she accepted. He also reserved a suite at the Hotel Del Coronado, in the hope that she would stay with him through the night. Their last encounter had been so special, so meaningful, he wanted more. He wanted to experience her, taste her, to know her hidden dreams. He felt like an eighteen-year-old again, and he liked the feeling.

He'd registered at the hotel earlier that afternoon, dressed for dinner and started walking the six blocks up Orange Avenue to the restaurant. He was dressed in dark denim jeans and a white shirt under a tailored black sports coat with soft black Prada lace-up shoes for comfortable walking. He was enjoying the stroll, not paying attention to anything, his mind on his date.

He should have been more alert, as two men stepped out from a doorway directly in his path and forced him to stop. Felix said, "Excuse me," and attempted to sidestep them. Again, they blocked his path. Then he felt the cold, familiar steel of a handgun pressed into his back. A third man had come up behind him.

He watched as one of the men in front opened his coat to reveal he was armed as well. The second man now held a semi-automatic close to his side in plain view. Almost immediately, another man crossed the broad avenue and stepped onto the sidewalk beside Felix, sealing off any opportunity for escape. Felix cursed himself for his lack of attention. In his business, that could prove fatal. He knew these men.

"Felix," the man beside him said, "Turn around and start walking. One wrong move, one wrong word, and I will kill you where you stand." He stepped close and patted him down as quickly and as unobtrusively as possible. Satisfied there was no weapon, he said, "Start walking."

Two men walked on each side, two more behind him. He was under their complete control. Felix could only hope for the opportunity to act. His inner senses were humming into the hyper stage prior to a violent act. A glance behind told him they were too far away to attack and too close to miss shooting him.

"Turn right at the intersection," the man behind him instructed. Forty yards further down the side street, an alley appeared that ran behind the length of the commercial district just before the street became a tree-lined housing neighborhood. "Turn right into the alley."

Felix saw a glimmer of hope now. If this was a straight up execution, they would have already killed him. They were taking him somewhere to make an example of him, probably because of what transpired at the Contreras home. The unwritten law was you avenged your own, especially your brother.

Another alley teed off the first, running behind the length of the homes situated on the long block that ran towards the Pacific Ocean. Felix could see their immediate destination was a white van parked 100 yards down the alley. He knew that once he was inside that van he was dead.

"Give me your hands," the man behind him instructed. Felix complied and the man affixed plastic ties around his wrists in front of him and zipped them taut, cutting off his circulation.

Before they could proceed, they heard the distinct click of high heels on pavement, gaining ground behind them. The indistinct outline of a slim woman in a dark skirt and white blouse was striding briskly towards the group of men as though they were not there. *A neighbor taking a shortcut home, maybe?*

"Raul, Arturo, see who the fuck that is and get rid of her," the leader demanded.

The two men complied, closing the distance between them and the woman at a rapid pace. Even though their posture and pace was plainly aggressive, the woman kept coming. When they got to within ten feet of her, she produced a silenced semi-automatic hand gun and shot Raul first, in the face. He was on her left and therefore capable of a quicker response as a presumed right hander, and then she shot Arturo in the throat and forehead from only five feet away.

Three muffled shots within one second and both men crumpled to the ground. Erika never broke stride. Felix had the advantage of previously witnessing her lightning speed. These men did not. Next, she shot the man to Felix's right, twice, center mass, and was about to shoot the other when Felix moved into him, grasping his gun hand by the wrist, stepping away in a counterclockwise spin, snapping the bone and dropping him on his back, the air whooshing out from his lungs on impact. Felix stomped on his face once, twice, three times while still controlling the man's wrist before Erika stepped up and put two rounds in his forehead.

She looked Felix in the eye, stepped around him to inspect the van to ensure it was empty, slid her gun back into the compartment built into her purse and returned. She unsheathed a four-inch black carbon fixed blade from the small of her back and easily snicked through the plastic cuffs. Twelve seconds had elapsed.

Felix rubbed his wrists, "Let's get out of here. Now," he whispered.

"Wait," Erika said. "If you trust me, do exactly as I say."

"Okay." Was there any other choice? She just saved his life.

She took his arm and led him at a normal pace to the north end of the alley, turned right out to the adjoining commercial alley and turned left at the side street back to Orange Avenue and turned left again.

"Where are we going?" Felix asked.

"We had a dinner date," Erika said, "unless you don't want to eat with me now."

He smiled down at her and shook his head, totally bewildered. "Whatever you say."

"That was the correct answer," Erika needled him. They were walking along the well-lit avenue, now teeming with pedestrians in the early evening. It seemed they were strolling along, two lovers with not a care in the world, but Erika's eyes were ever moving; her hand inside the slit of her purse was wrapped around the familiar silenced Glock.

"Why are we eating after that?" Felix asked.

"Because it's the last thing anyone would expect, and we have unfinished business there."

"We do?"

"Yes, Felix, this is what I do," Erika said. "Just follow my lead and do what I ask, okay?"

"Okay."

He'd been to Iraq and Afghanistan, killed scores of bad guys there, but here he was a babe in the woods. He trusted this strange beautiful woman as much as the Seals he'd served with in those dangerous places and situations. But he had no idea why.

They reached the now familiar restaurant and entered, Felix in the lead with Erika trailing as she requested. Her eyes studied the Maitre 'D and nearby wait staff for any "tells" and found what she suspected. The Maitre' D was the same handsome young Italian man that hosted them previously, this time clad in a cream-colored silk suit and tie that hung beautifully from his athletic frame.

"Ah, Felix," he greeted them. "Young lady, please allow me to seat you."

They followed him to the reserved table in the rear, secluded from the other diners and were seated. He offered menus and water, and then asked Felix if he would like his usual wine.

Erika interrupted him, "Excuse me, sir," she said. "Would you sit for a moment, please?" Her voice dripped honey.

The man replied, "Of course," and pulled up a chair for himself. "How may I help you, Madame?"

Erika produced a white business card with black print bearing a special phone number. Only she and Donny knew its purpose. It read *Homeland Security* and gave an 800 number below; nothing else.

The Maitre' D did not touch it. He read the print and looked up at Erika.

"Do you know what this is?" she asked.

"No."

"It's a get out of jail free card."

"I don't know what you mean," he said.

"Yes, you do." Erika held up her hand. "Don't speak. Just listen. By the time we finish dinner, I will know more about you than your own mother does. I will know if your parents are still alive, if you're married, if you have children. I will know your dog's name, if you have one. Same goes for any other pets. Where you live, where you party and who all your friends are. When I'm finished, I will be the only friend you have left in the world."

Her voice was serene, just above a whisper. She continued. "If a phone call, any phone call is dialed from this establishment while we're here, I will know it's contents ten seconds after that. Same with a text or email. When we're finished with our meal, a car will be waiting to retrieve us. If there is even a hint of interference, your life, as you know it, is over." She gave him her most sincere smile. "Now, do you understand what I said?"

On the verge of tears, "Yes," was all he could manage.

"Now, please, bring us a bottle of Sea Smoke Pinot Noir, slightly chilled to start. We'll order after that."

After he left, Erika turned to Felix. "Have you checked to see if that Beretta you picked up in the alley is on safe? The one in the small of your back."

Felix couldn't help but laugh. "No. You don't miss much, do you?"

"I try not to. Please check it under the table and safe it. I don't want you to hurt yourself."

Felix pulled it out and did as he was told, ensuring there was one round in the chamber of the semi-auto and the safety was engaged.

"Do you want it?" he asked.

"No, keep it for now. We'll get rid of it tomorrow."

"Tomorrow?"

"I assume that's okay with you," Erika said.

"You bet," Felix was beaming. This woman was making him think he should pinch himself awake.

They ate their meal without anyone being seated within earshot. The Maitre' D had been making himself as scarce as possible, but was careful to keep himself within Erika's sight as much as he could. He was completely unnerved.

Felix asked, "How did you know those four took me?"

"I was across the street parallel and a little behind you, and the one who walked up behind you, the whole time. I saw the first two brace you along with the one who appeared behind you. When the fourth man crossed the street, I crossed at the light."

"You were following me?"

Erika didn't answer. She gave him a blank stare. He took the hint.

"How'd you know they wouldn't shoot me right on the street?"

"That would have taken only one man, at most two," she said. "In any case, I would have been too late. Where do you think they were taking you?"

"Someplace where I would die slow. They would have made an example of me," Felix explained.

"Who were they?"

"The top enforcers of the four gangs in Barrio Logan."

"What will you do about it?" Erika asked.

"I don't know, think it through first. I can't afford a mistake now."

"Would you promise me something?"

"Anything, Erika," Felix replied. "You just saved my life. I will do anything you ask of me."

"Careful what you say."

"I stand by my statement," he said. "Name your promise."

"Talk to me before you retaliate. I may be able to help," she said.

"Consider it done," Felix said. "One more question. It was the Maitre' D who told them where I'd be, wasn't it?"

"Yes."

"What should I do about that?"

"Nothing, for now. Either your friends are going to kill him soon or I will have a use for him later. Better the devil you know," Erika explained.

"Where did I hear that before?" His chagrin was painted upon his face.

Erika only smiled.

After they finished, Felix signaled for the bill. The Maitre' D appeared instead of their waiter.

"Your meal is on the house," he said.

"Very kind of you," Erika said. "Please sit for a moment more."

The Maitre' D sat down.

Erika said, "When they ask, we were never here. Do you understand?"

"Yes."

"If anything happens to Felix because of what you've done, I'm going to kill you. If he trips and falls, I'm going to kill you. If he catches a cold, I'm going to kill you. Do you understand?"

"Yes."

"Good. Now open the alley door and we'll leave that way."

"Yes, Madame."

Felix just stared at the Maitre' D during the entire exchange. He said nothing. The blank look on his face inferred all he needed to say. The man wasn't certain who scared him more. He led them to the rear door and held it open until Erika scanned the surrounding area and nodded her assent. Felix joined her, and the Maitre' D closed the door quietly behind them.

Felix turned to Erika. "I thought we had a car arranged."

"No, that was just for his consumption," she replied, indicating the restaurant door. "The Homeland Security card is something Donny and I cooked up. It's a special number that is connected only to him. I fed him a line of total bullshit. "Besides, I'm not ready for our relationship to become public, you being a gangster and all." He didn't need any light to see the smirk with her comment.

"Let's walk down this side street to the beach and then walk to the Hotel Del," she said.

"How'd you know?"

"Know what?"

"That I reserved a room there."

"I didn't, until now," she said, "but it would be pretty dumb to stay in a room reserved in your name."

"So, you reserved a room too?"

"No, I reserved one of the private town houses next door to the hotel." Erika laughed. "Duh."

Felix stood there speechless.

"You coming, or what?"

"Oh, yeah." This evening was surreal.

She took his arm when they reached the side-street. "What was that thing you did with the flip?"

"Oh, the Seals. A Soo Bahk Do master was one of our trainers," he replied. "We got along well with one another, and I trained under him privately for over a year. It just happened."

"Nice. Now let's get to our room, and I'll teach you some other moves," she teased.

The rest of the walk was a blur.

Chapter 35

Petro had been on display, as per Leonid's instructions for over a week now. He'd visited the strip club almost every evening, eaten out on the Las Vega strip several times, even dined at the steakhouse inside the Four Seasons, where he knew his adversaries had stayed previously. He gambled openly at four different casinos, losing enough money to attract a crowd. Nothing.

His men were always nearby. One drove his car, one his dining companion, several just faces in the crowd. Maksima Orlov, who now managed the club, had accompanied him on two more of those dinner dates, sharing stories of home, growing up, and their time at University. He liked her, genuinely enjoyed her company. He understood why Leonid had installed her after the disaster that cost the lives of three of his friends. She was beautiful, a brilliant conversationalist, and a versatile politician, capable of charming anyone. He secretly hoped the relationship would grow into something more substantial.

There were worse duties, he knew, but his impatience ate at him like a cancer. It also put him on the razor's edge. He would be ready when it happened. And it would happen.

Chapter 36

Erika was sitting on the veranda of the Hotel Del Coronado condominium, watching the sun traverse the ocean from left to right. It made her realize the beach here faced south, not west. She was content, safe from the outside world and its pressures, wrapped in a terrycloth robe, alone with her thoughts. Earlier that morning, before sunrise, she'd emptied Felix's room of its possessions and returned to the condo with them. Felix was not happy she'd done it without informing him, but he already knew how futile a comment would be.

Her cell phone rang...Donny.

She was tempted to ignore the call, but she knew Donny never called unless it was important.

"Hello."

"Hey, Erika. We need to talk. There's a problem." Donny sounded worried.

"Something you can tell me now?"

"Yes. Mom was invited to a party with a famous politician in Montecito. I don't want her to go."

"Shit! Neither do I. When?"

"Two weeks from Saturday," he said. "Thirteen days from now."

Erika sat there for a moment. "Ok, I'll be up there early tomorrow. We'll tell her together. Set it up for us. Oh, and find out everything about the hostess, habits, haunts, everything you can think of."

"Okay."

"And not a word until I get there."

"See you tomorrow at 10am," Donny said.

"Count on it." She hung up.

"What's wrong?" Felix stood behind her in the doorway.

"Nothing," she said. "Business."

"Can I help?"

She looked up at him. An idea was forming, but it was terribly risky. She hesitated. "Let me think about that for a while, okay? I need a little time."

"Whatever you need," Felix said.

"Oh, one more thing," Erika said. "You should consider shaving the goatee and buying a pair of nerdy black glasses. A shorter haircut might not hurt either.

"What?" He didn't get it.

"The one second of hesitation could save your life. Mine too." Tact was not one of Erika's strong points.

"Do you have a place to go? Another car to use?" She asked.

"Yeah. Both," he answered.

"Great. Now let me sit here and think for a while."

An hour later Erika decided to trust Felix with her life. "I need to trust you with something. I have no one else to turn to," Erika said.

"You sound serious."

"I am. This is as serious as it gets. Look, I want to talk something out with you that could get me in serious trouble. I'll leave out names, but what I say has to stay in this room. This is literally life or death." Her eyes bore into his. "You sure you want to hear this?"

"After what you did last night, how could you even ask me that?"

"Be sure."

"I am."

Still she hesitated, trying to carefully frame her words. Felix could see her anxiety. He interrupted her train of thought.

"Erika, I've killed a lot of people during my time in the service of our country. Bad guys, for the most part. Some I'm not so sure of. I've murdered or ordered murders in this country and in Mexico. In my head and in my heart, they deserved it. I will probably, no, most likely, do it again. You saw last night how I live. One mistake is all it takes. This thing we have, whatever it is, I intend to pursue. Anyone gets in the way of that, I'll kill them too. Now do you understand?"

Her eyes were threatening tears. She'd never heard something so terrible sound so wonderful. This was turning out to be one really fucked-up relationship.

"Okay. Let me talk for a while. Then I'd like an honest appraisal."

"Go ahead," Felix said.

"A year ago, I was involved in an operation in Las Vegas with a Russian gang that bought sex slaves into this country under the pretense of becoming supermodels. They were threatened and turned out as strippers, whores, you name it. We snatched one of the girls as leverage, and as a result, a man I loved as a father figure was murdered right in front of me.

I killed three of those responsible then, and another one two weeks ago. I'm going to kill the rest of them. I work for that man's widow now, as part of a government agency that few people know exists. I love her, too."

Erika stopped. She then realized there was no stopping at this point. She continued, "A senator whose social habits included cocaine and Russian whores was videotaped as leverage, and he later maneuvered himself into the oversight committee that has financial control over our operations. In fact, he's the head of that committee—our liaison. Our organization is funded by an investment banker, a woman from Montecito whose sexual habits resemble a rabbit on steroids. She's also on tape with men, women—the works. The Russians have their hooks into her, too."

Felix, a veteran of many intricate ops in strange places absorbed the information with little effort. "How does this intelligence FUBAR relate to you?"

"What's a FUBAR?"

"Fucked up beyond all repair."

"Oh." She actually smiled. "Well, these Russians have me on tape, and my boss, too, when I killed several of them in a warehouse in Las Vegas."

"Can they locate you by those pictures?"

"No, but my boss's name was texted from a phone in Texas to this bitch in Montecito last week, and there's only one man who knows her name."

"The Senator," Felix said.

"Yes, but there's more. My boss was just invited—you could say ordered—to attend a social event and accompany the senator in Montecito. Two weeks from today," Erika said. "They will ID her there, maybe even take her."

"In that case, why would she agree to attend?" Felix asked.

"That's the problem. We know the Russians had our pictures. Now they have her name and she hasn't been told yet. That's what my phone call was about."

"Can she cancel the date with the Senator under some other pretext?"

"Not without severe repercussions to our agency," Erika replied. "I'm not even sure she'd believe she was in danger while she was escorting a United States Senator."

"Christ, I thought my life was complicated."

"Tell me about it," she commented.

"You can't let her go."

"I know. I'm going up there to talk to her tomorrow morning," Erika replied.

"Okay. Give me some time to go over what you told me. Call me after you meet. I may have a solution by then," Felix said.

"Okay, you do have a place to go? People you can trust?" She asked a second time, to be sure.

"Yes," Felix answered. "I have a place in Del Mar, on the beach. No one knows of it."

"No one?"

"Just you, now."

"What are you going to do in the meantime?" Erika asked.

"Shave. Get a haircut. Buy some glasses." Laughing, he pulled her into his arms. "One adventure after another." He kissed her.

Chapter 37

As she drove to Bel Air, Erika was preoccupied. The usual traffic jam at the immigration checkpoint, the area South of San Clemente, barely registered. This meeting would not go well, but she'd already made her decisions. If Sheila went to Montecito with the Senator, her life expectancy would be considerably shortened. And Erika would be next. Unacceptable.

When she arrived at the estate, Donny greeted her as she parked and escorted her directly to their casual meeting area behind the pool. There were lounge chairs and lemonade waiting.

Sheila was noticeably perturbed. There was ice in her greeting. "Hello, Erika."

"Hello, Sheila." They didn't hug and sat down immediately.

"Donny tells me you have something important to discuss with me," Sheila began.

"We do."

"And why is it that I run the agency and don't know the agenda before you two? I have other responsibilities to other operatives that are kept entirely separate from your cell for obvious operational security reasons. You do realize you're not my only two agents or responsibilities, don't you?" This was starting off badly. "If Richard were alive, you would not have dared to behave like this—either of you."

Donny was in it now, too.

"Look Sheila," Erika began. "Of course, we realize there are other cells and you have more than just us to deal with. And both of us have your best interest in mind. That's why we're here."

Sheila cut her off. "Did you ever consider it would be in

my best interest to know what my best agents and my best friends are up to? I'm running an agency here, Erika, not a junior high."

Erika had never seen her like this. The pressure she was under must be unbearable. "Okay, then let me talk. I'll fill you in." Erika attempted to shoulder the blame. "This was my doing, not Donny's. After you hear me out, I hope you'll understand."

"Before you start," Sheila interrupted, "Donny is responsible to me, not you. And he will answer to me, not you." She glanced at both of them. "Do you understand?"

Donny and Erika nodded their assent, tight-lipped, barely under control.

"Now, explain, please," Sheila said.

Erika shot right to the heart of the problem. "The Russians have your name with the city of Los Angeles attached to it."

"What?" Sheila was on her feet now. "How could they?"

Erika said, "Calm down, Sheila, and please sit. Now is not the time to pull rank." She waited a moment then said, "I'm serious, Sheila, this puts me in the crosshairs, too. It's not just you I'm worried about."

Slowly, the impact of Erika's statement seeped in. She sat down, took a deep breath and regained her control. "Okay, Erika. Let's start over. Tell me what's going on."

"There was a text message sent from an untraceable, prepaid cell phone, from Dallas to Rita Jackson in Montecito that read, "Sheila Gibbons, Los Angeles.""

"When?"

"Last week."

Sheila looked at Donny, the accusation plain to see. She didn't need to ask why she wasn't informed at once.

"I asked him not to inform you until I researched Jackson," Erika said.

"Let's not go there yet," Sheila said. "How did they get my name?"

"There's only one person who could have done it. Only one with access to your name and location: Senator Jerry Ross," Donny said.

"Any proof?"

"None," he answered. "But, the circumstantial evidence is overwhelming. Either one of us did it or he did. There's more," Donny said. "That information was texted to a cell phone, in Aspen, Colorado within five minutes. That phone is registered to a 270-acre ranch registered to a foreign corporation out of London."

"You think that's the Russians?" Sheila asked.

"I'm not sure yet. I'm looking into it."

"Where did you come by this information?"

"Our friends at NSA," Donny said. "I sent them keywords I was interested in, a huge list. Your name and Erika's, was imbedded in the text request randomly. We got a hit on your entire name and roughly 10,000 hits on Erika's—first name only. Nothing definitive to worry about regarding Erika, until now. Your full name, however, was used in context. Not good."

"What can they do with a name that I never use in public in a city the size of Los Angeles?"

"Not much, so far. But given enough time, they'll turn up something. They're not amateurs, Sheila. They're serious," Donny warned. "Just because you're Director now doesn't change what happened in Las Vegas."

Erika spoke up. "Rita Jackson relayed your name to someone in Aspen. We're sure of that. And now I understand you've been invited to accompany Senator Ross to a fundraiser at her home in Montecito? Sheila, I don't need any more proof. For my sake, if not your own, you can't go."

"Someone from this agency has to, Erika. These are not mere requests. It's how politics work. The source of funding and the Chairman of our Oversight Committee have formally requested a representative from our agency attends this function. That's me. I won't send someone who works for me knowing what could happen to them. I won't."

"Then cancel at the last moment," Erika said. "Wait until the day of the party and become violently ill."

"They will ask for a replacement; someone who knows me. Maybe even Donny. I'm sure of it," Sheila said. "And this won't be their last attempt, even if we somehow avoid attending."

Erika considered this. Sheila was right. They were playing defense and offense really was required here. She would have to view this predicament from an entirely different perspective in order to be effective.

"How much time do we have?" Erika asked.

"Thirteen days," Donny replied. "Then it's party time."

"Okay," Erika said. "Let's get all the intelligence on Jackson and Ross that exists and come up with a plan on Monday. Is that okay, Sheila?"

"What are we hoping to accomplish?"

"Coming up with an appropriate response," Erika said. "Let's not forget, we also have Petro strutting about in Las Vegas. They want a response. We need to come up with one they least expect."

"Ok, Donny, I see everything first. Do you understand?" Sheila asked. "And no one—I mean no one, acts without my explicit approval. Are we all on the same page?"

"Yes," Donny said.

"Yes," Erika chimed.

"Ok, let's do it."

Erika spent the rest of the day with Donny, accumulating every scrap of data on their targets, their habits, travel, phone calls, computer usage, credit card charges—everything. Once Erika was satisfied, she packed up everything and headed back to San Diego, a plan already forming. She called Felix after she was on the freeway.

"Hello," he said, noting the cell ID. "You miss me already?"

"Funny man," Erika replied. *I actually do miss him,* she thought. *A new feeling.* "Are you available tomorrow early?"

"Of course."

"Where can we meet?"

"How about you come to Del Mar beach early, about 8am? Park near 19th Street and walk out onto the sand. I'll find you there. Breakfast is on me," he said.

"Done. See you then." She ended the call, a smile on her face.

Chapter 38

The following morning, Erika parked her Mercedes on 19th Street in Del Mar, gathered up her purse and another satchel filled with intelligence documents she wanted to discuss with Felix, and walked out to the beach. A tall athletic man in a grey hoodie and black board shorts was waiting for her near the water. He pushed back his hood to reveal a clean-shaven face, shorter hair that still fell to his ears and nape, and black horn-rimmed glasses. He looked like a college professor every co-ed would have fantasies about.

She walked up and kissed him. "I like it," she said. "You look almost respectable."

"I was hoping you'd like it." He put his arm around her and directed her up the beach.

"Can we play naughty coed later?"

He couldn't help but laugh. "We can play whatever you like, Guapa. C'mon, I'll show you my place."

He led Erika to a sterile, white modern four-plex situated on the sand behind a concrete sea wall. It was the only one on the entire shoreline of ten-million-dollar private beach homes.

"I have the one on the top left," he said.

"Do you own it?" Erika asked.

"Actually, I own all four. The other three are on long-term lease. This one I keep for my private beach time. Once you're a Seal..."

"You need to be near the water?"

"Well done!" He laughed. "Now you're finishing my sentences."

He led her through the back entrance, up a flight of stairs and out the sliding glass doors overlooking the beach.

Looking out at the low overcast clouds and gray surf, he said, "It's supposed to warm up about 11am when the sun burns through."

"It's still pretty," she said.

"Yep, when I want to think about just how insignificant we human beings really are, I like to be near the ocean or in the mountains. It gives me perspective."

"A philosopher," she mused. "I haven't seen that side of you."

"That's the beauty of our relationship," Felix said. "We have so much to discover about one another." He kissed the top of her head. "Come on, I promised you breakfast."

The interior of the condo was white with splashes of color sprinkled throughout, utilizing pillows, wall art and accent furniture for contrast. The primary colors kept the eye roaming over the interior like paint on a blank canvas. Very nice.

She sat at the small counter separating the tiny kitchen from the living space while he retrieved eggs, bacon, and fresh bagels. "Over easy or scrambled?"

"Scrambled."

He gathered onions, tomatoes, bell peppers, mushrooms, and cheese and chopped them fine while the bacon crisped and the bagels toasted. "Want to butter those when they pop?" he said, indicating the toaster with a nod.

"Will do."

He cracked four eggs into a pan and added the remaining ingredients with effortless grace.

"You enjoy cooking?"

"I do. I cooked for Jorge when we were little, then again when I was deployed overseas. It calms me," he said.

"Good, because I'm better at eating than I am at cooking."

He set two steaming plates on the counter and poured a glass of V-8 juice for them both, while she brought the toasted bagels over.

"Let's eat," he said. "Then we can go over the material you brought. Afterwards, we can walk the sand all the way down to Black's Beach while the tide is out."

"You have a deal."

After they finished and put the dishes in the dishwasher, they sat at the dining table with mugs of fresh coffee. Erika began to spread the material on Rita Jackson across the glass surface.

"This is everything we have on the woman who funds our agency. She also texted my boss's name and general location to a ranch in Aspen that we believe is owned by a front corporation out of London for the Russian mob." Erika continued. "Now my boss, or someone from our agency, has been ordered to accompany a Senator with oversight of our budget and activities to an event in Montecito hosted by the same woman." She thought for a moment. "We also have incontrovertible proof that both the woman and the Senator have been filmed by the Russians, engaging in sexual acts with more than one partner, in her case, both genders. Liberal use of cocaine was also in evidence."

"I guess they like to party, huh?" Felix mused. "What's the immediate threat?"

"I don't want my boss to attend this function. She'll be identified or snatched. Once they have her, they'll come for me."

"Can't she send someone in her place?"

"Only me or another friend. It would be far more damaging for him to be captured because of the nature of his job. He supplies all the intel to us. And I don't want him hurt either. She won't delegate this to someone else without explaining the dangers, and since this is off the books, so to speak, she can't very well do that either," Erika said.

"Your boss seems to have painted herself into a corner," Felix said.

"Yeah, and I helped her do it."

"Well, if we can't cancel the date, perhaps we should concentrate on canceling the event itself."

"How?" Erika asked.

"Let's look over the intel for a weakness, maybe an opportunity. You said she likes to party, do a little coke. There are such things as accidents or overdoses. Let's look for any patterns of behavior."

They started organizing the material. After forty minutes, Felix asked, "Did you see these overnights at San Ysidro Ranch almost every two weeks?"

"Yes, I assumed it was where she went to treat herself to spa treatments every couple of weekends. It's not far from her house," Erika said.

"Then why would she stay there on Friday and Saturday overnight?" Felix asked. "Maybe she meets someone there for a little extra-curricular activity. Some of these dinner bills are too large for one person. Her husband?"

"No, they move in different orbits," Erika explained. "Our intelligence leads me to believe they lead separate lives. He is engaged in a long-term affair with his corporate secretary, and she has the morals of an alley cat in heat. She appears to be intent on sleeping with the entire population of California."

"Can you dig a little deeper?" Felix asked.

"Let me make a call." Erika dialed Donny and put her finger to her lips to shush Felix.

"Hello," Donny answered.

"Hi there. I have a question for you," Erika said. "I'm going over the intel on Rita Jackson, and I noticed she goes to San Ysidro Ranch about every two or three weeks and stays overnight. Why would she do that if she lives only ten miles from there?"

"That's easy," Donny answered. "If you reconcile her cell phone texts to her overnights, you'll see she meets a Brian Causwell from Santa Barbara there. Sometimes he brings a friend or another woman to spice it up, I guess. Apparently, he's her boy toy, pimp, and drug dealer all rolled into one."

"Do you have an address, picture, all that?"

"Of course, but I'll do you one even better. They have a rendezvous set up for dinner this Friday at the San Ysidro Restaurant, 7 pm. The room is registered under her name. No mention of him on the reservation."

"What's this place like?"

"Expensive. Great food. Great wine. Exclusive private cottages, salt water spas in the rear courtyards, private outdoor showers. Very romantic. Like that," Donny said. "You should Google it and see for yourself. Why? What are you thinking?"

"Nothing yet," Erika said. "Can you send me the info on Brian Causwell?"

"On its way," Donny said.

"Thanks, you're the best."

"You're welcome."

Erika popped open her laptop, powered it up, entered her password, and pulled up the information Donny had sent her on Brian Causwell. He was a good-looking surfer type, messy blonde hair bleached by the sun, 6'3", 200 lbs., and no facial hair.

He lived in a condominium complex just across the street from the beach volleyball nets on the Santa Barbara beachfront. No visible means of support, which meant he was being taken care of, or he was dealing. The address was owned by a corporate entity, probably not his, maybe owned by Rita. It didn't matter.

Erika turned to Felix. "Were you serious about doing anything to help me?"

"Yes."

"Even if it involves someone dying?"

"If it involves someone who intends to hurt you, in a heartbeat."

"You sure?"

"I'm sure. It's no more than you did for me. I'm in."

"This could go south," Erika warned.

"I'm not new to this, Erika."

She considered him for a few seconds. "Ever been to Santa Barbara?"

"Plenty of times."

"Want to go with me?"

"When?"

"Thursday."

"Okay."

"Just like that?" She asked.

"Just like that," he answered.

Her promise to Sheila evaporated in that instant.

Chapter 39

Felix spent the next day making arrangements that would dramatically alter his illegal business activities in the southwestern United States. He needed to operate through a series of cutouts to facilitate his personal security and his effectiveness as the major conduit for any contraband coming across the Mexican border. He knew of only one organization that could provide that level of service. He sent out feelers.

In the meantime, he gathered the items Erika asked him to bring to Santa Barbara: formal dinner wear to beach clothes, his personal weapon, a Glock .40, silenced, loaded with one ten round magazine and three extras. A fixed blade K-bar Marine tactical knife, a holdover from his past life as a Navy Seal, an ounce of pure Peruvian flake along with a sizable cocaine rock, a lid of highly potent marijuana, a two-ounce vial of Rohypnol, the date rape drug, with extra syringes, an air pressurized delivery system for the drug, and a lot of untraceable cash completed his inventory.

Erika was busy with plans of her own. She contacted Donny to request the most recent information on the Russians in Las Vegas, in particular the movements of Petro—the bait. She also requested all pertinent updates on the movement of Makisima Orlov and Oleg Yakovlev, the replacements for the strip club managers Erika killed in Las Vegas. He didn't question why the additional information was needed. He knew she would just give him a meaningless answer.

She also packed a selection of clothing similar to Felix's, her personal weapons, a blonde wig, large black framed sunglasses, small clear reading glasses and a professional movie make-up kit—and placed it all in the trunk. At 5am Thursday, she appeared at the rear of Felix's beach complex. He stowed his gear in the trunk, sat in the passenger seat, and kissed her hello.

"You ready for this?"

"Yes, and you don't need to ask me again," he chided her. "You couldn't chase me away."

He fired up the ignition and the big V-8 reverberated down the alley way leading to the street. She pointed to the Starbuck cup, grinned, and said, "Just the way you like it."

Within two hours, they merged onto the 101-freeway headed west. The westbound traffic was conveniently sparse while the eastbound lanes resembled a parking lot. The more she drove, the more she appreciated air travel.

When they arrived at the Fess Parker Doubletree Inn on the beach in Santa Barbara, Erika checked in alone. She'd reserved an oceanfront suite on the second floor with a huge veranda in the furthest building from the main complex. Felix remained in the car until she returned and drove them to their room. They quickly unloaded their gear and settled in for a nap.

Just before noon they dressed for a run and crossed the street to the sand. They jogged south along the shoreline, passing the beach volleyball nets and the condominiums across the street where Brian Causwell lived. They continued south for another mile until they ran out of shoreline and had to double back, retracing their steps.

Once again, they studied the condominium layout as they jogged past. They continued to the north pier, ran to the end of it and returned at an easy pace to their hotel room, easily covering the three-mile distance.

After a shower, they ate lunch in their room before dressing in shorts, sweatshirts, sunglasses and ball caps and walking south on the street fronting the beach, until they reached the volleyball courts. Eight of the ten courts were occupied by enthusiastic players clad only in bathing suits and T-shirts. Felix and Erika settled in as spectators.

In less than twenty minutes, Erika recognized the tall, blonde, athletic man dominating the game on the third court. She nudged Felix, who nodded his recognition as well... Brian Causwell. They watched him play without appearing to focus in on him. It was clear he was a regular by the number of players he was familiar with and the high level at which he played. They could hear bits of good-natured trash talk amongst the players. After his game finished, Brian high-fived and traded barbs with the team they'd vanquished.

Another skilled player called to him, "You coming down tomorrow?"

"Yeah, but I have to leave by four o'clock. I got a hot date," he laughed.

"All your dates are hot, man. Who are you kidding?" The man teased.

"Look who's talking." Brian shot right back, "the original beach bachelor."

"See you tomorrow Brian."

"Later."

Erika pointedly watched the other games as Brian passed by, ignoring him. As he crossed the street, Felix rose to shadow him, keeping fifty yards distant. He entered the condo complex in time to witness Brian as he unlocked his front door and disappeared inside. Felix continued to walk past the residence, noting the address and physical surroundings to confirm against the existing intelligence they had, and exited out the opposite side of the complex. He returned to the beach and sat down next to Erika.

"How'd it go?"

"Fine. The address is correct: a two-story stucco fronting the beach. The entrance is on the other side, facing the parking lot. It has about twenty feet of shrubbery lining the path to the door, providing pretty good cover. It's doable. Why don't you stroll through yourself, just to be sure? It's the fourth one on your right as you enter through the driveway behind us. Keep going and you'll come out down there." He indicated another driveway one hundred yards to south. I'll wait here."

She retraced his footsteps and returned within ten minutes. "If there are no complications, this shouldn't be too difficult," she said.

"Like what complications?"

"A visiting friend, a nosy neighbor—like that," Erika replied. "Absent that, I say we go."

"Okay."

"Let's head back to the hotel. I'm hungry," she said.

Chapter 40

After breakfast, Erika and Felix went for a morning run along the shore, then showered and moved onto the veranda to talk. They'd gone over each part of the plan until it was burned into their DNA. What to do if this happened—what to do if it didn't—contingencies upon contingencies. The entire operation was free-flowing and dynamic, abrupt changes could be required at a moment's notice.

Then there was the human component. They would need to get very close to their quarry to pull the operation off as planned. A lot of things would have to go their way to succeed. They did not know how Rita Jackson would react. This was definitely not a sanctioned operation. If something went wrong, they were on their own.

They rehearsed their roles again.

At 3pm, Felix and Erika left the hotel and walked down to the volleyball courts. Felix wore a ball cap, sunglasses, board shorts, T-shirt and flip flops. Erika wore a white bikini under an oversized gray hoodie she wore like a mini dress. The zipper pulled down enough to expose her bra top. She also wore sunglasses, a floppy straw hat and sneakers.

They settled on the grass in the shade to watch the games, easily spotting Brian among his friends on the same court as the day before. He was big and good looking. It wasn't any great stretch of the imagination to grasp why Rita Jackson had selected him as her lover. The couple didn't pay any more attention to Brian's game than they did the other contests. By 4pm the courts in use dwindled to three, and shortly thereafter, Brian's game came to its conclusion.

They watched him exchange high-fives with his competitors and cross the street. Erika gave him five minutes to get settled and followed him. Felix got up and walked one hundred yards south to where she should emerge from the complex.

Erika checked herself to ensure all was ready. She walked up the path to Brian's door and rang the bell. He quickly answered the door, looking down at the attractive brunette in a floppy hat and glasses. Her sweatshirt was unzipped to display a barely-there bikini top. A big grin erupted onto his handsome face, acknowledging his pleasant surprise.

"Well, hello," he said. "What can I do for you?"

Erika smiled back and shot him in the stomach with an air-propelled syringe full of Rohypnol she took from her sweatshirt pocket. He looked down in amazement at the dart protruding from his abdomen, then back at Erika as the grin on his face went slack and he staggered. She stepped through the doorway and gently guided him to the nearby couch. He complied meekly with her unspoken direction and sat down heavily. Erika turned him sideways and put his feet up on the couch, fluffing a pillow beneath his head. After pulling on a pair of latex gloves, she went in search of his keys, phone, and wallet, in an attempt to simulate a robbery if he was discovered while she was away.

Satisfied he was out for the night, she removed the dart, then her gloves and covered her hands with the sleeves of her hoodie, wiping anything she may have touched as she let herself out the front door. She casually walked through the complex without encountering anyone and found Felix waiting for her.

"Did it go well?"

"Perfect. Just like we planned," Erika said. "He'll wake up tomorrow with one hell of a migraine and a fuzzy memory."

On the stroll back to the Double Tree, Erika checked the battery from his phone to ensure it was charged and removed all the cash from his wallet. She kept the phone and dumped the wallet into a trash can after wiping it.

They returned to their room at the hotel to shower and dress for dinner. As they passed her Mercedes, Erika noted the new Arizona State license plates Felix installed the previous night. They would correspond with her new Arizona registration and driver's license depicting a young, blonde resident of Scottsdale.

Erika showered first. She finished blow-drying her hair as Felix appeared, naked and wet behind her in the mirror. He snuggled up to her, buried his face in her hair and caressed her neck and shoulders with his lips. She could feel him growing against her backside.

She smiled into the mirror. "I was going to ask of you were up for this, but I think I already know the answer."

"Hah!" Smiling back, Felix met her eyes in the mirror. "Sorry, I couldn't help it. I'm only human." He pressed into her backside.

"I'm warning you. Better save it. You're going to need your strength for later," she teased.

"You're sure about this, Erika? I don't want things to change between us."

"You have to trust me," she replied. "Nothing will change between us. It'll only get better. Look at it this way," she continued, "this is one of the many perks you get to enjoy when we're together."

"You're sure?"

"Positive." She turned and pushed him away. "Now go get dressed. I've got to finish putting on my makeup."

Felix dressed in gray slacks, black blazer and a black silk shirt, and then watched the news as Erika appeared in a lacy black thong and bra. She sat on the bed and rolled on black thigh high stockings before stepping into a chic, body hugging black dress.

"How do I look?" She asked as she pulled her blonde wig over her pinned up hair and smiled.

"You're killing me." Felix groaned.

"Just setting the mood, baby. You have everything?"

He patted his inside breast pocket. "All set."

"Let's go."

They drove to San Ysidro Ranch through a commercial section of strip malls and then past two public schools. The neighborhood morphed from middle class housing near the freeway into sprawling estates secreted behind solid walls as they climbed into the foothills. Coastal Oaks and dense foliage ensured the privacy of the residents as much as the gates and private security.

Erika passed the discreet sign that identified the San Ysidro Ranch without noticing it before doubling back to approach the security guard in the stone gatehouse. He checked off her name, Ann Snyder, against the dinner reservation and gave her parking instructions for the valet. She ignored his instructions and parked in the lower lot beneath the private cottages. The trip took just 17 minutes.

They held hands as they walked the grounds, examined the herb gardens, fruit orchard, and the pool-spa area. They noted the exits and entrances as they strolled the perimeter of the small property, taking their time, enjoying one another's company. They saw very few people and some staff members, all exceedingly polite in their subdued greetings, lending the entire resort an ambience of discretion. What happens in San Ysidro stays in San Ysidro.

They entered the restaurant at 6:30 pm and declined to be seated, opting instead to have a drink at the bar. The bartender served a glass of Chardonnay to Erika and Gray Goose Vodka with an olive on the rocks for Felix.

Rita Jackson appeared twenty minutes later, dressed in a tasteful red dress and heels, accessorized by a nine carat, diamond pendant necklace suspended over a plunging neckline. Three carat diamond earrings completed the package. At forty-something, she was stunning; her dark hair drawn up atop her head in a loose pile, with tendrils cascading around her pretty face. She was escorted to a candlelit booth in the furthest corner of the restaurant, presumably for privacy.

Within ten minutes of being seated, she was furiously

texting, her features lit up by the ambient light. Erika read the barrage of text messages on the stolen phone.

The first one read, "In the restaurant. Usual table."

Erika texted back on Causwell's cell phone. "Got it. Be right there."

Five minutes later, "Where are you?"

"Almost there," Erika texted.

Two minutes later, "What's taking you so long?"

"Something came up. I need to cancel."

"You're pissing me off." Rita texted.

"Sorry. Can't be helped." Erika replied.

"I don't give a fuck. You better be here in ten."

"Sorry, can't make it."

"Asshole."

Erika turned to Felix. "You're on."

He got up from the bar and walked towards Rita Jackson's table. As she looked up, their eyes met and Felix gave her his most engaging, full-of-interest smile. The irritated look on her face was replaced with a smile of her own. He continued on to the men's room. The bait was in the water.

He returned to the bar and spoke to Erika in low tones, very close to her ear. She noted Mrs. Jackson watching their exchange, then looked directly at her and smiled. Their quarry was circling the bait.

Felix motioned to the bartender. "Would you send whatever that woman is drinking to her with my compliments?"

The bartender looked over his shoulder to establish the guest Felix indicated and said, "Of course, sir."

If he was surprised at the request, it didn't register on his face or in his demeanor. He poured a glass of champagne and took it to her himself. There was a brief conversation, and then Rita held up the champagne flute in a salute to her benefactor.

Felix took the opportunity to slide off the barstool and

approach her table.

"Good evening," he said, offering her his hand. "Felix Mendez."

"Good evening, Felix. I'm Rita Jackson." *God, this man is gorgeous.* "And thank you for the drink. I'm charmed."

"You're very welcome. May I sit for a moment?"

"Please do." She looked over to where Erika was seated at the bar. "But won't your friend be a little jealous?"

"No, no. Anne and I have been together for a long time. She doesn't get jealous."

"How nice for you." She was still circling the bait.

Felix committed himself. "We couldn't help but notice such an attractive woman dining alone and wondered if you'd care to join us?" He gave her his most disarming little boy smile. "My treat. No strings."

"Hah." She laughed. "There's always strings." She considered the fact she was on her home turf here, surrounded by security and staff that had known her for years. She was perfectly safe.

"Are you sure your friend won't mind?"

"Of course not. She likes to make me happy."

"I'll bet." She hesitated for a beat. "Okay, why not? It appears my date is not coming, and I don't fancy eating alone. Please ask her to join us."

"Thank you." He rose. "I'll go get her."

Felix returned and made the introductions.

"Ann Snyder, meet Rita Jackson." They shook hands.

"Nice to meet you," Rita said. "Please sit."

Erika sat in the booth to her left and Felix to her right. She kept the center power position.

"Thanks for asking us to join you," Erika said. "You're beautiful."

Rita was clearly amused. "Well, thank you, Ann, but you're

quite the looker yourself," she said. "And he's pretty easy on the eyes, too." She indicated Felix.

"He is, isn't he?"

"Are you guys going to talk like I'm not here all night?" He laughed.

"Maybe," Rita answered. "I haven't decided what we're going to do with you yet." The hook was set.

"May I order champagne for the table?" Felix asked.

"Please do," Rita answered. "Dom?"

"Dom it is." He signaled the waiter.

They engaged in small talk designed to get to know each other better as the wine was poured and the food was ordered. They established where they lived, the industries they worked in: Rita, the banker; Felix, the importer; and Ann, the real estate investor. Each had amusing, authentic anecdotes to share and soon they were all laughing together like old friends. A second bottle of champagne with their meal loosened them up even more.

Rita took the bull by the horns after dessert was ordered. "Are you staying here at the resort?"

"No," Felix said. "I wish I'd known how nice it was. I would have preferred to stay here. We have a reservation at the Biltmore."

"You could still get a room here. I know the management quite well. You could cancel your reservation," Rita suggested.

"Are you staying here?"

"Yes. This is my private time, away from the world."

"Then it's settled. We'll stay here," Felix said. "Excuse me, I need to use the restroom and cancel our reservation."

Rita pulled out her cell phone and speed dialed the manager. "Hello, Robert? This is Mrs. Jackson. I have two guests who will be staying the night. Can you book them into 107, next to me? Put it in my name and I'll take care of it in the morning." She listened for a moment. "Thank you, that's perfect."

She turned to Erika. "It's done. Your keys will be on your bed. You're going to love it here."

"I'm sure of it, thank you so much. This is turning out to be quite the adventure."

"Can I ask you a personal question?" Rita asked.

"Of course, anything."

"Do you guys do this sort of thing very often? You know what I'm asking?"

"Yes, I think so, and the answer is no. In fact, very rarely. But occasionally I like to surprise him when he least expects it—give him a treat he'll never forget."

"Am I the treat?"

"I had hoped so."

"I guess I should feel complimented. How did you know I'd respond?"

"I didn't. I just hoped you like to party." Erika pushed one knuckle up against her nostril and sniffed through the other in a universal gesture that suggested cocaine. "You're quite attractive."

"Oh, my, are we ever on the same page. I do love a party," Rita said.

Felix returned and sat down. "All taken care of. Now we need to get a room here."

"That's taken care of," Rita said. "You're in 107, right next to me. I'm in 106. I'm going to show Ann around while you take care of the bill. See you in a little bit."

Rita and Erika wore huge grins as they slid out the left side of the booth and sauntered out of the restaurant, arm in arm.

It took another ten minutes for the bill to arrive. With the two bottles of Dom Perignon the bill came to almost $1,000. Felix dropped twelve, one-hundred-dollar bills on the table and left. It took another five minutes to locate room 106, situated on the north end of the property, behind ten-foot-tall hedges that ensured total seclusion.

He entered through a gate and followed a serpentine path through dense foliage and stepped up on the porch. Flickering light from the fireplace within, along with low mood lighting illuminated the sheer drapes as mellow jazz played in the background.

Felix knocked on the front door.

Chapter 41

Sheila and Donny were sharing a meal at Rico's, a small Italian restaurant in the Hollywood Hills. They weren't able to spend much time together on an informal basis, so when Sheila suggested they sneak out for dinner, Donny accepted immediately.

Sheila chose Caesar salad with Halibut in a spicy North Italian sauce. Donny decided on linguini with clams. Over coffee, the conversation drifted into familiar territory: Erika.

"You really think she's handling this Russian thing well? I mean, not too tightly focused on the one issue?" Sheila asked.

"If you mean revenge, yeah, she's tightly focused on that. I can't deny it, but that's what makes her who she is, that overdeveloped sense of justice. But overall, I think she has a clear perspective of what needs to be done, and if at all possible, she'll do it by the numbers."

"And if it's not possible?"

"Come on, Sheila, you know the answer to that. If she perceives any direct threat to you, me, or herself, she'll act."

"That's what scares me."

"It shouldn't. She's the best friend I ever had, and she's your friend too. She'd protect us with her life. How many friends do you have like that?" He chided her. "The person you need to be afraid of is this fucking Senator and that evil bitch you have to meet next week. I don't like any part of what that party is going to look like, Sheila. Erika is right. You should not attend under any circumstances."

"I will bring protection, Donny. Two teams. Nothing is going to happen to me. I promise."

"You better hope so," Donny said. "If something does happen to you, the Senator and the banker are as good as dead."

Chapter 42

Rita opened the door and pulled Felix inside the room. It was decorated in early California ranch style, with a comfortable seating arrangement in front of a crackling fire. An ice bucket of open champagne stood on the coffee table. Erika was sitting on the massive four poster bed packing a crack pipe with the purest rock cocaine she'd ever experienced. Her shoes were off and her dress was hiked up, exposing her bare thighs above the hose. Rita jumped on the bed, shoeless as well.

"Come and join us, Felix," she said. "Ann is busy ruining my character. You should help her." She was in full party mode. Erika took a deep hit on the pipe, held it for about six seconds, then melded Rita's lips with hers and exhaled into her mouth. Rita sucked the smoke into her lungs, holding it there before expelling the remainder in a rush of air.

She took the pipe from Erika. "Your turn, Felix. Come here." Rita took a drag on the pipe then pulled him to her on the bed. She locked her lips over his and slowly exhaled the fumes into his body, lingering on his mouth long after the smoke dissipated. Hook, line, and sinker.

Things got progressively more interesting after that. They shared more of the smoke with each other, taking turns. More champagne was poured, and soon they were snorting Peruvian flake off of each other's body parts, finally licking the remnants from each other's flesh and spreading it on their gums.

They lay back on the bed together and began caressing each other as more articles of clothing found their way to the floor. Erika excused herself to use the bathroom. "Be right back."

She used the facilities, noted steam rising from an outdoor Jacuzzi and returned to discover Felix shirtless with Rita astride him, her chic dress piled down around her waist and pulled up above her thighs.

"Hey," Erika said and peeled the little black dress down over her hips. They both swiveled their heads, taking in the athletic contours of her body in the flickering firelight. Erika knelt on the bed and pulled off Rita's dress. "There's a Jacuzzi in the courtyard. Anyone want to play outside?"

That's all it took. The rest of their clothes came off. Rita gripped the bottle of champagne. Erika brought the coke and pipe. Felix pulled two bath towels from the rack and draped them on lounge chairs around the bubbling pool, slipped into the steaming water and sat on the far side, the water almost up to his chest. Rita poured three glasses of champagne and handed one to Erika before entering the Jacuzzi with the other two glasses, offering one to Felix.

As he accepted, she turned around and snuggled her backside against his lap, feeling him grow again in response. She pulled his arms around her, draped his big hands over her breasts, and sipped her champagne. "Mmm," she murmured.

"Hey, wait for me," Erika teased. She set her glass on the rim of the pool and brought the newly loaded crack pipe into the water with her. With the pipe between her teeth, she waded over to Rita and insinuated her hips between Rita's thighs. She snuggled up to her pelvis, their bare flesh pressed against each other in the warm water. She put the pipe in Rita's mouth, and held a flame to it, watching the older woman slip into the false comfort of the drugs, alcohol, and the warm liquid cocoon as they caressed her. Felix took another hit, barely inhaling the smoke, as did Erika. She offered the pipe a second time to Rita who sucked greedily on the pipe, holding Erika's fingers to her mouth as she applied suction with her lips.

Felix and Erika exchanged a look as Rita exhaled the last remnants of smoke from deep in her lungs in an audible rush of air. Felix locked her in a bear hug, pinning her arms against her sides and submerged them while Erika locked her arms around her legs and forced them abruptly beneath the water. The pressure applied from their combined efforts, spread out over so much surface area applied to her skin, would leave no bruising. With his military training, Felix could hold his breath far longer than most humans would even attempt. Holding Rita beneath the water was child's play.

With no air in her lungs, Rita's first attempt to breathe drew hot, chlorinated water down her windpipe. She thrashed about wildly in an attempt to free herself, which only accelerated her drowning. She was locked tight until her struggles ceased. In less than two minutes, it was over. Felix held her under for three more minutes after he resurfaced to ensure her fate, and then turned her face down to float around the bubbling water. Jazz played in the background.

They left the champagne bottle with one glass by the Jacuzzi, along with the pipe and a sizeable chunk of rock cocaine. Erika washed and dried the other two champagne flutes and returned them to their original position at the bar. They both dressed and wiped down every surface they might have touched. Felix and Erika dried off with one towel, and dropped it in the swirling water. They returned the others to the towel rack as they found them. They were confident the chlorinated water would erase or render useless any DNA left behind.

Felix checked Rita one more time to ensure she could not be revived and double-checked the room before slipping out the door and locking it behind them. They encountered no one as they walked back to Erika's car in the lower lot, started it up, and cruised out the back gate. They were back at the Double Tree Hotel within twenty minutes. It was 1:45am.

Felix switched the license plates back to the original California plates and stashed the Arizona plates in his luggage while Erika changed into jeans, sweatshirt, and sneakers. She stowed the blonde wig in her luggage and met Felix back at the car.

He drove the quarter mile down to Brian Causwell's condominium complex and parked in visitor parking. Erika slipped out, donned another pair of latex gloves as she approached the condominium, unlocked the front door with Brian's keys, replaced the sanitized phone and put a sanitized baggie of the same Peruvian flake they used with Rita under the couch beneath Brian, who was snoring on the couch. He would have an interesting time explaining the drugs if the police discovered them. She slipped back out, relocked the door from inside and joined Felix in the car. They drove back to their hotel and went up to their room.

Erika produced a joint, fired it up, and said, "I don't know about you, but I'm wired."

"Me, too."

"What should we do about that?" she asked.

"I'll think of something."

Chapter 43

It took only four hours to drive back to San Diego. They both knew something profound had occurred during this trip, but neither wanted to put it into words. They had crossed a bridge—an important one that would require careful thought and honest communication. They'd engaged in sex with a third party and committed a murder that was not in self-defense. They didn't acknowledge this tectonic shift in their relationship, preferring to consider that evolution privately. For Erika, the sex meant nothing; she actually enjoyed shocking him. For Felix, it was complete confusion. Who on earth was this woman and what events had shaped her into this unexplainable force of nature?

Erika dropped him at the beach house. "Are you going to be alright?"

"Yes, I'm okay. I just…

"Just what? Come on, Felix. Tell me what's bothering you." Erika knew they had to talk now or the issue would fester.

"It's just that we've barely begun our relationship and now I've had sex with another woman in front of you."

"You knew that was a possibility going in, didn't you?"

"Yes."

"Felix, I don't view you as my property. And I'm not yours. What we did up there was freely given and necessary. As far as the sex goes, I hope you enjoyed it. I did." She could see the surprise on his face. "Besides, if this wasn't so serious, it would be hilarious."

"What do you mean?"

"We just murdered someone, and you're more worried about me watching you have sex than getting caught for a major felony."

Now it was Felix's turn. "Oh, I'm okay with the murder part. I just don't want to fuck up a great relationship before it's even started."

They both erupted at the absurdity of the remark. "Now who's a piece of work?" Erika laughed.

"What the fuck have I gotten myself into?"

"Stick around, big boy. There's more to come."

"I'll do that." He leaned over and kissed her.

"Now I need to ask you something. Are you going to be safe from your friends in Logan Heights, or do I have to babysit you?"

"Yes, I'll be fine. I've already taken some preliminary steps to deal with the men who tried to abduct me."

"I have some things to do," Erika said. "I may be a week or two."

"No problem," Felix replied. "I'll be busy too."

She kissed him. "Felix, you are amazing."

"No, Guapa, *we* are amazing." He climbed out of her car and she drove off.

Erika had not finished unpacking when her cell rang.

"Hey, Donny. What's up?"

"Hi, Erika. How are you?"

"I'm fine."

"You see the news this morning?" Donny asked.

"No, why?"

"It seems a friend of ours in Montecito has had a tragic accident," he said. "Mom wants to have a sit-down as soon as possible."

"Can you send me everything you have on this, Donny? I

don't want to walk in blind."

"On its way," Donny said. "The meeting is tomorrow at 10am."

"See you then." She hung up.

Erika finished unpacking, booted up her agency laptop, and sat down at the kitchen table to read the digital documents. There were numerous reports from several different sources, and speculation ran the gamut from the sordid to the tragic: from drug-induced accidental death, to suicide, to homicide. It was obvious from the discreet tone of the articles that someone in power had already exerted considerable influence over the flow of information. She would learn nothing more from these articles that would prepare her for tomorrow's meeting.

Sheila had arranged for the meeting to be held in the formal conference room, not in the backyard pool area. That was Erika's first hint. Sheila did not greet her or make an appearance until Erika and Donny were seated. That was her second hint.

Sheila sat down at the head of the table, in Richard's old chair. That was the last hint Erika required. Something important had changed.

"Good morning." Sheila greeted them collectively.

"Morning," Donny said.

"Morning," Erika repeated.

"Let's get right to it, shall we?" Sheila said. "There's been an interesting development over the weekend that's kept me busy for the last thirty-six hours, so forgive me if I'm a little brusque. Our esteemed Senator has been down my throat for much of that time, and I'm not sure exactly why, but I intend to get to the bottom of this today."

No one responded.

"As I'm sure you're both aware, Rita Jackson passed away

sometime Friday night or early Saturday at a very private resort in Montecito. The public information suggests a sordid affair, rampant alcohol and drug use resulting in an accidental death or possible suicide, maybe even a homicide. For now, it is being ruled an accidental death.

Still no reaction.

"Our investigation suggests this was a frequent meeting place for Mrs. Jackson and her lover. The only possible suspect that came to mind immediately was this Brian Causwell, a small-time drug dealer and Mrs. Jackson's occasional lover. There were several text messages sent to him the same evening that became increasingly angry in tone. The authorities found him at his condo, which Mrs. Jackson pays for, still groggy from apparent drug use. His entire life is about to get turned inside out." Sheila said. "You with me so far?"

Donny said, "Yes."

Erika only nodded.

"Here's where things get a little murky," Sheila said. "According to the restaurant manager at the resort, Mrs. Jackson was joined for dinner by a tall handsome Latino male and an equally attractive blonde woman on Friday evening. They shared an enjoyable meal together, drank two bottles of expensive champagne, and hit it off famously, as he put it."

Sheila had their full attention now.

"Apparently the two women left together, and the unidentified male paid cash for the meal and left on his own. There were no clear finger prints on the bills; unlikely in any normal circumstance. Coincidentally, Jackson phoned the manager's office and reserved the suite next to hers for some friends that were visiting. That room was never occupied."

Erika was desperately trying to hold back a grin that was threatening to erupt into a full-fledged belly laugh. Her torso was shaking and her hand covered her mouth in an attempt to stifle the sensation. It was to no avail. Donny thought she'd lost her mind.

Sheila turned on her. "What's so damned funny?"

That did it. Erika burst out laughing, trying unsuccessfully to stop. It was like laughing in church at the most inappropriate time. It just made it that much funnier and that much more contagious.

Now Donny was also trying not to break out in laughter, and he wasn't sure why. Erika had that effect on him. Sheila sat there, stone faced. She was not remotely amused. She waited until they were able to stop.

"Now," Sheila said, attempting to regain control over the meeting, "what's so funny?"

"I'm sorry," Erika replied. "I just couldn't help it. I kept wondering how much money you spent on your party dress!" She collapsed into laughter once again, amused by her own joke.

Sheila's face was now bright red. She was furious. Donny was concerned Erika had miscalculated badly.

It took several minutes before Erika regained her composure enough to continue while Sheila stared a hole in her. But she wasn't finished yet. "And now you tell me we have to investigate a blonde woman with a Hispanic partner!" She was laughing again.

"Why is that so funny?" Sheila demanded.

"Have you two looked in the mirror lately? You're already number one on my suspect list," Erika said. "Has the Senator ever met Donny?"

It took only a moment for the implication to dawn on Sheila. "Noooo..." She said. The ludicrous suggestion just grew teeth. "Shit!"

"Maybe you two could attend the funeral together," Erika suggested. She started laughing again, now joined by Donny, no longer trying to hide his amusement.

"Shit!" Sheila repeated. Even she had to admit the resemblance and the complications inherent in it.

"Not a good suggestion?" Erika was on a roll now. Defense had never been her strong suit. Putting Sheila and Donny on the defensive suited her much better. Erika sat silent while she watched Donny and Sheila run through the possible ramifications of her stated opinion and how it might be perceived. She did not like hiding anything from these two friends, but knew she had to in order to protect them all.

Donny waited a few minutes for things to settle down and addressed Sheila. "Do you mind if I give you my analysis before we go any further?"

"No, please do," Sheila said. "Maybe you can make some sense of all this."

"First, no matter how it transpired, we've been given a gift. The conduit to the Russians no longer exists. They still have your name and general location, but nothing else. The Senator has to be their next logical contact if they want you two so bad. Whether that evil bitch overdosed or was killed by her boyfriend makes no difference to me. We need to concentrate our efforts on isolating the Senator and finding the Russians," he said. "Nothing else matters."

"Donny, I can't argue with any of that. What concerns me is that this Montecito situation does not come back to roost within our agency," Sheila said.

"This agency had nothing to do with it," Donny said.

Sheila turned to Erika. "Do you have anything to add?"

"No."

"You're sure?"

"Positive," Erika said. "Oh, one thing..."

"What?"

"You won't be accompanying the Senator to any fundraisers or other functions anytime soon?"

"No, the fundraiser was cancelled and there are no other events planned," Erika said.

"Will you tell us if anything comes up?"

"Do you think I should?"

"Yes, this guy is dirty and my life is at stake, too. You have to realize that," Erika said.

"I know. You're right. I'll keep you both informed," Sheila said. "Now let's move outside for the rest of this meeting. Donny, please be certain there is no record of this discussion." Sheila took a moment to stare at both of them. She was not convinced. They gathered up their things and adjourned to the rear yard.

When they were settled, Donny started. "Okay, we think at least one, likely more of the Russians are holed up on the ranch in Aspen, Colorado. It's my opinion there's a great likelihood that it's Leonid himself. We'll have an observation team on the ground soon. Wherever Leonid is, Raina is likely to be there, too. We've got Petro living openly in Las Vegas, almost daring us to react. It's an obvious trap. Here's my problem," Donny paused. "They have to realize we know it's a trap. I just can't figure out the end game here."

"And there's only three principals left," Erika said. "Why risk one of them?"

"Exactly," Sheila said. "There's something else going on here…something we're not seeing."

"Could they have a large team there? Large enough to blanket the area? People experienced enough to spot you before you spot them?" Donny asked.

Erika was silent; thinking.

"This is a huge enterprise, hundreds of millions of dollars at stake. We have to assume they do have those resources," Sheila said.

"And they're just waiting for either or both of you to show your face there," Donny said. "The logistics alone are enough to make it implausible."

"What if they're using technology, facial recognition cameras, that sort of thing?" Erika asked.

"That could do it, but I doubt they have access to that sort of technology outside of the Russian military. No, my money is still on the Senator. I think the plan is for him to inform them when we mount an operation."

Erika spoke up. "Sheila, can I get everything on their operation in Las Vegas? All the businesses, all the personnel, everything we know? I want to take my time and look over everything—maybe develop a response."

"Yes, with one provision," Sheila said. "You do nothing until you clear it with me."

Erika smiled. "Of course."

"Okay. We meet one week from today. You two jokers can pitch me then," Sheila said.

The meeting was over. As Erika walked out, Donny shot her a look. It said, "I know you did it."

Erika winked.

Chapter 44

On the drive back to San Diego, Erika called Felix.

"Hello, beautiful," he answered.

"Hello to you, too," Erika responded. "I'm on the road and wanted to give you a heads up."

"About what?"

"I'm going out of town for a few days, so I'll be out of touch," she said.

"Not even by phone?"

"No."

"Okay," Felix said. "I'm kind of busy myself. If you recall, I have to attend to that problem with my four associates."

"Are we going to discuss it first?"

"No, it's better we don't at this point. I'm only in the planning stages at the moment. I've reached out to some old friends I trust implicitly, so for the time being, I feel quite secure. I'll fill you in the next time we meet."

"Okay, I should be back next weekend. I'll call you then," she said. "Bye."

"Bye."

When she arrived home, she booted up her computer and retrieved the data she'd requested on the Russians in Las Vegas. Erika knew a defensive posture would not advance her cause and might even get Sheila killed. She made her own decisions when it came to her personal safety or that of the people she held most dear. When she had a strategy she felt would achieve her objective, she put everything away, packed a bag with enough to last four days, selected a long rifle in a 7-millimeter caliber, with a mounted 4 x 12 scope, an automatic MPK7A1 submachine gun, and her Glock 9-millimeter pistol. She added several extra magazines, her black tactical fixed blade and a Kevlar vest, and stowed them in the secret compartment underneath her rear seat.

She rose early the following morning before sunrise, and drove over the crest of the Cajon Pass before 7am. She had about two and a half hours left before she reached Las Vegas. The two-lane black top stretched out over the barren desert. Its serpentine black ribbon wove its way through the purple hills and barren wasteland of pinion trees and scrub brush. The monotony gave her time to think.

She knew what she was about to do would change her life forever: professionally and personally. But there was no other way. Either she took the fight to the Russians, or she sat back and waited for them to find her. She was not very good at waiting.

Felix was another issue. There was zero possibility of them developing a normal relationship, given her unorthodox profession and his involvement in several criminal enterprises. She also realized the danger he was in now and had no idea how to help extricate him from it. She had to trust his judgment and experience. He'd proven his loyalty to her in Montecito with no hesitation. She'd done the same for him, and as a result, their relationship had gone from zero to a hundred in record time. She was terrified of what might happen when he learned about her past—what she'd done to survive.

She took the exit to Boulder City, just Southeast of Las Vegas, and pulled into a Hampton Inn. She paid for a room as Ann Snyder. She would operate from here, entering Vegas only when she was ready to act. She locked her car, stowed her gear, and settled in for a nap. It might be a long night.

When Erika woke, it was early afternoon and she began studying the aerial recon provided by a drone out of Nellis Air Force Base. Petro's residence was well guarded by both roving desert patrols and sentries in the nearby homes. The strip club and the warehouse had Russian members in and out at all hours and seemed just as difficult a target as Petro's home. Maksima Orlov, the new manager, was a non-player and lived in a gated and guarded golf community in a large modern, molded stucco and glass house where presumably she could entertain local business or political friends.

Oleg Yakovlev lived in a high-rise apartment a half mile from the Vegas Strip, two miles from the Gentlemen's Club. It was a secure upscale residence that fit his reclusive personality. He, too, was a non-player. She continued her intelligence review, probing for a weakness.

Once she exhausted every possible approach and discarded them as ineffective or likely to get her killed in the process, she concentrated on another one. If she couldn't get to them, she would force them to come to her. After a room service break, Erika began to study the intelligence Donny sent from a new angle.

After midnight, in her blonde wig, with the Arizona plates now attached to her car, Erika drove into Las Vegas, a city full of cameras. She wore a scarf that partially obscured her face along with black horn-rimmed glasses with clear lenses. She spent several hours reconnoitering the areas she was interested in until she was positive her plan would work. By 4am, well before daylight arrived, she was back in her hotel room, the *"Do Not Disturb"* sign hung in place.

She woke late the next day, had a light lunch by the pool, swam laps until she was satisfied she had pushed her muscles to the limit, and then lay in the sun for an hour. Back in her room, she showered and ate a light dinner before reviewing the Las Vegas intelligence photos again. She reconciled the photos to her reconnaissance from the previous night and began her preparations. Las Vegas was only twenty miles from her hotel and would take thirty minutes by surface streets to reach her destination. She set her alarm for midnight and settled in for a nap.

Dressed in blue jeans, sneakers, and a navy sweater, she was halfway to Vegas by 1am. She parked her car on the street in a location only two blocks from her intended destination, walked the last two blocks and entered an underground garage via the access ramp. She simply ducked under the restriction bar which required a gate code and walked through the cavernous cement structure without a sound. She found the spot she was looking for cloaked in shadow and hid behind a parked Toyota sedan to wait. It was 1:52 am.

At 2:30 am, a black Mercedes sedan entered the parking structure and pulled into the stall Erika had been watching. Erika squatted down and moved around the Toyota until there was only one vehicle separating her from the Mercedes. She crouched behind the vehicle until she heard the door of the Mercedes open and saw the interior light switch on. As the driver swiveled his legs around to exit the car, Erika stood abruptly and shot him twice in the head with her silenced weapon.

As he fell back into the driver's seat, she was right behind him. She reached inside the car and shot Oleg Yakovlev in the back of the head as he attempted to flee. He fell back into the passenger seat with his legs protruding from the open door. Erika shot him again.

She closed the driver's door, went around the vehicle and pushed Oleg's legs back into the vehicle and closed his door, too. She checked her surroundings one more time, then left the parking structure the same way she entered. She was back in her car, driving southeast through the suburbs of Las Vegas in ten minutes, careful to observe the speed limit.

By 4am, Erika was parked in a shallow wash out in the desert, a quarter mile from an exclusive golf course development. Unless you used the same dirt track she had, the car was concealed from view down in the gulley. The Glock was on her hip and a carbon blade at the small of her back, as she hefted the soft rifle case from her trunk along with a desert camouflage blanket. She had no trouble finding the low rise that led to high ground fronting the golf course she'd located the night before with only the fading moonlight to guide her. She unpacked the Sako 7-millimeter rifle, laid it on the soft case, pulled the camouflage blanket around her and the weapon and stared across the narrow ravine.

Below her, the manicured green fairway meandered in stark relief through the dusty brown hills. It was at least fifty yards wide and thirty yards below her. The ground rose another twenty yards on the opposite side, extending for forty more yards before ending abruptly at the waterfall of a disappearing edge swimming pool. Beyond the pool stood a modern estate of stucco and glass. The total distance between Erika and the house measured at 137 yards. She dialed in the distance on her scope and began her motionless vigil as the sky brightened.

By 6am, the grounds crew had inspected the fairway for debris and rolled the greens smooth in anticipation of the usual early golfers. At 6:45, Erika watched the first foursome appear, and then follow their shots down the fairway in their electric carts.

At 7am, the curtains in the estate were drawn open and the sliding glass doors were shunted aside, opening the entire living room to the outdoors. Maksima Orlov appeared, wearing a tasteful ankle length dressing gown, holding a cup of coffee. Erika could see steam rising from the cup through her scope. Maksima was talking on her cell phone while leaning against the fence railing that separated her estate from the golf course.

A man dressed in a suit and tie, Russian security, appeared in the living room behind her and came out to stand in the shade provided by the veranda. Erika took him first with a center chest shot. The silenced weapon made no noise, but the sudden disturbance behind her made Maksima turn to see what caused it. Erika shot her through the side, a classic heart and lung shot just behind her right triceps. She dropped in a heap. At that range, there was no need for a finishing shot on either target. They were gone.

She slid backwards off the crest of the hill, stowed her weapon and walked quickly to her car. She drove down the wash for almost a mile before she reached the blacktop, then used surface streets until she reached the highway at Boulder City. She was back at her hotel by 8:30am, in time to order breakfast. She napped for most of the day and checked out by 4pm. She drove her car, still with Arizona plates, southeast on Highway 93 on the direct route to Phoenix. It took Erika two hours to reach Kingman, Arizona, where she turned southwest and crossed over the state line to Needles, California. From there, she headed due south on Highway 95 to Blythe, then west to Palm Desert, California. It was a circuitous route that took almost eight hours to traverse, but was also the safest and least predictable path for anyone trying to find her. She pulled off the highway at a deserted rest stop and switched back to California license plates.

It was after midnight when she pulled up to the gates of the Vintage Golf Club where she maintained a two-bedroom cottage. She wasn't much of a golfer, but the resort boasted the best security in the desert, and was extremely protective of their residents. It served as a bolt-hole, unknown to anyone, if Erika ever needed it. The gate guards at the meticulously manicured entrance greeted her by alias and passed her through security. The need for some private time would be her alibi, if she needed one.

She spent the next two days on the property, running the desert trails in the early morning, before the heat of the day set in, swimming laps and even hitting golf balls at the driving range. It was the calm before the storm. Once the news reached the agency, as it most likely had already, there would be hell to pay. She was concerned because Donny had not called her already.

Early Sunday morning, she pushed the big V-8 up the hill on Highway 74, putting the car through its paces on the twisting mountain roads before catching Highway 79 into Rancho California, then Interstate 15 South to Escondido and Del Dios Highway to home. She pulled into her garage in Rancho Santa Fe just before 9am.

Chapter 45

The local news station in Las Vegas broke the story early Friday morning. National news picked it up Saturday, and by Sunday, the story was sensationalized internationally. The reports suggested crime organizations originating out of Russia were involved in turf wars over drugs and prostitution in Las Vegas, Nevada. Four Russian nationals had been assassinated during the early hours Thursday morning, and the FBI and other intelligence agencies were swarming over C-Side, a Gentleman's Club, managed by one of the deceased.

As expected, when she opened her agency laptop, there was a brief message requesting her presence at the Bel Air residence at 10am Monday.

This time Donny escorted Erika out to the pool area. Apparently, this meeting would be off the record.

"Good morning, Erika."

"Good morning, Sheila." No hugs or kisses.

"You know why we're out here?" Sheila asked.

"So that we're off the record."

"Correct. Now would you mind telling me what's going on behind my back?" She was seething.

"Look, Sheila, I understand you're angry with me, and you have every right to be," Erika said. "But please hear me out before you make any final decisions."

"Go ahead."

"First, you granted me autonomy in the field—the same latitude you enjoyed as an operative. I exercised that judgment in the past, most notably in Brunei and Haiti, not to mention last year with you in Las Vegas. Sometimes it's necessary."

The reference to Las Vegas was intentional. Erika and Sheila had exercised wide latitude in the application of deadly force during that encounter, in an attempt to rescue Sheila's husband, Richard. They had broken every rule of engagement. They had also lost him in the process.

"As you know, there's not always time to go through channels. Opportunities can be wasted when time is of the essence. I went to Las Vegas to obtain first hand intelligence. I needed to see it myself. They set a trap, hoping we would stumble into it like a bunch of naive school children. They also murdered one of our agents and left us a message. I returned the favor in New York. Now they parade Petro publicly in Las Vegas. For what? To incite us—to hope we send someone to deal with him. It was a ploy to capture one of us. Don't forget, I have a very personal stake in this, and I don't want to get killed because some fucking crook of a senator has his ass in a jam."

Erika was displaying more emotion than Sheila had ever seen before. Her anger was rising. Sheila now realized Erika was terrified for her own life. "When I acted in Las Vegas, it was not in pursuit of a personal vendetta. I hurt them. I hurt their business interests and put them in an international spotlight. They are going to have so many national agencies crawling up their ass for the foreseeable future they will not be able to operate. And with your permission, I intend to up the ante—to cause the same sort of grief wherever I find their business interests. New York comes to mind."

Sheila sat there, stunned. She'd never experienced this side of Erika. Every time she attempted to gain control of her, she provided one more reason to trust her judgment. Her plan was solid—at some point the Russians would have to respond. Her tactics were flawless. Every local and national agency, along with the press, was investigating this as an international drug war, and now, this group of Russians was under a microscope. Erika may have done more damage to their organization in one night than the agency had done in the past year. Donny kept silent.

"I'll concede the effectiveness of your actions in Las Vegas. They are going to have a very difficult time explaining who they are and why their management was slain. The press is going to do a far better job of exposing this group than we could have," Sheila said. "But I still can't have you making decisions that affect this agency and my future without my knowledge. I have to trust your word and I can't. This has to stop."

"I'm not sure I can promise you that. If the opportunity arose to remove any of the principals that took Richard, I'd kill them out of hand," Erika said.

"That's different."

"No, it's not," Erika countered. "I'm an operative in a fluid situation. If I can't make an independent decision that might save your life or mine, then I can't do this job anymore."

"I hope you don't mean that, Erika."

"I'm afraid I do."

Donny finally intervened. "Look, both of you have a point and both of you are being obstinate for no reason. Neither one of you could do the other's job. Why don't you stop to appreciate what the other has to deal with and find a way to help each other? It seems to me we've gotten caught up in petty internal disagreements when we should be focused on the Russians—and the operations we should be engaged in."

The women were still staring at one another, but their expressions had softened considerably. Sheila broke first. "You're right, Donny. I keep getting caught up in who's running the show instead of how effective it is. God help us if our oversight committee ever discovers who's really running this agency."

Erika softened, too. "I agree. And for my part, I'll do my best to keep you in the loop on everything I do here. But I also want you to understand that sometimes it will be after the fact."

"Okay," Donny interrupted. "Let's get refocused on the Russians. Petro is gone now. I believe he left by private jet to Aspen. We may have them all together in one place. We need real time intelligence on their ranch. Sheila, can I task a drone over that area for a week—10 days—without the Senator becoming aware of it?"

"I'll find out." she replied.

"There were several passengers on that private jet. Petro took six friends with him."

Donny produced a file folder with pictures of the men boarding the plane. There were also pictures of their gear being loaded on the tarmac. Several of the bags did not appear to be clothing containers. Erika didn't have to guess what was inside. She'd seen many cases just like those when shooting with Ray and Jim in Owens Valley.

They were preparing for war.

Chapter 46

Petro and six other men deplaned from the Citation X at the General Aviation section of the Aspen Airport. The flight from Las Vegas took over ninety minutes, buffeted by high winds the entire way. They'd fled Vegas quickly before the authorities could rope them into the investigation. Everyone felt raw. They were hard men, trained for combat, and leaving the field with their tails between their legs and dead comrades behind did nothing to improve their mood. They stored their gear in the Suburbans that pulled up to the jet on the tarmac and departed without exchanging a word.

The late summer winds brought the chance for an afternoon storm to Aspen. Thunder, lightning, and billowing clouds bumped up against the 13,000-foot peaks, accentuating the mood. The sun was bright and hot, threading its way through the accumulation of cumulus as though it could hold off the impending storm. The temperature dropped fifteen degrees and the cloud cover thickened and won the battle over the retreating sun as they approached the ranch.

The ranch was shaped like a drunken rectangle, the west side nearly a half mile long meandering along a twenty-foot-wide creek that swelled to a small river when the snow melt from the hills above augmented the natural flow by a factor of ten. The northern boundary featured steep rock formations, caves, and sudden ravines that scarred the gentle slopes leading up to towering mountains beyond the ranch borders. The eastern boundary fell off for two hundred feet to the valley below, leading to a gradual slope down to the town of Aspen. The main lodge of wood, stone, and glass took advantage of the incredible vista laid out below, perched only fifty feet from the mesa rim. The entry to the ranch resembled the pole of a flag lot, with a long half-mile easement of paved asphalt that gradually broadened like a funnel as it approached the stone pilasters hung with ten-foot iron gates. After accessing the gates, the north and south borders spanned more than a third of a mile.

There was a small lake in the center of the property and several smaller ponds surrounding the main house that marched downwards like sentinels for four hundred yards to feed the lake in a series of small waterfalls. Summer or winter, it was an incredible work of nature that needed no enhancement. It was a perfect place to meditate or wander, allowing the natural beauty to provide an inner peace. It was Leonid's favorite spot on the ranch.

Fir trees and stands of Aspen covered the Northern hills and Western slopes down to the river with mountain meadows dominating the central portion of the ranch. The stables, located in the southwest quadrant could easily accommodate fifty animals and currently housed a dozen quarter horses, mountain-bred animals accustomed to the altitude. They had plenty of grass in the surrounding pastures cross-fenced with lodge-pole pine, divided into four different areas, allowing some pastures to rejuvenate while the horses grazed on the others.

There were five additional guest cabins spread around the property—one in the northern forested hills, two in the center near the lake, one at the entrance gate, and one more overlooking the northeast rim of the mesa. It was one of the major properties in the Aspen area.

Before the contingent from Las Vegas arrived, four guards inhabited the cabin at the ranch entrance, sharing security duties at the main gate. Two more guards were posted at the main house, living in the guest lodging above the seven-car attached garage.

Petro would stay in the main house with Leonid, Raina, and her pet, bringing that total to four. The other six Russians were divided up, two to a cabin. The two lake houses would accommodate two in each and the mesa rim cabin two more. Everyone was told the northern mountain cabin was uninhabited and off limits. So far as they knew, there were sixteen Russians occupying the ranch. No one else was welcome.

The six new security personnel would be split up and paired with the six permanent estate security guards so that they could learn the layout of the ranch during their roving patrol assignments. There were always three two-man teams roaming the property and another three pairs stationed at the entrance, the main house and the lake. They rotated every four hours around the clock, day and night.

Leonid and Petro sat at the bar in the great room, Leonid nursing a Scotch, Petro with his tea. "Are you sure they will come?" Petro asked.

"They will come. They have no choice. They intercepted the name somehow. They know we have it. That's why they killed the lady banker and disrupted our Las Vegas operation. Either they put a stop to us or eventually we will find this "Sheila Gibbons" and then the other one. They know we are here. They will come." Leonid said.

"And you're sure they killed the banker?"

"All but certain." Leonid hesitated for only a moment. "It's precisely what I would have done. And it's too much of a coincidence. I would have killed the Senator, too."

"How many do you think?"

"Not many. If they mobilize a task force, the Senator will know. And then we will know. And then we will disappear and attend to this another day."

"I am glad," Petro said. "I consider this a blood feud. It is no longer just business. It is good to know you feel the same way."

Leonid took a sip. "That is how it has always been. There is no other way."

Petro rose and donned his coat against the evening chill. "I will go and inspect the security arrangements. Good night."

"Good night, my friend."

Chapter 47

A week had passed and Donny finally managed to station a drone over the Aspen ranch without alerting the Senator. They were back in the Bel Air conference room. Aerial photos of the Aspen ranch were on a large video screen that depicted captures of heat signatures downloaded from the drone.

"It's a shame we couldn't have had a drone on station before they arrived," Sheila said. "We could have isolated the new arrivals from the permanent residents. I want to know if Leonid or Raina are there. Can we get high resolution shots in daylight?"

"Yes," Donny said. "But only if we get a lucky shot at an angle that's recognizable and well lit."

"Let's keep trying," Sheila said. "I think they are there and want us to know it."

"It's a shame that drone is not weaponized," Erika said.

"On U.S. soil?" Sheila remarked. "That's not going to happen. Military assets being used against civilians in the Homeland? That's over the top, even for you, Erika."

"Just a thought," she said.

"Kind of like Leavenworth is a thought," Sheila answered.

Donny intervened. "They have to know we saw them leave Las Vegas and know where they landed. They're not hiding. They want us to come. I just haven't figured out why?"

"There's only one reason for it," Erika said. "Somehow the Senator is in their pocket. He is their cover."

"Why do you think so?" Sheila asked.

"Come on, Sheila. He set you up for this party at the banker's home. You never would have made it out of there. And eventually, you'd have given me up and gotten yourself killed. He needs a message sent to him as well." Erika was pissed.

Sheila considered what Erika said. "Okay, I get it. If he was willing to go through with the party, covering for this group is a simple decision compared to that."

"There's also a big cash payment somewhere. Donny needs to find it. Off shore, somewhere is my guess," Erika said. "He's not doing this without a large reward."

"I'll get right on that," Donny said. "But first we have to figure out how to deal with the Russians on this ranch without alerting Senator Ross."

"That won't be easy," Sheila said. "If I request any assets outside this immediate group, the Senator will know. He signs off on all inter-agency ops."

"I still don't have a clear picture," Erika said. "Here's what we know…..somehow Senator Ross is in their pocket. He set you up at the party; therefore, he has a replacement for you in mind; himself or someone he knows he can control. It has to be him. There's no other way he can keep a lid on whatever we do in Aspen."

Donny said, "If he plans to retire as a Senator and go into intelligence work, he could set us up for failure at the ranch, get us all killed, and take over the agency. He gets paid for giving up Erika and Sheila, probably a tidy sum, and the ability to make ongoing monies by overlooking future activities. I think the Senator is planning on moving in and making a fortune by doing so."

"It's starting to make sense," Sheila said. "That arrogant prick!"

It didn't take long. Two days later, Sheila received a request for a face-to-face meeting from Senator Ross to discuss the events that had occurred in Las Vegas. He further requested the meeting be held at the agency headquarters, a request that was not only unusual, but also never granted to anyone not directly involved in operations for security reasons. Erika had already departed for San Diego where she was preparing for the inevitable trip to Colorado. Donny was still in residence, trying to formulate an assault plan that would be hidden from the Senate Oversight Committee. It was not going well.

Sheila stepped into his basement office. "You're not going to believe this."

"Believe what?"

"Senator Ross just called requesting a personal meeting here," she said.

"Here? This is operation headquarters. He can't visit here. That's a complete breach of security." Donny was incensed. "Who the hell does he think he is?"

"The ranking Senate Democratic Chair of the Intelligence Oversight Committee is what he said. He's pulling rank, Donny."

"Fuck him. We know he's dirty. Maybe Erika is right. He needs a message delivered."

Sheila had never heard Donny speak with such vehemence. "Whoa there, Donny. What's gotten into you?"

"I'm so sick of these self-serving sons-of-bitches enriching themselves and their friends at everyone else's expense. They join Congress as unemployed attorneys and leave there as millionaires. They stopped serving the American people decades ago. This is simply organized graft at its most sophisticated. Now he wants to put all of us at risk to promote himself to a position where he can extort huge sums of money from international criminals."

"You don't have any proof of that, do you?"

"How about twenty-two million dollars in seven different overseas accounts controlled by the Senator?"

"What?"

"You heard me."

"You can prove that?"

"Not in a court of law," Donny said. "But this also is not a problem that will be resolved in the courts. Sheila, I'm positive. Ross is on the take, big time. He's been protecting this group long before we stumbled on to them."

The enormity of the statement stopped her in her tracks. *How long? How far? Was Richard's death related?* She sat down heavily, all her strength gone.

"Donny, what do we do here? I have to meet with him, and he wants to see where we operate from. I feel like I'm in way over my head."

"Set up the meeting for next week, maybe ten days from now. We'll set up an operations center for him. It just won't be here. We'll also bring in personnel. This town is full of actors—he'll never meet a real operative." Donny almost laughed.

Sheila considered his suggestion for a few moments. "You really think you could pull this off?"

"Yes, as long as you control what he sees, who he talks to."

She was smiling now, warming up to the idea of pulling the wool over the Senator's eyes. "I know of a nice estate property that's still owned by our agency. Will that do?"

"It sure will." Donny knew she was referring to the home where they originally met.

"In the meantime, I want you to trace all payments made to Senator Ross, get evidence of his ownership. See if it leads back to payments in other countries, to other people in power. Two can play this game," Sheila said.

"I've already identified officials in Russia, Great Britain, Italy and South Africa. If these bank accounts are part of a protective scheme, this organization is far larger than we ever anticipated. There's almost one hundred million dollars involved in these accounts and several others I haven't identified yet."

"Keep pushing. I want as many of these people identified as quickly as possible. We're going to hurt them—all of them. In the meantime, I'll set up a meeting place for the Senator, and get Erika back up here tomorrow. As usual, her instincts were right on target. Eventually, we will need a permanent solution."

Chapter 48

Erika was lounging on the upper veranda of the Del Mar beach house owned by Felix. She faced the late afternoon sun retreating over the Pacific dressed only in a black bikini—the Indian summer heat painted a sheen of perspiration across her body. Felix slid the patio door open and reclined in the chaise next to Erika. He was wearing only boxer shorts and offered her an iced tea, which she accepted.

"When are you leaving?" he asked.

"Day after tomorrow."

"How long this time?"

"A week—ten days."

"I don't suppose you can tell me where you'll be or what you're doing?"

"Afraid not," Erika said. "You know the routine. Even if we worked together, it would be need-to-know only."

"You think we could ever do that—work together?" Felix was serious.

"I never gave it a thought. Why? What are you thinking?"

"You know my situation, Erika. In a lot of ways, it's not much different than yours. The same dangers exist. The stakes are incredibly high. I've given this a lot of thought, and I've made a few major decisions about my business practices. Things I need to change."

"I'm listening," she said.

"For most of my life, I thought my future revolved around being Hispanic. That was my heritage, my destiny. I thought that my people were the only ones I could trust," Felix explained. "Now I know that's not true. They sold me out, my brothers. There's only one rule. The strongest one makes the rules. So the solution is to become the strongest, the most feared, the most ruthless."

"So, how do you accomplish that?"

"Well, the most ruthless men I ever met were all in the military," he said.

"The Seals?"

"Yes. There are over a million service members returning to civilian life over the next five years. Some of them are Seals, and they are only trained to do one thing. They don't know how to operate within the strict confines of law and order. I served with a lot of them. I know them: their strengths, how they think, what makes them tick. They're adrenaline junkies. I had an army of highly-trained, competent warriors at my disposal all along."

"You already contacted them, didn't you?"

"Yes."

"Are they all Seals?"

"Yes."

"All men you can trust?"

"With my life."

"That's what you will be doing."

"That's what I've been doing, Erika. This is an upgrade."

"You're sure?" she asked. "How do you know they will work with you? Doing the sort of thing you do? Drugs, violence, and smuggling are not really career choices?"

"I don't. But I'm also thinking of making some changes along those lines, Erika"

"Like what? Don't tell me you're going to go straight now. Are you?"

"I don't know about all that yet. It depends on how things work out. There are a lot of variables to consider. I don't have a handle on all of them yet," Felix said.

"Are you sure you want to go in that direction?

"Yes."

"Then do it," she said.

"It's that simple?"

"Most things are."

"That still doesn't answer my original question," Felix said.

"Which was?"

"Do you think we could ever work together?"

"You mean doing what you do? Erika asked.

"No, doing something different. I'm not sure what. There's been too much blood. And there's going to be more. The people who tried to take me out have to pay or I will be looking over my shoulder for the rest of my life. There is no other way."

"What is it you're proposing?" Erika had been giving her future some thought lately too. It was the perfect time for Felix to offer a suggestion.

"When you get back I'll have a better idea about where this is going. We'll talk then, okay?"

"Okay," Erika said. She lay back and sipped her tea, putting the future out of her mind. She just wanted to enjoy her time with Felix for now.

Chapter 49

It was early evening and Leonid, Raina and Petro were seated before the immense plate glass viewing window overlooking the twinkling lights of the town of Aspen below. Late September was a perfect time to enjoy the warm sunshine in the daytime and cool sleeping weather at night. The town was devoid of tourists, allowing the locals freedom of movement and ease of obtaining dinner reservations that was rare.

"The Senator assured me that the agency could not mount an operation against us without his knowledge. He has consolidated his power over this Sheila Gibbons's agency and will, in fact, be conducting a personal visit to their offices as a prelude to an investigation into their activities. Apparently, the death of our lady banker hit too close to home for the Senator. Our colleague has set his sights on the directorship of that agency. Once he has accomplished that takeover we will be able to operate freely within this country," Leonid explained.

"How reliable is this information?" Petro asked.

"Ninety-five percent," Leonid said. "No one gets one hundred percent in our business, but I now have a direct line to our new partner through an email account he and I share. No one else has access. We don't send any email from the account; instead, we compose drafts, read them, and then delete them."

"And how much will this new relationship cost us?" Raina asked. "Assuming, of course, he is able to take over this agency."

"He wants one million dollars per month once he heads the agency paid into revolving overseas accounts managed by a third party, same as before."

"A million dollars? Per month? That's quite a pay raise," Raina said.

"It's nothing compared to the freedom to operate that it will buy us. That doesn't amount to one percent of the narcotic traffic alone that we will control. Besides, we have leverage to apply to the Senator once he is in place. We can bargain with him at that time," Leonid replied.

"Can we work similar deals in Russia and Europe?" Petro asked. "Brazil, perhaps?"

"I'm already working on it," Leonid said. "And once we land a few more intelligence agencies in those countries, we can operate at levels no one has ever dreamed of."

"But first, we must deal with this Sheila Gibbons and Erika," Raina said. "What have you done about that, Leonid?"

Leonid grinned as he unveiled his new strategy. "If we can't get to them, he will bring them to us. The Senator will bring forth new intelligence that pinpoints us here and recommend an operation to eliminate us. He will share that information with us, and we will be waiting for these women to appear. We will take them long before they get to this ranch, that I promise you."

"We can take them on the road anywhere between here and the airport," Petro suggested.

"If we don't need them alive, we could take them out of the sky before they ever arrive at the airport," Leonid said. "That would be safest. However, the crash investigation would inevitably conclude a surface-to-air missile was used. That would become national news immediately."

"So we take them here?" Petro asked.

"Here, at their hotel, or at the airport before they leave Los Angeles. I will decide once the operation is mounted. We need to be patient and flexible, as always," he answered.

Raina shuddered involuntarily, that spark of insanity reappearing in her eyes. "Remember your promise to me, Leonid."

"Yes, Raina, you need not remind me again," he said.

Chapter 50

Erika sat at the Bel Air rear yard meeting area, drinking coffee from an insulated travel mug. She was not happy.

"Since when does this asshole dictate when and if he visits a closed operations facility?" she said.

"Since he wrote the oversight charter and had it ratified by the Intelligence Oversight Committee. I never saw it coming," Sheila said. "He can pretty much call the shots, according to the document he sent over."

"So, what do we do now?" Erika asked.

"Do you remember the estate where we first met?" Donny said.

"Yes."

"We still own it. We'll set up offices there next week so that the Senator can visit," he said.

Erika went from angry to happy in the blink of an eye. "That's too funny," she said. "I guess we can have more than one office."

"And no one specified which one," Sheila said. "It's time we both played this game."

"What do we do about our Russian friends in the meantime?" Erika asked.

"Anything we do has to be off the record or they'll be waiting for us," Sheila said. "We don't know how they'll be communicating with the Senator, but we know they are communicating."

"Donny, you can't figure out how?"

"Not yet. They have to have some kind of closed system. Nothing shows up on any computer network or phone that I can detect."

"So where does that leave us?" Erika wanted to push the conversation regarding the Russians. She had some of her own ideas.

"Can you work up an action plan that leaves all of our support agencies out of the loop?" Sheila asked.

"I think so. Can I use any of our in-house personnel or assets?" Erika asked.

"In-house only: Donny or me. Any of your trainers or transportation assets are also acceptable. But you clear it with me first. Who are you thinking of as personnel?"

"I don't know. Let me think about it," Erika said. "What about transportation assets? Won't the Senator figure that out?"

"We can't risk using our usual methods of transportation. We do have the budget to contract it out to charter carriers, so that's no problem." Sheila replied.

"Okay, let me work something up for your approval."

Donny had doubts about Erika's plans, but wisely remained silent.

That afternoon Erika landed at Independence Airport in the Owens Valley. Ray and Jim were waiting on the tarmac in the familiar gray suburban. Erika deplaned, unloaded her gear, and hugged both men before the trio headed south to their private shooting range.

The temperature was barely sixty degrees in the sunlight because of a cool breeze swirling out of the mountains. They all wore padded shooting vests to ward off the chill.

"What's up?" Jim asked after they were settled at the picnic table.

"I have something to discuss that is delicate. I have authorization to speak with you and I may need to share some operational details that have to stay strictly between us."

The men shared a glance. Ray said, "Go on."

"It concerns Sheila," Erika began. She shared the background on the Russians, how Richard had died, the lethal situation Sheila found herself in, and after further encouragement, what she intended to do about it. She left out the details regarding Rita Jackson and referred to Jerry Ross only as "the Senator."

"Who would run this operation?" Jim asked.

"The three of us," Erika said. "I couldn't very well ask you to put your careers—and your lives—on the line without giving you planning and operational authority," she added.

"Once I see the operational parameters, I may have to add personnel," Ray said.

"Sheila said I cannot add any personnel without her express approval. Sorry, guys."

Ray looked to Jim. "Go ahead," Jim said.

"Erika, Jim and I come from Special Forces. I think you realize that by now."

"I know you didn't fall off a turnip truck," she said.

"You also know Sheila runs many cells and that none of them are aware of the others?" Jim asked.

The light bulb went off in Erika's head. "And you're one of them?"

In answer, they simply shrugged. Jim added, "Don't worry. I'll clear everything with Sheila first."

"Does this mean you're in?"

"It's what we specialize in."

"What's that?"

"Cleaning up details left intact by other cells. Sometimes, a ransom payment only encourages the kidnappers to do it again. We're the team that discourages them permanently from a repeat adventure," Ray explained.

"I guess I came to the right place," Erika said.

"Especially since the ambitions of the Senator could threaten us personally–our families, too," Jim added.

"Eventually, he has to go, you know."

"I know," Erika said. "I will see to that personally, once this is done."

"Okay, and as to any other personnel required, you leave that to us. Are we in agreement?" Jim asked.

"Absolutely."

"Do you have time for some target practice?" Ray asked.

"You bet."

Chapter 51

When Erika arrived home, she collected all the data on the Russians, along with every physical detail on the ranch in Aspen and sent them via courier to Ray and Jim. The men would develop the initial assault plan and come up with the number and type of personnel required. Erika had soon realized the two men were experts at combat tactics. She could not have done better in selecting an assault command structure if she had the full resources of the agency at her fingertips. Once they came up with an effective plan, they would act.

Erika dialed up Donny. "Hello."

"Hello."

"Do you have time for a strategy session?" Erika asked.

"Now?"

"As soon as you can."

"I'm setting up a new operations facility for a visit. You ought to see it. The last time we were here, you and I didn't see very much of it. It's nice," he said.

"Look, I hate to interrupt this walk down memory lane, but I need to discuss a future venture with you." Erika was being as cryptic as possible over the phone, as was Donny.

"With or without Mom?" he asked.

"With."

"Then why don't you come up here and look over the old place. It wouldn't hurt for you to become familiar with our agency offices before the unveiling."

"Okay, set up a meeting for the three of us. I'll come up in the morning, early. Send me directions, please. I've forgotten exactly where it is."

"Will do. See you tomorrow."

Erika dialed the house from her car, and the ten-foot-high iron gates opened to admit her. She'd never seen this estate in daylight. Both times she'd met Donny here had been at night.

The home was a large two-story structure in the Spanish Hacienda style; it boasted a red barrel tile roof over white stucco and fifteen thousand square feet of opulence. A circular stone driveway arced around a twenty-foot-wide fountain featuring cherubs pouring water from stone carafes to fill the pool beneath them. A massive double door, ten feet high, framed the front entrance up three steps from cobble stones. The home oozed wealth and power.

Erika parked in the circle facing away from the home and approached the front door just as Donny opened it.

"Good morning," he said. "How was the drive?"

"Great. How are you?"

"Fine, Erika." He kissed her and led her into the house.

"So this is what the front entrance looks like." Erika said. "We always used the service entrance, didn't we?"

On the two occasions Erika had visited the house, she had been a young prostitute accompanying Donny. They'd used the garage entrance into the kitchen. Circumstances had changed radically since then.

"See! Proof positive of our ascendance into the top management," he said with a wave of his arm. "C'mon, Sheila is in her office waiting for us."

"This looks like you've been working here for years," Erika said. She hugged Sheila. "You've done wonders for the place."

Sheila stifled a laugh, but the humor in the situation was too hard to ignore. "I just hope the Senator is impressed with this old complex," she said.

"Do you really think he'll believe all of this?" Erika asked.

"Why not? It's not too different from the real thing, and

he's never visited a clandestine operation center quite like this before. Officially, this place does not exist," Donny said.

"Is it wired for sound and imagery security?" Erika asked.

"Yes. I updated all that over the past two days. It will be activated the morning the Senator arrives," Donny replied.

"Why not activate it right after you give him the address?" Erika said.

"Damn, I hadn't thought of that," he answered. "Once he has the location, there's nothing stopping him from sharing that information. And if he wanted something to happen to this place, he'd want it to occur before he visits, rather than after."

"I would activate it as soon as he knows the location," Erika said. "Otherwise, it gives him a deniability factor he won't have after his visit."

Sheila turned to Donny. "Set it up to record and download in real time to the Bel Air location. Then we'll know if anyone shows up that's not invited."

"I'll get right on it."

"Now, let's get to our presentation, Erika," Sheila said.

The trio sat at a comfortable furniture arrangement in one corner of Sheila's office rather than at the desk. Once they were settled, Erika began. "I've contacted a couple of agents, downloaded the physical layout of the ranch to them, and now I'm waiting for them to formulate an assault plan along with a request for additional personnel and equipment needed."

"I'm curious. Why did you contact the man who called me?" Sheila asked.

"At this point, I think it's better you don't know," Erika replied. "I'm not usurping your authority, Sheila. I just want to outline our approach in general terms while leaving you unaware of any details that could come back to hurt you. If you're put under oath, you can truthfully answer you were ignorant of an operation conducted without your approval by a rogue agent. It gives both us cover."

"How does it cover you?"

"It'll give me time to disappear."

"What?"

"If something goes wrong, you're going to need plausible deniability," Donny interjected. "She's right. You need to be insulated from this operation–especially since this is the group that murdered your late husband. They will call it a reprisal if you're aware of the operation before the fact."

"Then these requests for personnel and equipment cannot be processed through our system," she said.

"I know. Donny and I will handle all that outside the lines," Erika answered.

Sheila said, "Give me an hour to consider what you've proposed. I'll give you my answer then." After a moment's hesitation, she asked, "Erika, you wouldn't really leave, would you?"

"If I had to."

Donny and Erika rose and left Sheila alone to think.

Ninety minutes later, they returned to Sheila's office and retook their seats.

"Okay, here's how I see this. We have two very serious, very distinct problems to solve. The obvious one is this Russian gang operating with impunity inside our borders. They've committed murder on top of prostitution, drug smuggling, money laundering, corruption of public officials, and God knows what else. There can be only one group response for this. They have to be put down permanently. If you can eliminate this group in Colorado cleanly, I can protect you afterwards. I do not want to know anything until *afterwards*. Is that clear?"

"Yes," Erika said. She knew her approach would now be accepted.

"Yes," Donny echoed. He knew there was no other way. This gang had to be eradicated.

"The second issue is our esteemed Senator. He has to remain in the dark until after we have dealt with the Russians. Then he has to be addressed," Sheila said. "I will let you know how I want that handled when the time comes. Understood?"

Erika had a malicious grin on her face. No answer was required.

Sheila ignored the look and continued. "Okay, as of now this is an operation that is not under my direct supervision. I want complete deniability on this issue. Are we all in agreement?"

"Yes."

"Yes."

"Good. Let's go to work, people."

Donny and Erika filed out.

Chapter 52

It took five days before Jim contacted Erika by encrypted e-mail. It read "operational details complete–Bel Air meet set for 0700 Tuesday–see you then."

Erika packed her car with enough gear to fill her trunk and rear seat. She included the .50 caliber Barrett Rifle with all the accessories, an MP7A1 submachine gun with six 30 round magazines, and two personal handguns, both 9-millimeter Glocks, all equipped with suppressors. She also put a .380 automatic in an ankle holster along with her carbon fixed blade. If things didn't go well in Colorado, she could always start a small war somewhere else.

When she arrived at the Bel Air estate, Donny, Jim, Ray, and two more men were waiting in the conference room. They had turned off all video and recording equipment and Sheila was conspicuously absent.

She hugged Donny, then Jim and Ray. She walked up to the other two men in the room and introduced herself. "Hello, I'm Erika."

They shook hands. The tall one, easily six foot five, said "I'm Smith and this," he indicated the other man, standing all of five foot seven, "is Jones. We're not here."

Erika smiled her gratitude. "Understood." Smith was not only tall, but wide in the shoulders and chest, with legs that looked like tree trunks. He wore a white t-shirt that looked like there were two bowling balls stuffed in where his shoulders should have been. His skin was coffee colored, his nose and lips were broad, his eyes mere slits under a shaved head. His face bore the marks of a life spent in a boxing ring at some point–definitely not the lightweight class.

Jones, an Apache, wore his long black hair in a ponytail that accentuated the hard-edged planes of his face. He also wore a white T-shirt, and his body, though slight, appeared chiseled out of granite, not an ounce of it wasted on fat. His black eyes took in everything and gave away nothing. He didn't speak. He just shook her hand without applying any pressure and nodded. Erika pegged him as a dangerous person.

"These gentlemen, and I use the term loosely, have graciously agreed to accompany us on that short vacation we discussed. Smith can handle any sort of heavy weapon and is quite handy in any type of physical combat. Jones is recon. He has a peculiar talent for popping up where people least expect him and has a wealth of knowledge about living outdoors for an extended period of time. He could track an ant through a jungle. You can trust them both with your life," Jim said.

"Gentlemen," he turned to them, "this is Erika, no last name. The people we are going to visit are desperate to get their hands on her. Believe me when I say she has no equal with a handgun." Before Erika could bask in the compliment he added, "But her long-range shooting needs some work." Then he took the sting out of his comment. "You can trust her like you would Ray or me. We both do, and she's no rookie. She'll stick."

"Donny will serve as our control. You've all worked with him before. We will have direct voice contact with him at all times once we're in the field. If you don't want him to hear your transmissions or you don't want to hear him, turn off your com equipment. If you want him to hear you, but not make any noise, put your com on channel 7, that's a passive circuit. He can hear you if you find yourself in a situation, and he will know what to do about it. Trust him. I have many times in the past and he's never let me down. Any questions?"

The team had a lot of questions. They spent several hours poring over terrain maps of the ranch and surrounding area, selecting ingress and egress entries, areas of responsibility, fields of fire, and building locations. Donny summarized their approach.

"You'll be flying into a small airport down valley from Aspen and driving an hour from there. The assumption is that they will be looking for a team to land in Aspen, Vail, or Grand Junction. Denver also is a possibility, but since that would be a five-hour car trip, we're not choosing that route. Your cover story is a hunting and fly-fishing trip north of Rifle near Meeker, Colorado in the White River Valley. Please familiarize yourselves with that area so that you are conversant about the elk herds, mule deer, and fishing spots. You'll find that in your packet," Donny said.

"Once you're in Aspen, you will approach the ranch from the North through the hills. There is sufficient cover in the trees, large rock formations, and a fast-moving stream to the west. The east side is a steep cliff face that overlooks the Town of Aspen. If you need to exit in that direction, you'll have to grow wings. The south collapses into the mouth of a funnel where the highway fronts the entrance to the property."

Jim took over from there. "Smith and I will occupy the high ground after we clear the two cabins in the tree line. We will establish a clear field of fire and wait until Erika is in position at the main house and Ray is at the front gate.

"Jones will recon the two cabins around the lake and confirm how many Russians are there and how many are on patrol. He will communicate with me to direct your movements when and if that becomes necessary."

He looked over the group. "That puts two long-range shooters on high ground, two expert combat specialists with short guns at the cabins, and a recon rover to help where needed. Everybody clear?"

They nodded their understanding.

"Ok, let's saddle up."

Chapter 53

Erika surveyed the open country around the Rifle Airport. Mountains stood sentinel far to the east and north, rolling hills occupied the south, and the western approach fell away beneath the huge mesa where the airport was built. The sun was bright with few clouds to shield the group as they deplaned. A light breeze took the edge off the warm midday sun, but Erika knew it would be near freezing overnight. Weather in the mountains was always unpredictable and even more so in late summer and early fall when it was not unusual for temperatures to swing forty degrees in one day.

Two Suburban four-wheel drives waited for the group at the airport. They stowed their gear within and left. Jim drove one of the rentals with Erika and Ray as passengers. Smith and Jones took the other Suburban. Ninety minutes later, they arrived at a rental home at the base of Snowmass Mountain near the Two Creeks ski lift. It was a five-bedroom luxury house that easily accommodated the group. Each individual retired to their rooms to assemble their equipment and rest up for later. Tonight, they would get into position for the early morning assault. It was important to be prepared and to get as much rest as possible before the long night in the field.

In late afternoon, the team reloaded the Suburbans with their gear and drove down to Highway 82. They crossed over the main road, traversed an old wooden bridge that spanned the Roaring Fork River, and headed into the hills below the ranch. They continued on a circuitous route that took them away from the compound before doubling back on an old Forest Service road blocked by a heavy chain attached to two steel posts imbedded in concrete pilings.

Jim and Smith were in the lead vehicle, prepared for just such an eventuality. Jim got out and attached a sturdy length of chain to one of the posts and the tow bar on the Suburban. Smith put the vehicle in all-wheel drive and reversed back up the dirt road until the post bent from the applied force and evacuated the hole it was buried in. Jim set the post and chain aside, retrieved his tow chain and climbed back in the passenger seat. From there, the two vehicles followed the abandoned road up into the mountains above the ranch.

They parked two miles from the ranch on the backside of a ridge that shielded them from view. They would have to traverse the valley on the other side, climb a steep hill, and then descend for almost four hundred yards through dense trees before reaching the property, all without being detected.

Jones snaked his way to the ridge top to observe the opposite ridge while the other four unloaded their gear. He made no noise.

Erika watched as Jim and Smith donned Gilly suits, coveralls that utilized random camouflage attachments of leaves, twigs, and bushes that distorted the outline of the human figure, rendering detection difficult, if not impossible. She knew the human eye expected to capture a recognizable shape stored away in the brain, not some shapeless conglomeration of branches and leaves. Camouflage face paint completed the deception. The two men guarding the high ground would be, for all practical purposes, invisible.

Erika and Ray would take the main house and the cabin at the gated entry. They were dressed similarly to the roving patrols they'd seen on video. She wore jeans, a beige fishing shirt under an army green tactical vest that would protect her vitals from small arms fire and carry extra ammo, and tucked her long brown hair beneath the battered old ball cap Jim had given her years ago.

"My lucky hat," she told Jim, tipping it to him.

"Let's hope you don't need it," he replied.

Ray wore the same vest over a camouflage shirt and green pants with a dirty brown ball cap. Both of them wore comfortably light hiking boots that were the equivalent of mountain sneakers. Jones, lying up on the ridge, was invisible, wearing full camouflage with a Gilly hat, face paint and no vest. He did not want to be constricted in any way. Jim and Smith both carried .50 caliber Barrett Rifles without the BORS system, as it would only be an impediment to hitting a moving target. And both men were so proficient with the weapon that it simply wasn't needed.

They carried personal handguns holstered at their sides and an M7A1 submachine gun strapped on their backs. All the weapons were silenced. Each carried enough ammo to arm a small country.

Ray carried two Glock semi-automatic handguns in .40 caliber, an MP7A1, and a K-bar Marine tactical knife.

Erika holstered one Glock 9-millimeter handgun on her right hip and another under left armpit in a shoulder rig. Her black carbon blade was sheathed in the small of her back and her MP7A1 submachine gun was clipped to her vest in a ready position.

The Apache scout carried two 9-millimeter Glocks and a fully camouflaged MP7A1. She assumed he also carried a fixed blade or two, but none were in evidence.

Everyone was ready as dusk began to soften the contours of the mountains. It would be dark soon, allowing them to get into position before daybreak. The Apache reappeared like an apparition.

Together, they performed a communications check. They inserted ear buds and adjusted a wire microphone positioned to the side of their mouths. Each spoke in turn to the others, including Donny. He then checked each person for both passive and active communication reception. Once everyone was satisfied, the Indian reported on his recon.

"There's no guards stationed in the woods on the high ground, but there was a roving two-man patrol that walked the property line along an old game trail just below the ridgeline on the other slope. I almost took them out, but I figured they would be in communication with the main house. And I was right. I followed them down to the lake in the middle of the compound where they met another two-man patrol. So, there are four rovers at any one time, maybe more if they patrol the entry area too. I would bet on it," he said.

Jim spoke into his mike. "Donny, can you confirm?"

"Yes," Donny's disembodied voice came over everyone's earpiece. "The drone picked up three teams of two. One patrols the lower region that Jones did not encounter. Another loops a circle through the upper woods. They occupy the northeast cabin overlooking the city just below the tree line. There is a second two-man team from the west-central cabin near the lake that patrols the center area of the ranch. The lower patrol came from the cabin at the entry gate. The upper cabin in the northwest corner appears unoccupied, but it is suspicious for that reason. Check it first."

"Where are the others?" Jim asked.

"There are two guards living above the garages at the main house. If Leonid, Raina, their pet and Petro are in residence, that makes six. Two are always at the gate house and two more are in the east central cabin by the lake. Add the six on patrol for a total of sixteen. And again, I don't like the idea that no one is living in the northwest cabin in the trees. I do not have eyes on that cabin. It's too deep in the trees," Donny said. "Check it."

"Will do," Jim replied. "We'll move out at midnight as planned. Jones will recon the northwest cabin for occupants when we move in. Everyone get some rest."

By 10:00 p.m., the Apache had vanished into thin air. He crept through the dark woods aided by a night vision monocular that operated on heat signature generated by other mammals. He assumed that the roving patrols were equipped with the same technology. Whoever detected the other adversary first would have a distinct advantage. He intended it would be him. This technology was the main reason the assault would begin at first light. By then, the advantages of night vision would be

negated and natural biorhythms would be at their lowest. He watched the northwest cabin for over an hour and detected no lights or movement within. He found it even more surprising that the patrols never passed through this area at all; it was as though they had been instructed to stay away from there. Something was not right.

He clicked his mic twice to alert the team. "No movement at the northwest cabin and no patrols. I'm going down to take a look."

"Careful," Jim said. The comment was superfluous. The Indian moved like a ghost, taking advantage of every shadow, every bit of cover. He skirted the cabin, looking for any sign of occupancy and found nothing. He peered through every window, using the monocular to detect any heat source within. The cabin was deserted. Not even the hearth held a heat signature. It was stone cold.

He did pick up on recent boot impressions in the soft earth leading away from the cabin—large impressions, bearing a lot of weight.

He clicked his mic twice. "No one home, but someone very big was living here. Their tracks are deep and extra-large, about a size 17 boot."

Erika said, "How old are the tracks?"

"I can't tell until daylight. It could be weeks. It could be days." The Indian's voice was a whisper. "Do you want me to enter?"

"Is there a security system?" Jim asked.

"I can't tell. I have to assume so."

"Then leave it," Erika said. "I think that one is out of the game."

"You sure?"

"No. Donny, anyone other than Fyodor that big?"

"No, just him."

"I don't like it," Jim said.

"Me neither," said the Apache.

"Stay on it. Do not enter until we're there."

"Roger that. I will recon the rest and get in position on the north ridge before you start."

"Roger."

"Out."

Based on Donny's observations, the patrols would change personnel at 6:00 am, an hour after daybreak. The two men from the entry gate would switch with the other two housed there. The east-central cabin team would switch with the west-central two-man team, and the northeast cabin would return for sleep. Only two teams of two would operate in daylight. They were not expecting company then. Jim and Erika intended to have everyone in position before the shift change.

"Let's move out," Jim spoke to all of them through his mike. "Jones, are you there?"

"All set," he responded. "I have your twelve."

The four agents descended to the valley that separated the two ridges. With the aid of night vision, they ascended the opposite slope leading to the ranch. Jones watched them and the property behind him, alert for any patrol, and alternating his attention between focal points every ten seconds. When they were within fifty yards, he whispered, "Everyone find cover and hunker down. Patrol on approach."

Each agent scrambled to find a boulder or a tree to shield their bodies. Cover was plentiful on the slope and everyone was in position as the pair appeared on the ridgeline peering out over the valley below. They never even looked at the area where the four agents were hidden so close to them before continuing on their patrol. Jones rotated around the trunk of a large tree, his Glock in his hand, to protect his heat signature from detection as they passed within ten yards of him. Once again he considered shooting them, but it was still too soon.

"Okay, they're gone. Come straight up over the ridge. I'm twenty yards to your right."

The group did as instructed and met him at the top. Using hand signals, he led the troop down slope through the trees until they neared the northeast cabin in the trees. Jones whispered, "This cabin is empty. I will take these two when they return, then go directly to the low cabin in the woods. Jim, Smith, come with me. You two stay here."

He led Jim to a position above the east-central lake cabin and situated him with a clear field of fire that encompassed the cabin, the entire lake, and in the distance, the main house, almost 700 yards down the hill. Jim settled in as Jon led Smith to a position 500 yards above the west-central cabin, the lake, and only 300 yards below the empty cabin where he'd found the large boot prints. "Be careful. The empty cabin is 300 yards above you in the trees. It will take me ten minutes to get there and check it once the party starts. There's no one on your six until then."

"Understood," the big man said. They bumped fists before Jones disappeared back into the trees.

He returned to Ray and Erika, and signaled them to follow. They walked slowly and quietly, stopping every twenty yards to listen and scan the terrain around them before moving on. It was a slow, deliberate process, used since ancient times to hunt game, so it took almost two hours before he situated Erika beneath the stairwell leading to the quarters above the garage. There were two large trash bins parked there as a convenience for the large trucks that came to empty them. Erika wedged herself between them and settled in to wait.

Ray followed his Indian guide back north away from the house before turning west, skirting the south side of the lake, and approaching the large cabin at the gated entry. He positioned Ray just ten feet off the path that the returning patrol would use, in a shallow depression rimmed with boulders. He disappeared once Ray was settled.

Chapter 54

Donny had eyes in the sky, watching over his team as light seeped over the eastern horizon. Once the rising sun cleared the flat mesa top, it shone like a spotlight over the ranch. It would create a blind spot to anyone looking back toward that direction.

Jones sat behind a bush just twenty feet from the door of the northeast cabin. The rising sun would cast a brilliant glare towards anyone approaching the cabin. Donny spoke into his earpiece to warn him. "Twenty yards out, one behind the other, three paces apart; rifles slung on their backs, heads down."

The Apache rose into a crouch; his senses vibrated, but his body relaxed. The two men neared the cabin, their body language already closing down in anticipation of the end of their shift. Jones stepped towards them on silent feet, his MP7A1 pointed at the pair.

He loosed a three-round burst into the first figure, knocking him to the ground, and shot the second man from only ten feet away. That three-round burst stitched a line from his throat to his forehead, killing him instantly. With no hesitation, he fired another silent three-round burst into the head of the fallen guard, reducing his face to pulp.

He keyed his mic twice so that everyone could hear him. "They're wearing Kevlar body armor. Use head shots." Jones dashed into the cabin to ensure no one else was present. A quick reconnaissance and he was on the move again. "Two down, northeast cabin empty," he said.

Seconds later, Donny spoke again. "Jim, your two replacements just exited the east-central cabin headed uphill."

"Got 'em," he replied.

The two men were abreast one another, walking up the slope towards Jim. With a .50 caliber Barrett rifle in hand, the

Kevlar vests would not be an issue. He waited until they were in an open meadow before he shot the man on the right, dead center of his chest. He crumpled forward, collapsing into a crouch before keeling over onto his face.

The second man froze, trying to assimilate the sequence of events, when Jim shot him in the chest, a little higher up, throwing him backwards as though a tremendous force had been abruptly applied. The .50 caliber rounds punched right through their protective armor, pushing bits of it through their bodies and out the back as if it were tissue paper.

Jim double clicked his mic, saying, "Two down, east lake cabin. Going down to clear." He stashed the .50 caliber rifle, swung the MP7A1 submachine gun around to the ready position and advanced on the cabin, 300 yards down slope. The northeast section of the ranch was clear.

Smith had a tactical problem. The two guards approached the west lake cabin from below, one of them shielded from view whenever the other was in the open. He keyed his mic twice. "Do not have a shot on both targets. One only. Am I clear to fire?"

Jones answered. "Wait, Smith, almost there. Watch your six. That cabin is not cleared yet. Give me thirty seconds."

The Apache drew on skills honed by generations of his ancestors to sprint through the trees and over boulders, struggling to maintain his balance as he ran headlong downhill, attempting to beat the pair approaching the west cabin from below. He slid to a stop with seconds to spare, coming up against the north wall of the log cabin. Breathless, he keyed his mic, asking, "Smith, do you have a shot?"

Jones peered around the corner of the cabin as the pair approached, just three or four yards from the front porch when he heard the big man respond, "Yes."

"Take it."

The lead guard stopped as though he'd walked into a wall, then fell in segments, first to his knees, then sat on his haunches, then keeled over on his left side. His partner immediately fell to the ground and rolled behind the south wall of the cabin, his mind frantically trying to interpret this latest sequence of events.

"One down." Smith keyed his mike. "One loose."

The Apache raced around the east wall of the cabin and peeked around the corner just in time to see the second guard snatching quick looks uphill from behind the south wall. He crept up behind him, weapon at the ready, until he was only three feet behind him. He fired a three-round burst into the base of the guard's skull, killing him instantly. He keyed his mic. "Number two down. Checking west lake cabin. Smith, watch your six. I did not clear that cabin. I repeat. I did not clear that cabin."

"Roger that, Jones. I have my six. Be careful. You're on your own."

"Roger that. On my own." The Indian entered the cabin like a ghost through the rear kitchen door. He went room to room until he confirmed that only two men had occupied the dwelling. He activated his mic to let the team know. "West lake cabin clear. Two down."

Jim heard the message as he was entering the east lake cabin. He pushed the front door inward on well-oiled hinges, hearing no sound until the door bumped against the stop. He risked a quick look before retracting his head back behind the log wall. No response. He ducked below the windows and jumped off the front porch, skirted the south wall, and approached the rear entrance. He tried the knob, but found it locked. Not good. Decision time. The team would need him as backup at the main house and gate house within minutes. He selected full auto on his MP7A1 and propped an Adirondack chair beneath the rear doorknob to seal off that avenue of escape before returning to the front door.

He risked one more peek around the front door jamb before sliding into the front room on his knees, spraying the interior from right to left as he slid along the wood plank floor. He killed the furniture, three walls, several pictures and two windows before dropping the empty magazine and slapping another one home. Sweat was pouring off his brow. He was too old for this. It took a full minute before Jim knew the cabin was empty. He was careful while inspecting the two bedrooms, closets and bathrooms before keying his mic. "East lake cabin empty. Moving to the Northwest cabin. Smith, I'm on your three."

Smith responded. "Welcome back. I'm on the cabin's six, one hundred meters out."

"Roger that. Jones, get to the entrance ASAP! If any of these guys contacted the main house, they're going to need you there. We'll clear this cabin and follow."

"On my way," Jones replied. Once again, he was running downhill.

Jim retrieved his Barrett rifle and got into position 150 yards out from the northwest cabin where he had a clear view of the front and rear doors as well as the entire west side. "Smith, cover the south and west sides. I have north and east."

"Roger that," Smith responded. "Moving." It took only a minute to get into position. "I have the south and west."

"Sit tight," Jim said.

"Roger that."

Six men were down, but the situation was quite different for Erika and Ray. She had potentially six targets and none had appeared yet: two in the upstairs garage rooms and four in the house. Her skill with a handgun, along with her very personal interest in the outcome of this operation, dictated she shoulder the responsibility for the main house. Similarly, Ray had opted to face the four guards at the entrance to the compound, based on his combat skills. Waiting in hiding did not sit well with either of them and they squirmed as they listened to the action through their earpieces.

Donny's voice broke into her thoughts. "Ray, two guards returning fifty yards out on your left. Get set."

"Roger."

Ray stood on the right side of a massive willow trunk as the pair approached from his left. There is a point where honor departs and survival takes precedence in any combat situation. Ray shot both of them from ambush, in the temple, from only ten feet away, dropping them within a second of one another. It was hardly a sporting tactic, but it was effective. The .40 caliber rounds exploded their heads like cantaloupe from such close proximity, sending them to the gravel path like bowling pins.

He keyed his mic. "Two down, entry cabin." Then, "Oh, shit. That hurts. I'm hit."

Several things happened at once. Erika heard Jones say, "Stay down. I'm fifty meters out. He's spraying the trees with a silenced weapon. Say again. Stay down."

"Roger that. Fuck."

At that moment, Donny's voice tickled Erika's ear. "Erika, they're coming down the stairs."

She crouched between the dumpsters; only her eyes above the rim, watching their legs descend the stairs from beneath the stairwell. The gaps between the steps were bereft of risers, giving Erika the opportunity to time her movements to perfection. As the first man passed by, the second one was on the last step, turning to his right to follow his companion. She stepped out between them and shot the trailer in the forehead just above the bridge of his nose from two feet away. She swiveled on her right foot and shot the first man in the back of the head. These were the two men Petro had remembered from Rome. Both died without knowing who shot them. To be certain, Erika put one more round into the back of their heads where they lay. She keyed her mic. "Two down at the main house."

"Do not enter. Repeat, do not enter. Cover exits and wait. We'll be there in five," Jim said.

Jim knew Erika would be chafing at his instructions, but he had to clear the upper northwest cabin in the woods before he could advance on the lower houses. Two guards were still alive at the gate house, and four more occupied the main residence. Those were not odds he wanted his team to take chances with.

Jim said, "Smith, cover me. I'm going in the back."

"Got it. You are covered," he replied.

Jim used the trees as cover until the last twenty yards. He discarded the Barrett rifle and pulled his MP7A1 into position on full auto before sprinting across the open area and backing up against the wall of the log cabin. He risked a quick look through the window. Nothing.

He pushed open the unlocked rear door and peered inside. The cabin was silent. The gloom inside prevented him from seeing any detail, but there was no heat in the cabin, no lights on, no dishes out on the sink. It looked deserted. He entered the small kitchen, gun at the ready, then the great room, both bedrooms, closets, and bathrooms and found no evidence of recent habitation. He spoke into his mic. "Smith, all clear. Coming out."

"Roger. All clear."

Jim retrieved his Barrett, and the two men trotted down past the lake until they neared the entry cabin. He asked into his mike. "Ray, how are you doing?"

"I'm fine. Under cover. I took one in the hip. I think it hit my pelvis then went clean through my side. Everything's numb. I could use a hand," he said.

"Jones, you see him?"

"Yes."

"Can you reach him?"

"Yes."

"Okay. Smith has the entry cabin covered on the north and east side. Take the south and west, assist Jim and either kill 'em or bottle 'em up. I'm going to Erika. Erika, you copy?"

"I copy. Welcome to the party. I got the south and east. Take north and west and tell me when you're ready," she answered. "The two guards from the apartment are down. The main house is still active: all four."

"On my way."

Chapter 55

The house was in a panic. It was 6:00 am and all hell had broken loose when a call from the entry gate woke the household. The guard was speaking quickly, his voice garbled over the closed intercom system. Leonid shook the sleep from his brain and stopped the monologue with a shout. "STOP! Speak slowly. What is happening?"

"I have two guards down. Someone shot them only twenty yards from the house. I saw it happen and closed down the perimeter. Demitri and I are locked in the cabin." He was gulping air as he spoke, clearly rattled.

"How many?" Leonid asked.

"I don't know. They were under cover."

"Where are the others?"

"I don't know. I radioed everyone and you are the only one who replied," the guard answered.

"Okay, stay inside and relay any further information as it occurs. This line will stay open," Leonid said. He turned to Raina and Petro, who'd emerged from their rooms and overheard the conversation. "We're under attack. Most, if not all of the guards are dead. It's time to move. Get some clothes."

Raina, wearing a blue silk dressing gown, was disrobing as she left the room without a word. Petro wore pajama bottoms with a white t-shirt. He said, "Go. I will take care of this." Leonid, dressed in boxers and t-shirt, turned and headed back to his room.

Two minutes later, Raina appeared dressed in blue jeans and a black sweater pulling Stasja, dressed similarly, behind her. They ran to the basement stairs. Leonid appeared on their heels, dressed in blue jeans, sneakers and sweatshirt. "Come with us now, Petro."

"No, you go. I will surrender after you're safe. Come back for me."

"That is a promise, Petro."

"Go."

Leonid ran down the stairs, certain he would never change Petro's mind. If Petro survived, he would move heaven and earth to rescue him.

The hidden doorway, secreted behind the basement movie theater screen, stood open. Leonid ran through the opening, activating the closing mechanism as he passed. He ran down the metal stairway, descending fifty feet before emerging outside the cliff, seventy feet below the mesa rim onto a game trail leading down to the town. He caught Raina and Stasja halfway down the slope leading to a townhouse they owned on the outskirts of Aspen. They went directly to the garage, started an M-class Mercedes SUV, and drove to the airport. The pilots had been alerted from the ranch house and forty minutes later, they were in the air, accelerating through the light cloud cover above Aspen. Raina hadn't said a word all morning.

Chapter 56

Jim spoke into his mic. "Erika, I have north and west covered."

"Okay, what now?"

"Stay in position. We will clear the entry cabin and then the main house. Smith, Jones, Ray—confirm."

"Roger that," Smith replied.

"Roger," from Jones.

"Understood," said Ray.

Jim said. "Erika?"

"Confirmed," she answered in a flat voice.

"Ray, how are you holding up?" Jim asked.

"I'm fine, but it hurts like hell. I have the entrance cabin in sight on the northwest corner. I can give cover fire from here."

"Okay, Smith, your call."

Smith said, "I'm gonna put some .50 cals through that cabin and see what falls out. Ray, Jones, take anyone that comes out."

"Roger."

"Roger."

The Barrett rifle did not look so imposing in the big man's hands. He handled the weapon with the same ease a normal-sized man would handle an M-16. He extended the tripod at the front of the rifle, rested it on a boulder in front of him, and lined it up on the front door.

With the absence of a normal report, dulled by the suppressor, the weapon sounded more like an irritating, ratcheting, metallic grind. The front door erupted as though by magic. A four-inch hole appeared in the center of the wood planks as the kinetic energy of the BMG .50 caliber round expended itself on the three-inch thick door before traveling through the house. Both guards fell to the floor in search of cover. Smith sent the second round through the cabin only two feet above the floor, and the guards realized the ground offered no cover. After seven more rounds penetrated the cabin, they began to see beams of sunlight pierce the interior. They were acutely aware of the awesome power of the weapon employed against them.

As Smith removed the empty magazine and replaced it with a fresh one containing ten rounds, one guard took advantage of the brief lull in the action to sprint out the back door. Jones was only twenty yards away. He fired a three-round burst that hit the man's Kevlar vest and flung him backwards to the ground. The Apache quickly advanced on the fallen man and finished him with a burst to the head.

He turned at the sound of a black Suburban crashing through the garage door towards him. The other guard had made it into the attached garage in a frantic attempt to escape and intended to use the two-ton vehicle as a battering ram. Jones scrambled for the protection of the trees, not certain he would make it.

Smith heard the engine and sound of something heavy slamming through a panel of sheet metal. He tore through the woods to the cabin and saw that the guard was trying to run over his partner and fired three .50 caliber rounds through the engine block, immediately disabling the vehicle, causing it to creak to rest—almost upon Jones.

He put three more rounds through the front passenger door, perforating the driver with each shot from right to left through his torso, converting flesh into hamburger. The driver died instantly.

Smith triggered his mic and said, "Two down at entry gate. We're clearing the cabin now."

He and Jones cleared the entry cabin and went to help Ray. Smith handed his Barrett rifle off to his teammate, and examined Ray. "Are you going to make it?"

"I'm good, but I don't think I can walk," Ray said. Smith looked at the wound and then applied a compress from his backpack and duct-taped it to his torso. Then he gently lifted Ray up in his arms. He carried him to the cabin and deposited him there with his weapons to act as lookout until the rest of the ranch was neutralized.

"Are you gonna be okay?" he asked Ray.

"I'm good. Go get the rest of them."

"We'll be back," the big man said. He clicked his mic to report to the team, "Entry cabin is secure. Ray will stay in the cabin. Jones and I are approaching from the west. Try not to shoot us."

That did it for Erika. She did not want anyone to enter the main house before she did. This was too personal. She also did not want to get shot by one of her own. She keyed her mic. "I'm going in the back, Jim," she said.

"Wait for backup. Two more minutes," he replied.

"That just gives them more time to set up. I'm already there," she said. She was on the rear porch, stealing glances through a kitchen window. There was no sign of anyone in the room.

"I said wait, Erika."

"Too late," she said. "I'm in the kitchen. It's empty. Take the front." She swiveled the MP7A1 to position on her back and pulled her Glock. It was her weapon of choice in close quarters, just an extension of her will. Hours and hours of practice in combat scenarios and dozens of operations distilled to the real thing in seconds. There were no ribbons or medals for this type of work. Survival was your reward.

"Wait there, Erika," Jim said. "Backup is here. I'm coming in the front."

"Okay, I'm waiting," Erika said as she passed through to the great room. She had no intention of waiting one more second.

It was lucky for Jim that she disobeyed.

"Jim, stop!" she screamed into her mic. "The front door is booby-trapped. C-4. Do not enter."

Now she understood why they abandoned the kitchen and great room. When her team opened that door, everything in the adjoining rooms would be obliterated.

"Roger that," Jim answered. "Coming around the back. Thirty seconds."

Petro heard Erika scream. He had been waiting downstairs for the front door to blow. He was already angry he did not have the opportunity to rig both entrances. He chose to rig the front door, assuming the attackers would breach that door first, or at least simultaneously, with the rear. Once he heard the door blow, he could either flee through the passage below or stay and mop up the carnage. Once again, that bitch upstairs had ruined his plans. He snapped. He would take her now, no matter the consequences.

"I give up," he yelled. "I give up. I'm unarmed."

Erika keyed her mic. "Jim, do not enter. I have one coming up the stairs. I don't know if he can detonate. I say again, do not enter."

"Holding on the rear porch. Jones and Smith, hold the perimeter. Erika, keep your mic open."

Erika triggered her mic to stay open so that everyone, including Donny, could hear. Sheila, as they had agreed earlier, was not on premises in Bel Air and not involved. Erika was on her own.

She yelled down the stairwell, "Walk slowly up the stairs with your hands up, palms facing forward."

"Don't shoot me! I give up," Petro repeated.

"Start walking." Erika her weapon trained on the advancing figure when she realized who it was. "I have Petro," she said.

"Be careful," Jim warned.

Erika did not answer him. She zoned in on Petro coming up the stairs. When he was near the top of the stairwell, Erika stepped back to keep a safe distance, her weapon trained on his midsection.

When he gained the top of the stairs, Erika backed away some twenty feet, fully aware of this man's capabilities. She said, "Hands on your head and turn around slowly."

He did as ordered.

"Any weapons?" She knew the question was a waste of breath, but asked anyway.

"Why don't you frisk me? See for yourself," he chided.

" Turn around."

Petro turned to face her, closing the distance by a couple of feet as he did. If he could get within ten feet of this bitch, she was his. He inched forward a bit more.

Erika held the Glock loosely in her right hand. "You stabbed the agent in the stomach at the Westlake house, didn't you?"

"Yeah, I did. And I broke Richard's nose as well. Then I twisted it around to get his attention. I enjoyed it, but he screamed like a child." His smirk was infuriating. He inched forward some more. Just a few more feet closer and he would strike. He'd never missed downing and disarming an opponent once he was committed to doing so. His knife was sheathed in the small of his back, ready for use once she was down.

This woman was the one from the Las Vegas warehouse video. He was certain of that now. She didn't seem to notice him shrinking the distance between them as they talked. He noticed the silenced semi-automatic dangling from her right hand. Perfect.

Erika knew he was trying to antagonize her, throw her reaction time off and confuse her. That was fine with her. The outcome would be the same. She watched the distance shorten every time he casually talked and moved.

Petro asked, "Didn't you invade our warehouse in Las Vegas and murder my friends?" He inched closer.

"Yeah, I did. I also shot Sergei in the face. He was your

friend, wasn't he?" Now she was goading him. "He didn't scream like a child. He didn't scream at all. He just died like the dumbass he was."

"Yes, Sergei was my friend," he said, struggling to contain his anger. "He was honorable, loyal. He was the best sniper in the world. You tricked him."

"He was the second best," she goaded him further, "because I shot him." Erika took notice each time he inched closer. It would happen soon.

"And that crazy little bitch; was she a friend of yours too? Or that fat fucking pimp that liked to torture girls? Was he a friend of yours?" Erika could see the rage building behind Petros' eyes.

"Yes, they were my friends. The girl belonged to Raina, her pet. You will pay dearly for that insult," he replied. He was at the required ten-foot distance for an attack. One more distraction and he'd have her.

"Wait until you see what we do to your girlfriend," he sneered. "She will take a long time to die, I promise you."

Erika didn't care about his words. She could not be distracted by thinking about the threat to Sheila. She would not spare time to react to what he said. It takes the brain almost a full second to recognize a stimulus and another second to send a message through the neural pathways to the joints and muscles required for action to mount a defense. Those are key moments for a highly trained combatant.

Conversely, a reflex is the result of practicing a response to a given stimulus. It is ingrained in the neural pathways, muscle, bone, and tissue. It is an organic, living part of the individual who practices. It is instantaneous.

Petro exploded into a blur of limbs, dropping below firing level to a prone position and using his left hip as a fulcrum; he pivoted and jetted his right leg in an arc to sweep Erika off her feet. He launched his deadly attack in half a second.

He was a quarter second too slow. Erika shot him in the right hip when he dropped, her gun moved so quickly he didn't see it. He did feel the piercing pain in his right hip as he attempted to slide his extended right leg toward her ankles, though.

The leg never made it that far. She shot him in the right knee. The same awful, piercing pain immobilized that joint as well. Furious, he tried to rise on his left leg to catapult his body forward in an attempt to grasp this slender female and crush her throat in his hands.

She backed away calmly and shot him in the left knee as he bent it to rise, collapsing him back to the wooden floor. She wasn't talking now. She did not want anyone on the communications system to realize what was happening until she was ready.

She shot him again, this time in the right elbow. The fixed blade that he wanted to bury in her torso clattered to the floor. Then she shot him in the left arm for good measure, leaving him helpless on the floor. Petro was no longer a foe to be feared. He was writhing in agony, but not a sound came out of him.

"And this is for Richard," she said as she shot him between the eyes, a cold-blooded execution.

Jim looked on from the kitchen doorway, a strange expression on his face. Unable to allow Erika to face their enemy alone, he'd entered the kitchen door knowing they could both be killed in the blast. He'd watched most of what had occurred. He was having trouble reconciling what he'd witnessed with his understanding of the young woman he'd trained. But now was not the time to engage in psychoanalysis.

Erika locked eyes with him as she dropped the magazine out of the Glock into her hand and inserted a fresh one. Her expression was blank.

She heard Jim address everyone on the communications system. "Smith, stay put. Jones, come in the rear door through the kitchen. The front door is armed with explosives. We have one bad guy down and out in the great room. We need to clear this house."

Smith said, "Roger that."

Jones reported, "On my way."

Jim looked at Erika thoughtfully, still trying to figure her out. Erika's face remained blank.

The Apache appeared in the kitchen, looked through the doorway at the bloodied corpse on the floor of the great room and walked to the front door to examine the device attached to the block of C-4. He ignored the body; it was just one more corpse that morning. The explosive was a more immediate concern. He pored over the lead wires, inspected the simple trip mechanism attached to the door jamb, then simply removed the wires leading to the explosive brick, picked it up, and set it on the bar counter. He opened the front door.

"That was enough C-4 to bring down half this house," he said. "Somebody is seriously pissed."

He didn't remark on the fallen Russian or what he'd heard in his earpiece before Erika executed the man. That comment was personal between her and the man on the floor. "Let's get this house cleared and get out of Dodge."

The trio went room by room. They could tell that the occupants had left in a hurry. Open cosmetics, toothbrushes left out, and expensive jewelry and clothing strewn on the floor told the story. Once they were sure no one else was in the house, they left the home and approached the entry gate.

Jim warned of their arrival by microphone. "The main house is clear. We're on our way to your location. Let's get Ray out of here."

They located the keys to one of the vehicles from the ranch, bundled Ray into the back seat and drove back to their rental home in Snowmass. On the way down, they retrieved their vehicle and left the commandeered Suburban in its place. They repacked their weapons and personal effects, called in the charter pilots, and drove down the valley to the Rifle Airport. They returned the rental vehicles, loaded the Citation X, and were on their way back to Los Angeles within thirty minutes of their arrival at the airport. Jim had training as a battlefield medic and stabilized Ray as best he could, but he wanted to get him professional medical attention as soon as possible.

Before the plane departed, Erika called Donny on the secure com line. "You're going to need a large cleanup crew. Thirteen down. We're wheels up in five minutes."

"I'll take care of it."

One of the pilots asked about the fishing trip when they landed at Burbank Airport. Jim said, "It was terrific until my partner fell on a rock and injured his hip. We caught a lot of fish, but we let a couple of big ones get away."

Jones and Smith disappeared after brief handshakes all around, except for Jim, who hugged each man hard. They didn't need to say a word. Erika wondered at their past. She had the impression these men would come whenever Jim called, no matter the circumstance. There was an undeniable bond between them that would never be broken. She would do no less for him.

Ray was taken by ambulance to a local hospital that had an agency relationship that ensured their cooperation and discretion. Erika and Jim were finally alone. "I assume that was some unfinished business," he said.

Erika knew he was referring to her execution of Petro. "He was the one that abducted Richard and killed the two agents in Westlake."

"Well done, then," Jim said.

Erika approached him and he took her in his arms and held her for a few moments. When they separated, she said, "I'm going to take you up on that hunting trip next year."

"You do that, young lady. You do that." Jim gave her one last look and walked away.

Erika watched him leave without a backward glance, then retrieved her car and drove away from the airport. She and Jim would never speak of the incident at the Aspen ranch. He knew this was personal for her and she suspected he had some ghosts of his own. They all lived with emotional scars. It came with the territory.

One of those scars haunted Erika at that very moment. She had Leonid and Raina in her grasp and let them escape. She was seething inside.

Chapter 57

Erika drove south on Interstate 405 from Burbank so she could drop in on Donny at the Bel Air Estate to fill him in on the operation in Colorado. She exited on Mulholland and climbed the winding grade up to the wrought iron gates. She buzzed the intercom at the entrance, aware she was on video. She waved at the circular glass eye that contained the camera.

Donny's voice came from the intercom. "Hey, Erika. Come on up."

Donny opened the front door for her and came out to greet her. They hugged and Donny said, "Nice work, Erika. Now there's only two left."

"Thanks, Donny," she said. "You haven't located them yet, have you?"

"No, we suspect they took a private jet out of Aspen about the time you were on the ranch property. I kept the drone on your operation, so I'm not sure who was on the jet. There were at least three passengers and two or three crew members according to the manifest," he said.

"Well, I know one person who was not on that jet," Erika said.

"Who?"

"Petro. I paid him back for everything he did to Richard—and then some," she said.

She was not boasting. She was aware that Donny knew Petro had been eliminated. She just wanted Donny, and soon, Sheila to understand she had exacted a certain amount of revenge before sending him to hell.

"Where's Sheila?" Erika asked.

"She's not here," Donny answered. "And you're not going to like where she went."

"Where?"

"To lunch with the Senator."

"What?" Erika was incredulous. "Why didn't you tell me?"

"He called while you were in the air. I was hoping you would contact me. I couldn't very well send a message like that through an unprotected communication link. Besides, he didn't come here. He visited the fake operations center. Two of our best security personnel, his driver and his security agent accompanied her to lunch. She'll be safe."

"How long ago?"

Donny looked at his watch. "Twenty minutes ago. The Senator arrived at the house less than an hour ago."

"Shit."

"Erika, what is it? Why are you so upset?" Donny asked.

"Because, when I was at the ranch house, Petro waited for me. He threatened Sheila by name. He wired the front door to blow if one of us entered that way. It was just dumb luck no one did. He wanted to kill me even if it meant his death or capture. I can't imagine the Russians wanting her any less. Donny, I'm worried," she said.

"I'll call her," he said. "We'll put her two guards on high alert and find out exactly where she is right now."

"Do it," she said. "And call me in my car and keep me informed of anything unusual. Anything at all." Erika ran to her car.

The big V-8 rumbled back to life as Donny was contacting Sheila on his cell. Erika was out the gate and headed down the hill by the time Donny connected with Sheila.

"Yes?" she answered.

"Sheila, our friend just returned from Colorado with some new information that suggests you may be in danger right at this moment," he said.

"Is it serious?" Sheila asked.

"She thought so. She's on her way to you. Where are you now?"

"We're heading east on Sunset on our way to the Bel Air Hotel." Sheila replied. She tried to look unconcerned as the Senator looked askance at her. She held up a finger to indicate she'd be right with him.

"Are you in the car with your two agents?" Donny asked.

"No, the Senator arranged a limo for us. The other car wasn't necessary."

"Tell me they're following you," Donny begged.

"Yes, of course. They will pick me up after lunch and I'll see you about 3 this afternoon, in plenty of time for our appointment."

"Erika is on her way," Donny said.

"Very good. I look forward to seeing her then." Sheila hoped she was acting sufficiently unconcerned under the steady gaze of the Senator.

"Is there a problem?" the Senator asked as she shut her cell down.

"No, just the office reminding me I have an important meeting at 4 this afternoon. I'm sure I'll be there in plenty of time."

"Good. I've been hoping to spend enough time with you to get a better handle on some agency matters that have been troubling me," Senator Ross said. "And to get to know you a little better, too, of course."

"Of course," Sheila answered. "That shouldn't be too hard for us to accomplish in short order." She gave him her most encouraging smile. She'd forgotten more about manipulating men than he ever knew.

Senator Jerry Ross viewed Sheila as an obstacle to overcome—one more bump in the road. Sure, she was attractive and bright. She was gaining insight and experience on an almost exponential basis. But, now she was just someone to be used. It was a shame this beautiful young creature had to be disposed of before the Senator could realize his dream. It could have been a far more pleasant ride with her by his side. What a shame!

Two days ago, he had been instructed to invite Sheila to a lunch date at the Bel Air hotel. A Russian operative would take charge of the matter from there. He was further instructed to disappear once that man was in position.

The doorman at the Bel Air Hotel opened the rear door of the limo and helped Sheila and the Senator out of the back. He asked his security agent to escort them to their cottage. They walked through the lobby and out past the gardens and swimming pool to Senator Ross's suite. When Sheila raised an eyebrow at the obvious impropriety of entering a hotel room together, no matter how chic, the Senator said, "Not to worry, Sheila, we've set up an informal brunch out on the patio where we can talk without being overheard. I hope you don't mind."

"Not at all, Senator," she said. "I was just a little surprised."

"Are you sure this is okay?"

Sheila surreptitiously punched a speed dial on the phone concealed in her purse that was connected to Donny. "Of course, it's okay. I'm not concerned about dining in your private suite. I was more worried about your reputation than mine. You are a senior Senator, after all." She hoped Donny heard every word.

He unlocked the door, stepped aside, and invited her to enter. The suite was huge and situated just beyond the swimming pool. It backed up to the private street bordering the hotel grounds and was protected by an eight-foot stucco wall. The hotel staff had set up a lunch table on the rear patio of the living room area. Sheila waited in the plush environs until the Senator closed the door and led her through the open patio sliders to their dining table.

"I hope this meets with your approval," Senator Ross said.

"Yes, of course, Senator," she said. "It's beautiful."

"Call me Jerry, please. There's no need for formality now."

"Okay, Jerry it is."

He turned to his security guard. "You can go now, Dennis. Grab some lunch with the driver and be back in an hour. We shouldn't take longer than ninety minutes."

Dennis grinned. He had accompanied the Senator on several of these assignations in the past. This was normal procedure. "Yes, sir. See you in one hour."

Sheila heard the exchange. It raised all sorts of red flags for someone in her position. It must have been obvious to the Senator. He said, "No worries, Sheila. We'll be fine on our own for an hour or so." He led her to the patio.

He held her chair out for her to be seated and then pushed her into position close to the table. He sat opposite her. The sun umbrella covered the entire seating area, allowing them to enjoy the warm weather without baking in the sun. There was a vibrant display of flowers in the center of the glass table and a gleaming service of silver and crystal.

"I'm impressed, Jerry. You do know how to put on a lunch."

"Good, I've accomplished my first goal," he said, taking his seat. He poured them each a glass of sauvignon blanc. "I do like to take a glass of wine with a meal." He offered a toast. "To new beginnings," he offered.

Sheila clinked his glass and said, "To new beginnings." She shifted in her chair. "Now, Jerry, how can I help you?"

"Very direct," he said. "I like that." He hesitated a moment before speaking. "I'm concerned over these recent events in Las Vegas regarding some unsavory Russians. Apparently there is a feud beginning between two rival factions attempting to gain control of certain rackets there."

"Yes?" Sheila encouraged him. "What does that have to do

with our agency?"

"Didn't your agency get involved in an operation there last year that resulted in your husband's death?"

This was still a painfully raw subject for Sheila to discuss, but it seemed the Senator was intent on picking at that scab. "You were there in person, weren't you?"

Her radar was pinging continuously now. Still she didn't speak, forcing the Senator to continue. "Wasn't there another female operative involved in that operation with you?"

The hair on the nape of her neck stood on end. "If you read the reports, and I assume you did so before confirming my nomination, you know that identities of operatives are not included for security reasons, Jerry. That would constitute a major breach of our charter security and make it virtually impossible to recruit from the other agencies."

"So I'm not to be trusted even though you report to me?" The Senator's thin veneer of civility was beginning to fray, adding to Sheila's growing concern.

"It's not you specifically, Senator. There are aides, assistants, and several other individuals that have been responsible for outing agents in the past. Valerie Plame comes to mind. If you recall, she was exposed as a CIA agent by a politician who unwittingly used her name and title in a public document. I don't intend to make the same mistake."

"Come now, Sheila, there are just the two of us present. You won't even confirm who was with you in Las Vegas?" the Senator chided.

"I haven't even confirmed I was there, if you think about it. And what kind of Director would I be if I shared any information with anyone, for any reason, Senator?" Sheila was getting hot now. How dare this cretin lecture her on security matters!

Senator Ross, the veteran of many disagreements in his twenty-four years in the Senate was unfazed. "Really, Sheila, we're on the same team here. It's not like I couldn't gain access to that information on my own."

"Then that's what you will have to do, Senator. Go through the proper channels. Get it on your own." Sheila hoped Donny was hearing their exchange and had alerted her two security agents. What she did not realize was that it would not have made any difference.

Chapter 58

The two agency security personnel were instructed to follow the limousine carrying Sheila and the Senator to the Bel Air Hotel and then wait in the parking lot until their business lunch was concluded. They did as instructed.

There was a silver Mercedes parked a few spaces over, closer to the exit gate; one of two access points to the walled-in lot. The driver opened the door and got out to stretch his muscles, raising his hands over his head, reaching for the sky while rotating his neck muscles to relieve the tension. He was obviously waiting for his passenger, just as they were. The agent in the driver's seat couldn't help marveling at the limo driver's size. He tried to guess—250, maybe 270 pounds–and that oversized block of a head atop the huge hulk of a body. He looked like a large refrigerator on legs.

He walked over to the two agents, a wide grin plastered on his face. The driver lowered his window. "How're you doing?" he asked.

"Fine, fine," the big man replied in an unusual accent. "And you?"

"I'm good," was all he managed before Fyodor shot him with a silenced weapon. The bullet caught him in the temple, spraying bits of bone, flesh, and blood over his companion. Fyodor leaned in the open window and shot the other agent twice in the back as he was attempting to flee the car.

Quickly, Fyodor pulled both men from the vehicle with no more effort than picking up a bag of groceries and stuffed them between the rear bumper and the security wall. Satisfied they would not be discovered, he left them and entered the hotel grounds.

Erika pulled into the entrance drive of the hotel, shut down the engine, and approached the valet. "I'll only be a few minutes. I'm picking up a guest."

"What is the guest's name, please?" the young man countered.

"Senator Ross," Erika responded with as much self-importance as she could muster and kept walking. She had her earpiece in and Donny on the other end of the line. "Okay, where are they?"

"In the bungalow behind the swimming pool," Donny answered. "Enter the pool area and continue on through the rear gate. There are two cottages. You want the one on the left, 113." He'd hacked into the reservation system of the hotel and Sheila had a microchip implanted in her inner arm that could locate her within several feet.

"Okay, stay on the line." She was walking through the hotel grounds following the signs for the swimming pool. She strolled through a pool deck full of sunbathers and an older man swimming slow laps in an otherwise empty pool, and exited through the rear gate. The concrete path meandered left and right through the foliage surrounding the two cottages. Erika went to the right, bypassing the cottage. She continued to the rear of the property where it ended at an eight-foot-tall block wall covered in the same salmon-colored stucco as the cottage.

She consulted Donny on the com line. "Is the cottage next door occupied?" Erika asked.

"Hold on," he said. Ten seconds later, he said, "No one is registered. It should be empty."

"Going over the wall," Erika said. She jumped vertically, grasping the top of the rough surface and pulled her head up over the edge to scan the small patio. No one there. She scrabbled up the wall, swiveled her hips over the top, and dropped into the yard.

She could easily eavesdrop on the conversation between Sheila and Senator Ross; it was like being on the patio with them. She carefully moved a patio chair over to the wall separating the two yards and stood on it without making a sound.

The next bit of information from Donny echoed in her ear and chilled her to the bone. "I can't raise the security team, Erika. Something's wrong."

Next, she heard Sheila say, "Senator, I will not share the identities of my agents with anyone, and that includes you. Politics and Intelligence have been separated for as long as I've been involved for good reasons. You should know better."

In a voice Erika barely recognized because of its threatening tone, Senator Ross replied, "Well, *that* is about to change. You're going for a ride with this gentleman. He has a dear friend that is dying to meet you. And you have another girlfriend they want to meet. You'll need to tell them all about her. I'm sure you will all get along famously." The Senator's face formed the most hideous grin Sheila had ever seen.

Erika tried to look over the wall, stretching to her limit on her tiptoes. The information Donny had relayed about Sheila's security team not responding troubled her because it meant there were other players in the field—ones who did not have their best interests in mind. On the one hand, she needed to check on the security team, and on the other, she did not want to leave Sheila, her Director and friend. Sheila screamed; the sound cut off abruptly.

She leapt to the top of the wall, scraping the underside of her forearms as she scrabbled up yet another rough stucco surface. She pulled her weapon as she perched atop the wall, taking in a scene that defied her comprehension. Fyodor was holding Sheila aloft.

How was that possible? She had shot him dead center in New York. She saw him fall from the impact of the big .50 caliber round. *It couldn't be.*

The Senator was still seated at the table, his back to Erika, unaware of her presence. Fyodor, however, looked up when she appeared, causing the Senator to turn around to see what had attracted his attention. Erika dropped to the patio floor, gun in hand.

Fyodor lifted Sheila like a ragdoll, using her as a human shield. Up close, he was not only intimidating; he instilled a terror that rose up in her throat like a solid blockage. Erika felt her knees wobble at the sight of him holding Sheila like a play toy. He fixed his gaze on Erika with a hatred so intense that she could feel it across the patio as a physical sensation. It did not, however, prevent Erika from a violent reaction.

As she rose from a crouch, Senator Ross turned in his chair to see what Fyodor was staring at and Erika hit him square in the mouth with the Glock. The silencer, along with the weight of the loaded weapon broke several of his teeth before he toppled over backwards. He was not a factor in this fight.

Erika ignored the fallen man and concentrated on the giant holding her friend. She leveled her weapon at the pair of them. He had one massive paw clamped over Sheila's mouth to silence her; his other arm encircled her abdomen just below her breasts, squeezing her breath from her body. Sheila was turning pale with the pressure being applied to her lungs, her ribcage compressed painfully.

His voice, seeming to emanate from the depths of a cavern, startled her. It sounded like a cement mixer filled with rocks. "You're the other bitch from the warehouse." He spat the word 'bitch.'

Erika stared back at the monster; only fifteen feet separated them. She knew she could not allow him to advance on her. If he got his hands on her...

"That's right, Fyodor," Erika said, mocking him. She'd decided what to do. "Who was that dumb fuck I shot in New York, your fucking twin?"

An outpouring of animal rage erupted from the giant. He squeezed Sheila even tighter, cutting off her oxygen through pure strength, turning her into a lifeless rag doll. His strategy was clear. Even though he was under strict orders to deliver this woman to Raina so that she could pry every last bit of intelligence out of her, he would continue to squeeze the life out of Sheila, using her as a human shield until he could get close enough to snatch Erika up in the same lethal bear hug. A blue tinge appeared on Sheila's lips. It would not take much longer before the young woman suffered permanent damage or worse. He took a step forward, still hugging Sheila tight to his body, moving closer yet.

Too close. Erika shot him through the right foot; a tiny hole appeared on the instep of his black boot. He faltered; his grip on Sheila loosened just a tiny fraction. Then he continued moving forward, slightly favoring his right leg.

Erika shot him again—this time higher up in the right shin, dangerously close to Sheila's feet dangling lifelessly in front of him. This time he reacted, hopping onto his left foot as the impact to his shin registered, stifling for a moment the primordial need to crush this woman who murdered his brother. Wounded or not, he would have her.

Sheila, mercifully unconscious, shifted in his grasp, exposing his right shoulder. Erika snapped off another shot, hitting Fyodor squarely in the joint where the two major bones met. She was rewarded by a grunt of pain, nothing more. But he halted his forward momentum for a moment to assess his injury. He looked at the wound and then moved forward again—an unthinking, unfeeling automaton, intent only on destroying the only thing that mattered. Eight feet separated them.

It was a war of attrition; Fyodor continued squeezing the life out of Sheila and Erika could only wound the advancing behemoth unless she risked killing her best friend. She knew what she had to do.

She shot him in the left foot, noting the long trail of blood behind his right boot, marking his forward progress. Again, he stopped, still holding Sheila's limp body in front of him, the wound to his foot a momentary impediment. He shuffled forward now, mere inches with each movement, but closer with each effort.

Erika shot Sheila this time, from only six feet away, the nine-millimeter bullet passed through the flesh of her right side, above the hip bone, striking Fyodor in the ribcage and deflecting downwards into his abdominal cavity. He stopped.

Erika held her ground, all her senses tuned into this

moment in time; nothing else existed. The next few seconds would determine if they lived or died.

Fyodor exploded forward like an NFL fullback carrying a football through the opposing defensive line; only he was carrying Sheila and there were no opposing linemen, just Erika.

She dove to her right, the only option available to her as Fyodor drove himself and Sheila directly into the stucco wall, smashing her between his bulk and the rough, unforgiving surface. The skin on her forehead, cheeks, nose and chin blossomed red at the impact. The monster bounced backwards, still on his feet as he relinquished his grip on Sheila and turned to his left to make a grab at Erika.

Erika tucked and rolled on her right shoulder, completing a half somersault and rising to one knee in a combat stance. She fired her weapon, muffled by the silencer, as the giant roared in frustration. She shot him in the left hip as he turned, spinning him counter-clockwise to expose his torso, and then unloaded her weapon into him. Nine more rounds hit him from the sternum to the center of his chest in the space of three seconds; and yet, he maintained his forward momentum against the brutal onslaught of lead.

Erika, her weapon jacked open on the empty magazine, could only look up at him in horror. He lunged forward, clubbing her with his fist where her neck joined her trapezium muscle, knocking her backwards with his weight and pinning her to the Mexican tile floor. He took in one large gasp of oxygen and attempted to rise up, blood gurgling with air bubbles from his lungs. He raised his fist to deliver another blow to the fallen woman, and then an odd look of comprehension replaced the pure hatred on his face as he realized his own death. He collapsed on top of Erika. Her shoulder and neck numb from the blow, she couldn't arrest his fall. She took his full weight, the impact of his fist connecting with her left shoulder again, even in his death. Her arm felt like it had been dislocated from her body. *Damn, that hurt!*

She slipped one leg out from underneath his enormous weight and pushed the dead Russian off her as she clambered backwards away from him. With her good arm, she reached back behind her to retrieve a fresh magazine for her weapon. She dropped the empty magazine at the push of a button, but had to hold the gun under her left armpit to insert a fresh one with her right. With two good hands, she could accomplish a magazine change in under a second. The numbness in her left arm caused her to take considerably longer to accomplish the same task. She jacked a round into the chamber by hitting the slide release and stood. Senator Ross rose unsteadily to his feet, and Sheila appeared to be breathing on her own, her chest rising and falling in a shallow rhythm.

Now that she was free, she approached the Senator, intent on finishing the job. She lurched forward and kicked the Senator's feet out from underneath him, sending him to the tile floor once again. She put the gun to his forehead and said, "Now you know who I am, asshole. You won't need to ask anyone ever again."

"Erika, NO!" Erika turned at the sound. Sheila was sitting up, her bloody face a mask of horror at discovering Erika about to terminate the Senator. She kept the gun pressed to his forehead.

"Why not? This asshole is just going to fuck us over every chance he gets. I say we end this charade right now."

"No, I said." Sheila rose to her feet. "We can use him to get to them." She was furiously trying to come up with any sort of reason that would prevent Erika from taking his life. "Once you pull that trigger, you're no better than they are."

"Like I give a fuck." Erika put up her weapon and stepped away from him. "But you're the boss."

"Thank you."

Erika returned to the fallen Russian behemoth and searched him for weapons. She found a silenced semiautomatic handgun, retrieved it from his belt, jacked open the action, and sniffed the weapon. "It's been fired, very recently. Your security team is not answering Donny," she said. "You know what that means, don't you?"

"Erika," Sheila shouted. "I said no!"

"Fuck it." Erika took two long steps towards the Senator and then shot him twice in the forehead. The silenced weapon made less noise than the little man falling back over his chair as death took him.

"Goddamnit, Erika, you just shot a United States Senator," Sheila was apoplectic. "Are you out of your mind?"

"No, a Russian gangster shot the Senator. You, in spite of your life-threatening injuries, shot and killed the murderer before he could kill you, too. You're a hero now, Sheila." She took the gun back to Fyodor and pressed his right hand around the grip. The sausage-like fingers were still warm to the touch. She dropped it next to his outstretched hand.

"I can't allow an agent working for me to do this sort of thing, Erika. You can't just execute someone without the benefit of a trial."

"He's a United States Senator, like you said. He would have weaseled out of this somehow and you know it. He tried to kill you, and he would have eventually killed me. Now he won't be killing anyone. I just stepped on a roach, Sheila, nothing more."

Erika knelt down in front of Sheila to examine her injuries. Her face was a mask of abrasions, and her right cheek looked oddly out of symmetry, suggesting a fracture. Her forehead, nose, right cheek, and chin were scraped so badly that a plastic surgeon would need to repair the damage. Her right side was bleeding where the 9-millimeter round had passed through her flesh. "You need a doctor, boss. Your face is a mess." Erika extended her weapon, butt first, to Sheila. Sheila just stared at it.

"What are you doing? I'm not taking that," she blurted.

"You have to. This is the gun that put down that monster after he shot you, and you're the only agent left on the scene. I'm leaving, Sheila. Take it."

"What do you mean you're leaving?" Sheila looked down at her side and realized for the first time she'd been shot. "How did I get shot? Did you shoot me?"

"Take the weapon, Sheila." Erika was not about to answer

her last question. She just stared at her boss and friend, mentally willing her to take the gun. "Please, Sheila, take it. It's the only way."

"I will take the weapon, Erika, but I'm ordering you to stay on scene," she said. Erika handed the gun to Sheila, making sure she wrapped her fingers around the handle by wrapping both of her hands over Sheila's.

"Then I quit," Erika said. "I don't mind facing honest criminals who want to kill me, but I draw the line at taking shit from people like that." Erika indicated the fallen politician. "They're more dangerous than real felons. They are wolves in sheep's clothing. I won't be a party to this any longer." Erika turned and jumped up, grasping the top of the wall with both hands and pulled her body atop it. She turned and stared at her best female friend in the world, memorizing her features. She loved Sheila and it broke her heart to leave. But it was the only way and it was time for Erika to go.

"Erika, please don't," Sheila pleaded.

Erika dropped down on the other side.

She went directly to the hotel parking lot and found what she feared. She examined the bodies for a sign of life. Both agents were dead of gunshot wounds.

Chapter 59

Erika retrieved her car without incident and spoke to Donny as soon as she was motoring down the narrow street leading away from the hotel.

"Erika, what's going on? I could hear fragments, but not enough to figure it out. Then you went silent." He was frantic. "Sheila just called in the incident and said you left. Where are you?"

"Never mind where I am, Donny. Listen carefully. Fyodor was there with the Senator. He killed both agents. They're behind their car in the parking lot. He also shot the Senator and then Sheila killed Fyodor. She's been hit and beaten pretty badly. That is the official story line. You got that?"

"Yes, I got it, and Sheila agrees. Now where are you?"

"Don't ask me again, Donny—not if you value our friendship," she answered. "Now listen to me. Empty the Senator's bank accounts. Same deal as before."

"We only steal from dead people. That was the deal."

"It still is. Move the money, Donny."

Chapter 60

"Felix?"

"Erika, is that you?" he answered.

"How many women do you have?" It was a poor attempt at a joke.

"What's wrong?" he asked.

"Everything," she said. Torment was obvious in her voice.

"I'm at the beach house. Come on."

"One hour."

Felix was waiting in the street in front of his house, with the door to his empty garage open. He waved her in. She parked her car inside and he hit the switch to descend the door and opened her car door. She got out and he enveloped her in his arms. Yes, she thought, yes, I have a place to go; someone to take care of me. She just stood there like that, feeling the strength of his arms around her. Yes.